I quoted the Bamarre greeting: "Soon, across the Eskerns."

"Yes."

"Why do people say that?" I was enjoying this rare openness between us.

She took a long breath. "The saying means we want to live in Old Lakti."

"With monsters?" But the Bamarre were weak! And cowardly. After only a few battles, we'd wrested the kingdom from them, and they'd rebelled just once, more than a century ago.

She shrugged. "Free. It's just a saying."

Also by GAIL CARSON LEVINE

NOVELS
Dave at Night
Ella Enchanted
Ever
Fairest
Stolen Magic
A Tale of Two Castles
The Two Princesses of Bamarre
The Wish
Ogre Enchanted

THE PRINCESS TALES
The Fairy's Return and Other Princess Tales
The Fairy's Mistake
The Princess Test
Princess Sonora and the Long Sleep
Cinderellis and the Glass Hill
For Biddle's Sake
The Fairy's Return

PICTURE BOOKS
Betsy Red Hoodie
Betsy Who Cried Wolf

NONFICTION
Writing Magic: Creating Stories that Fly
Writer to Writer: From Think to Ink

POETRY
Forgive Me, I Meant to Do It: False Apology Poems

THE
LOST KINGDOM
OF
BAMARRE

GAIL CARSON LEVINE

HARPER

An Imprint of HarperCollinsPublishers

Library of Congress Control Number: 2016949989
ISBN 978-0-06-207468-3

Typography by Katie Klimowicz
18 19 20 21 22   CG/BRR   10 9 8 7 6 5 4 3 2 1
❖
First paperback edition, 2018

To my editor, Rosemary Brosnan,
whom I cannot thank enough or often enough

THE
LOST KINGDOM
OF
BAMARRE

CHAPTER ONE

Before the Lakti betrayal,
And their swords clashing,
And their flaming arrows flying,
And their siege engines rolling,
The Bamarre built the cities—
Our towers upheld the sky,
Flutes day and night playing,
Wind's whisper praising.
The sun's eye opened wide.

MANY YEARS BEFORE I penned these lines, Lady Klausine leaned over my little bed. I was just a year old and asleep.

"Her name is Peregrine?" Lady Klausine shifted the green tassel on my baby cap, which had hidden half my face. "A long appellation—"

"It's because she's always moving"—my mother squeezed her hands together—"peregrinating. So, begging your pardon, we call her Peregrine—Perry."

"I wonder you didn't name her Hair, she has so much."

Lady Klausine's Lakti guard, her Lakti maid, my father, my mother, and even my sister laughed dutifully. My parents' and my sister's green tassels swayed, the tassels we had to wear to mark us as Bamarre.

"Do you think her hair will stay that color?"

My hair was and is a shade between auburn and black, although my parents had locks the dark brown of damp earth, and my sister's hair is the tan of old parchment. The three of them had curls, but my hair has always been as straight as silk thread.

My father squinted. "The red may fade."

"Have you more children?"

"Only Annet." My mother pointed her chin at my sister, who was nine years old, small for her age, and painfully thin.

"How unfortunate no other relative was here to warn the goodman against foolhardiness." Lady Klausine fell silent.

Years later, I speculated about this quiet moment. Did she decide then, or earlier, as soon as my father stammered out his reason for stealing from her garden?

Would she have wanted any child? Or did my small fingers wrap themselves around her longing? Perhaps my curling eyelashes fanned her desire.

Or did my hair, as straight as hers, and the firm set of

my mouth suggest a resemblance between us? Practical considerations always weighed heavily with her.

She ended the silence. "Soon you and your goodwife will leave town. I'll find a place for the two of you, but your daughters I will keep. The elder will—"

"My baby!" my mother cried.

My father pressed his body between Lady Klausine and my bed, but the guard tugged him away and held him.

My mother wailed and called vainly for a fairy to come to our aid. My sister clung to her mama.

I rolled over and burrowed deeper into my dreams. Finally, my mother ceased screaming and my father stopped struggling. They couldn't have succeeded in keeping us. Power was all with the Lakti.

Lady Klausine continued. "I suppose the sister is not given to peregrinating?"

My father shook his head. Annet was as steady as a good donkey.

"She will be her sister's nursemaid. Hers will be a better life than you could have reasonably expected."

No one answered. Lady Klausine couldn't guess what a Bamarre father wishes for his child.

She lifted me out of my bed. "Good night, Goodman, Goodwife. Rejoice that it did not go worse for you. Come, Annet."

My sister balked.

"Move, girl." The guard took her elbow.

She shook him off. Our mother whispered into her hair, "Please care for Perry as I would."

She didn't say, Love Perry as I would. Perhaps she knew not to demand the impossible.

Lady Klausine carried me through the iron gate, which my father had climbed to commit his crime, down the torch-lit cobbled garden path, through a long castle corridor, to the empty nursery. I didn't waken. Despite the purloined fruit I'd been fed, I was a scrawny thing and mustn't have been heavy—but had I weighed as much as a young ox, Lady Klausine would have managed. The Lakti, as I learned again and again, were strong and resolute.

Annet followed with the guard and the maid. In the nursery, Lady Klausine lowered me into a gilded crib that had been kept ready for fifteen years. Its linen sheets were fine and clean, but the mattress was as thin as my old one had been and the blanket no warmer. Lakti children enjoyed the trappings of wealth but not the comforts.

I didn't whimper, merely continued my sleep.

Lady Klausine smiled her serious smile. "Peregrine is a Lakti in nature if not birth." She dismissed her guard and, in a low voice, gave instructions to her maid, who left also. When both were gone, she bade Annet attend her at the window alcove.

"If she isn't supplanted by children of my body"—

Lady Klausine still harbored hope—"and if she proves herself worthy, your sister will be our heir. If you prove worthy, too, you will stay at her side after she no longer needs a nursemaid. You'll be as safe and secure as a Bamarre may be."

Either the light was too low for Lady Klausine to make out Annet's expression or my sister hadn't yet perfected her sneer.

"You must never tell Peregrine or anyone else she was born a Bamarre. Never, or you both will suffer. Be kind, but do not coddle her."

The maid returned with a bundle. Lady Klausine herself replaced my threadbare diaper with new cloth, slipped a linen baby gown on me, and exchanged my cap with its green tassel for a bonnet. She must have been gentle, because, half-awake, I accepted her hands without complaint.

She straightened. "I've posted guards at the door and window. I expect my daughter to be well in the morning and you in attendance." She swept out, followed by the maid.

My sister stood over my crib. She must have hated me. Our father wouldn't have stolen from the castle garden if not for me. An older child can go without, but a baby has to eat.

Annet would soon find mothering and fathering

among the castle servants, most of whom were Bamarre. That night, however, she had no comfort. I imagine she wept, and her tears woke me and started me wailing. When she finally picked me up, I doubt I got much solace from her arms.

CHAPTER TWO

ANNET KEPT LADY Klausine's secret. I remained igno-
rant of my origins.

I had no recollection of being told I was adopted, but
I always knew I had been. This is the earliest story told of
me by Lady Mother, as she preferred to be called: "We'd
had you only a month. You were a determined walker for
one so young. . . ."

She recounted the saga so often—to spur me on, to
explain my successes, to induce guilt when I failed—that
I came to feel I remembered it.

I was fourteen months old. Lord Tove—(not *Lord
Father*)—had been waiting on the king ever since the
border war had stopped for winter. When he was free to
travel, Father came home, and of course I had to meet

him. Lady Mother—tall, stately, unbending—flanked me on my left. On my right, tassel swaying from her cap, trudged my nursemaid—sullen, with a frown line already forming. (My imagination supplied the details about Annet.) I trundled along, once almost slipping on the rushes scattered across the floorboards but catching myself, an important moment in Lady Mother's recital. As I careened with my baby gait, she murmured, "Prodigious. She will be a credit to us."

The distance was a quarter mile. I accomplished it without falling. If I had fallen, I sometimes wondered, would she have found another child to adopt?

The cold stone walls of the corridor were hung with linen, embroidered by Bamarre artisans, that depicted Lakti warriors in pitched battle. Slitted windows near the ceiling let in light enough. Lady Mother wouldn't allow lamps to be lit during the day.

Enthusiasm carried me across the threshold of the study, where Father looked up from his account book to watch. Now that I had a clear destination, this handsome, smiling man, I held out my arms and toddled on. But halfway to him, I came down on my bottom.

He laughed at my astonished face.

After a moment, Lady Mother laughed too.

I struggled to stand, accomplished the feat, and completed my journey.

Lord Tove set me on his lap facing him, where I believe I felt instantly at ease. I expect he spoke baby talk to me, because I later saw him hold lengthy nonsense conversations with other castle babies. He probably let me explore his short brown beard, pull his long nose, and touch his silver brooch, which was stamped with the face of a snarling wolf.

The image didn't trouble me, another happy sign to Lady Mother.

Father, who had no idea I'd been born a Bamarre, didn't test me at every turn. He was pleased with me and with almost whatever I did. If he had been present more often, my childhood would have been happier.

He was a nephew of our king Uriel—a son, a daughter, and an older nephew removed from the throne. Father commanded the Lakti forces against our enemy, the Kyngoll. We wanted their silver mines, but we would take their entire kingdom if we could. The Lakti were always bent on conquest.

Lady Mother's version of my parentage presented me as the daughter of a knight, who, along with his wife, had died in an outbreak of the pox. Their relatives considered me unlucky and wouldn't keep me. Lady Mother's maid heard of my plight from a cousin, a laundress. Out of respect for the grieving family, Lady Mother told one and all, she kept the identity of my birth family to herself.

According to this account, Annet had been a servant in my parents' manor. Though I could hardly believe it, I was told I'd been very attached to her and had wailed when Lady Mother tried to separate us.

Often, when I disappointed Lady Mother, I pictured my dead parents. Such kind faces they had, with deep smile lines, sympathetic eyes, soft features. When Lady Mother scolded or, worse, fell silent, I called them up in my mind and wished they had lived.

Annet was an occasional comfort, though she didn't mean to be. Lady Mother's reasons for disapproving of me meant nothing to her, which gave me a fresh way to think about whatever I'd done.

At night, Annet recited poetry, which I loved. If she'd known I was awake, she probably would have been silent. My memory, especially for poems, was excellent. One poem seemed to be a favorite. She'd sit in the window alcove and say it in a voice that surprised me with its sweetness.

> *A pewter moon glints on statues*
> *Of tasseled laborers guarding*
> *A garden where only owls are free.*

When I was six, my education began in earnest—tutors for two hours, the rest of the day devoted to physical education. A Lakti child might be slow with figures, might blink and think before penning a paragraph, but she mustn't falter at her games of war.

Of course I excelled at footraces. Older runners, taller runners, more experienced runners—none could catch me. Lady Mother gloried in my every victory. She said little, merely favored me with a nod when I looked for her approval, which I always did. A nod from her equaled an embrace and a garland of laurels from anyone else.

> *Lady Mother nods. At night*
> *I dream the nod and race again.*

Whenever he saw me race, Father waved his arms and shouted and laughed as I surged toward the finish line. My happiness at his pleasure surpassed even my joy at winning.

I lost only once. It happened in my first year of training.

Mistress Clarra, our instructor, a small, energetic woman, conducted monthly tournaments and matched each of us according to a system of her own. On this occasion my opponent was Varma, three years older than I but just two years stronger and one year taller. I was confident I could best her.

According to Lakti rules, one contender chose the

kind of contest and the other selected the place.

A coin toss gave me first pick. "A race."

Varma smiled smugly. "We'll run through town, from north gate to south, Beef Road to Barrel to Longwall and out."

I'd never been through town! Lady Mother didn't let me go alone and Annet had never taken me. I'd have to stop for directions. I had lost before I began.

Mistress Clarra drove home the lesson by saying, "A Lakti warrior anticipates."

I turned to Lady Mother, bracing myself for her rebuke.

But she merely presented another lesson. "Varma knew you'd call a race," she said. "A Lakti warrior should be unpredictable."

I would remember.

With application, I did well in all the outdoor skills. In swordplay I loved to dance forward, glide back, feint, thrust—always in motion.

Even skill with the rope snare came when I was hardly big enough to toss the noose over my opponent's head. At archery, my aim was true—though I wished I could be the arrow, flying to the target.

Mistress Clarra's other charges were the children of knights under Father's command. Once a tournament began, I cared about none of them, but when we trained I wanted their friendship, and after I defeated them, I wanted—ridiculously, unrealistically—their congratulations. If I'd known how to joke or even how to be friendly, they might not have minded me, but I was awkward and blundering.

Those old enough to see ahead to when I might succeed Father were pleasant. The younger ones, however, blurted out their feelings. They hated me.

When we weren't competing or practicing, Mistress Clarra encouraged games to build our skills and foster the cooperation we'd need on the battlefield. One game, Lord's Captive, gave the children their revenge.

We were divided into a guard team and a rescuer team. The rescuer team picked their It, who would be imprisoned within a circle of guards. A freedom pennant—a blue rose on a green field—would be planted thirty yards from the jail. The rescuers' objective was to free It, and the guards' task was to contain It and take more prisoners by tagging them. The special objective of the It was to reach the pennant without being tagged.

The first time a team picked me, I was chosen because I could outrun everyone. The rescuers expected to win the round.

As soon as the circle of guards closed around me, my temples began to throb. My chest felt as if a giant hand were squeezing it. I couldn't see through the haze across my eyes.

Before a minute passed, I burst through the circle, tagging myself by touching guards and causing my team to lose.

From then on, I was made to be It whenever someone was angry enough at me to sacrifice a round.

Mistress Clarra never saved me. "This is weakness, Peregrine," she said. "Conquer it."

I tried. I wanted to stop suffering, but my peregrinating nature couldn't tolerate imprisonment.

CHAPTER THREE

ONE CHILD DID befriend me—my cousin Willem, Lady Mother's nephew. He and his parents lived with us for much of the year, though they had their own home south of our castle, a manor house in the middle of New Lakti. His father, Sir Noll, was Lady Mother's brother-in-law and Father's lieutenant, his second in battle.

I couldn't remember a time without Willem. He dined with us, sitting halfway down the long feast table. Before I was old enough to participate, I watched him and the other children train. I noticed him in particular because he waved to me. Wherever he was, at whatever distance, if he saw me, he waved.

He didn't need my friendship. All the children liked him.

I continued to watch him, even after I could join in. When I reached a race goal, he was the one I turned to see.

He always finished in the middle, never right behind me. Full of goodwill, I studied his running. His light build should have given him an advantage, but his method had flaws, and I wanted to tell him about them. At least I knew better than to give him advice in front of everyone.

A month passed before I found the chance to speak with him privately, when Mistress Clarra set up an archery target in a meadow beyond the outer castle curtain. A stiff wind was blowing, and everyone's arrows flew wildly.

Willem shot first, I fourth. With luck (and skill) my arrows fell, as his had, in a stand of pine trees. When Mistress Clarra sent us all to gather them, naturally I went with him. I was eight years old and he ten.

He spoke first. "The wind has made neighbors of our arrows, Perry." His black hair whipped about his face.

Feeling shy, I nodded.

He went on, "If this were a real battle, the wind would have to blow our enemies, too, so they'd be where our arrows could strike them."

It took me a moment to understand. Then I had to laugh, which made me feel more at ease. "They'd look funny, being blown in full armor." Working in the subject of speed, I added, "Your arrows were as fast as mine."

"Unlike my legs." He sounded regretful.

We reached the trees.

In a burst, I said, "You could run faster. I can tell you how."

"Really?" He crouched to pick up an arrow. "Yours."

Mine were fletched with peacock feathers, everyone else's with goose.

He handed me the arrow without looking at me.

I forged ahead. "You twist when you run."

"I'll try not to, Lady." He handed up another arrow.

No one called me *Lady*. I wouldn't be a lady for years. I thought something had gone wrong but didn't know what. "Here's one of yours." I picked it up.

"Don't trouble yourself, Lady."

"All right." I found one of my own arrows and plunged on. "It's because your arms almost—"

"I think Mistress Clarra is the one to tell us what—"

I almost shouted. "But I run faster than she does!" In exasperation, I added, "And her legs are longer!"

Finally he looked at me. His dark face had flushed even darker, but after a few seconds his frown smoothed and he laughed. He had a lopsided, likable mouth. "Perry . . . Cousin . . . you can teach me how to run better if I can teach you how to talk to people better."

I'd never thought about it that way, but that was exactly what I wanted to learn. "Yes. Yes! I wish I could be like you."

He stared at me. I thought he was pleased, but I wasn't sure.

He bowed, and I was sure.

"You first," he said. "Show me what you mean."

I bent my arms at the elbow and closed my hands into loose fists.

"I do that," he said, frowning again.

"But you don't keep your arms at your sides. Your hands almost touch. They make you twist and slow you down. You should lift your knees higher, too."

He nodded. "I see. I'll pay attention next time."

"My turn." I gave him one of his arrows to see if he'd take it—to make sure he'd forgiven me.

He accepted it. "You shouldn't criticize people unless you're sure they want to listen."

But I just wanted to help. "I—"

"Not even if you don't mean to hurt their feelings."

Oh.

"What else?"

He started to answer, but then his eyes shifted to a point above my shoulder.

Mistress Clarra arrived to order us to rejoin the others.

Willem was a faster runner after our conversation and often ended a race right behind me. I learned only the lesson about giving criticism—which was helpful more than once. We both tried to speak alone together again, but Lady Mother kept me apart from the other children, and Mistress Clarra allowed us no free time. Willem and I exchanged yearning looks. I could have helped him with his fencing, too, and I was sure he could make me the girl I wanted to be—liked and admired by all.

> *True friends, Lakti to Lakti,*
> *Kept apart but never forsaking,*
> *Willem and Perry, Perry and Willem.*

I loved linking our names.

Six months after our friendship began, Willem had to leave dinner with a stomachache. I turned to watch him run from the great hall, knees high, arms held tight to his sides, a performance I was sure was for my benefit, and I grinned.

But his stomachache turned out to be the first sign of the pox. The next morning, his parents took him to their home in hopes that others might be spared infection.

I was beside myself with fright. Would the pox steal my friend as it had robbed me of my parents? I plagued both Lady Mother and Annet with questions. Would he recover? Could our physician be sent to treat him? Did it hurt to have the pox? Why did he have to catch it? Might a messenger be sent to find out how he was faring?

Lady Mother answered each question once and without softening. In life there was no certainty; the pox killed many but not all. Our physician would stay with us in case any of us fell ill, too. Willem's head might ache, and his muscles would be sore, nothing a Lakti couldn't bear. A messenger would not be dispatched for such a trivial reason. As for why he'd caught the pox, such foolishness didn't deserve an answer.

That night, I couldn't sleep. A half hour after Annet blew out the candle next to my bed, I sat up.

"Annet?" She slept on a pallet next to my bed.

Moonlight streamed in through the casement window. I saw her raise herself on one elbow.

"Do the fairies cure Bamarre children who get the pox?" Fairies occasionally visited the Bamarre, never the Lakti.

"No."

"Why did he get it and I didn't?"

"You still may." Pause. "I may, too."

I hadn't thought of that. "Oh."

If Willem had given me more instruction, I would have known to tell Annet I hoped she didn't get sick. I did hope that, but I didn't think to say so.

She added, "Would Lady Klausine's physician treat me if I got sick?"

"A Bamarre physician would treat you."

"We don't have physicians." She might have added that the Bamarre had healers, who were sometimes better, sometimes not.

I said, "I'd tell our physician to take care of you," though I doubted he would.

"Don't worry. The pox kills or it doesn't." She seemed determined to give me no comfort. "Nostrums never cured anyone. Go to sleep."

"I can't!"

"Then don't."

CHAPTER FOUR

ALTHOUGH NO ONE else in our household fell ill, the pox struck the king's castle. His Highness himself caught the disease and recovered, but both his children died. Father's cousin Canute became crown prince, and Father moved up in line to the throne. If anything befell King Uriel and Canute, Father would rule.

Distant tidings to me, although I heard Lady Mother and Father discuss the change.

The three of us were striding in the snow-dusted outer ward, a mile's march that Lady Mother called health-giving and Father called bone-chilling. I loved the movement and relished having them to myself. And their company helped me stave off worries about Willem.

"Long life to Uriel," Lady Mother said. "Canute isn't

fit to rule." Even I had heard that the crown prince was weak-minded.

"He means well, darling. Uriel has a soft spot for the Bamarre. Canute would be firmer."

"You mean, *you* would be firmer." She favored him with a sweeter smile than she usually bestowed on me. "Canute dotes on you."

"Nonsense." But Father sounded pleased. "Perry, I want you to be there for the audience with Einar next week. Klausine, she'll see what we put up with, and she can entertain Dahn."

Einar, who was king of the Bamarre, had a son, Prince Dahn, the same age as Willem. I'd never entertained anyone, and I doubted I could. Still, I was delighted to be part of Father's plans. "I'll do my best."

"You're a credit to us both." He squeezed my shoulder through my thin cloak, and happiness warmed me.

Lady Mother said, "You must be polite and gracious, Perry." The castle's stone battlements seemed to echo her words.

Though the Bamarre had their own king, they had to obey Lakti law, and our king ruled them in everything important. I understood King Einar to have a pretend title.

He lived in a house only a league from our castle and ran his enterprise from there, sending Bamarre-made shoes across New Lakti in the eight carts he owned. The task of meeting with him generally fell to Father. Every year, as well as when edicts were issued, he called King Einar in for an audience.

The week passed. No word about Willem. I ate little for worrying until Lady Mother noticed. If I put down my spoon, she said, "Eat, Perry," and I obeyed without enjoyment.

The evening of the audience came. Father gestured to the guard—a Lakti, as all guards were—to admit King Einar and his son to our great hall. When the royals entered through the distant double doors, I glanced at Father. His expression smoothed, as if he had put on a bland mask, and his smile held no warmth, a smile that made me uneasy.

The king, who was a decade younger than Father, looked regal in his gray wool cloak, sewn by a Bamarre tailor to fall in soft folds and to show off the width of the royal shoulders rather than the slightness of the royal frame. The faces of both father and son had an indoor pallor. Lady Mother, Father, and I wore no cloaks in the castle. We Lakti could withstand cold.

King Einar merely nodded and didn't return Father's smile, as if this meeting were a favor he had granted.

Prince Dahn possessed a small round nose, big gray eyes enlarged by spectacles, and thick lips, which, after he annoyed me, I decided were blubbery.

The two mounted the dais and halted a few feet from the row of chairs where the three of us sat. After a pause long enough for me to count to ten slowly (an insult of a pause), both bowed.

Father and Lady Mother rose instantly. I followed their lead. We bowed or curtsied without hesitation.

"Soon, across the Eskerns," King Einar said. Another insult, as even I was old enough to realize. He'd spoken the traditional greeting from one Bamarre to another, but we were Lakti and wouldn't allow the Bamarre to cross the mountains and leave New Lakti.

Father's eyes hardened. "Lady Peregrine will entertain the prince."

"Follow me." I led him behind a screen that had been placed to hide the servants' corner, where trestle tables, benches, and sleeping pallets were stacked. I'd had the servants set up two chairs and a low table, which held a yellow ball, a set of knucklebones, and a game of Nine Men's Morris—items to help me be polite and gracious. "Do you like to play these, Prince Dahn?"

"No, begging your pardon."

The Bamarre—excepting Annet—were always begging people's pardon or saying other polite phrases the Lakti hadn't time for.

"What games do you play? Can you teach me one?"

He shrugged. "No, begging your pardon."

"I'll teach you mine."

"Excuse me. We Bamarre don't play Lakti games."

"What do you play?"

"If you please, we play Bamarre games."

"Teach me one."

"No, begging your pardon. You're a Lakti."

I thought, He's only a Bamarre. He probably doesn't know he's rude. "Do you like to race?"

"Never!" His green tassel flew to mark his vehemence. "Begging—"

I thought of making him eat the tassel. "What do you do all day?"

"I write down the accounts for Father, and I read."

During the rest of our half hour together, ungracious or not, I occupied myself by playing knucklebones against myself and hated the prince for making me fail my parents. When the audience with Father ended, we were called out to share refreshments, which included delicacies rarely served even at a Lakti feast: dates, figs, almond-paste candies, and preserved cherries in ginger and honey.

After the Bamarre royals left, Father wiped down the front of his tunic. "Sweetheart, I had better bathe. I start to itch when Einar's here, as if his Bamarre bugs jumped from him to me."

There were Bamarre bugs? In addition to the lice and fleas that plagued everyone? I scratched my chin. "Can I get Bamarre bugs from Annet?"

"They aren't real insects," Lady Mother said, glancing sharply at Father.

Father put his arm around me. "On our Bamarre servants, the bugs stay where they belong."

I understood that a Bamarre king discomfited Father, while Bamarre servants didn't.

Out of shame for my performance, I tried to forget the audience. What I never thought about, because I'd seen it hundreds of times, was the embroidery on the screen the prince and I had sat behind, which depicted the last free Bamarre king kneeling to a victorious Lakti ruler.

My first news of Willem came two weeks later—from Annet, who was brushing my hair, always a mass of tangles in the morning.

"Ouch!"

"Your friend is better."

I twisted around, which hurt even more. "He is?" Why hadn't Lady Mother told me? "Ouch! Really?"

"Am I a liar?"

"Oh!" I had been taught not to be affectionate or effusive, but I hugged her awkwardly around her chest and an elbow.

She grunted and wielded the comb again.

Willem alive and getting better, when I feared that he'd died!

"How do you know?" I watched her in my vanity mirror.

"A messenger told me."

Most messengers were Bamarre. This one had carried a letter to Sir Noll, Willem's father, and had returned with word that Willem was recovering and Sir Noll would arrive in a day or two to plan the spring campaign against the Kyngoll.

Alas, the pox had departed with much of Willem's hearing. When he returned to the castle a month later, he was a changed boy. He no longer waved to me, though I waved to him. I continued to try, with even greater desperation than before, to get close to him. If he had been entirely deaf—and blind, too—I wouldn't have liked him less. I imagined him legless as well and I his only friend. I didn't wish disaster on him, but I longed to prove my faithfulness.

He kept his distance.

I received no nods from Lady Mother for my performance as a scholar. I could barely sit still long enough to learn anything, even in the subjects I liked, which were just geography and Lakti history (mostly battles). My lessons were held in the upper chamber of the castle's southeast tower, where the windows beckoned and the walls tormented.

Lady Mother herself, rather than a tutor, attempted to teach me oratory, at which the Lakti nobility were expected to excel.

At these lessons, I perched on a high stool, separated by a table from Lady Mother, whose eyebrows arched, giving her a surprised look—rarely a happy surprise during our lessons. Soft cheeks and not much of a chin belied the grim set of her mouth. Her nose, her best feature, was short and straight; the nostrils flared when she was gripped by feeling.

My worst performance came on a day when I was nine years old. Annet sat in the west window seat and stitched tulips on linen that would become a wall hanging. Father wasn't home, but he would have stayed away in any case— he hung back in domestic difficulties.

I had been swallowing tears since we climbed the stairs. I didn't let them fall, but they thickened my voice and made my task even harder.

"Begin, Peregrine." Ordinarily, Lady Mother called me Perry; during lessons, I was always Peregrine.

The night before, supervised by Annet, I had copied out three paragraphs that Lady Mother had chosen. Strangely, they concerned a scourge of boils on the elbows of Lakti men two hundred years ago.

Now I had to declaim what I had copied. Since I wasn't a strong reader yet, to shout words that I could barely sound out—to do so in this confining tower with Lady Mother glowering—was beyond me.

I swallowed. "A plague of—"

"Louder, Peregrine." Lady Mother's voice was patiently pained.

I eked out a little more volume. ". . . plague of fur-furun-furunsells—"

"Fur*uncle*s, Peregrine. 'Uncle' like your uncle Aleks." Father's younger brother. "Still louder."

". . . fur-furuncles reflects not on—"

Lady Mother stood and paced, nostrils flaring.

I tried a diversion. Sometimes this succeeded. "Did the speech make people feel better?"

"Orate!"

". . . not on Lakti character, but tests . . ." I looked up.

Lady Mother loomed over me across the table.

I knew what would come next. She'd declare her disappointment. I'd disappointed her twice this week already. Another time was more than I could bear.

I bolted, pelted down the tower stairs, and raced across the inner ward. A stableman caught my arm, but I squirmed free. Elation replaced dread. No one could catch me.

In five minutes I had crossed the drawbridge. On the other side of the road, I entered a small wood, where I climbed a low-branching oak tree. Thoughts of escape—stealing a horse, or running until my legs gave out—kept me company, but in truth, I was waiting to be found. My exhilaration drained away.

A guard returned me to the tower, where Lady Mother delivered three sharp strikes to my knuckles with her sheathed knife.

The thought I had nurtured while I was being brought back erupted. "If I were a Bamarre, you wouldn't treat me this way." The Bamarre didn't have to declaim, and I'd never seen Lady Mother strike a servant—though other Lakti did.

Annet hissed, a quiet sound that seemed to slither around the tower.

Lady Mother lifted me by my shoulders and shook me.

Still defiant, my voice rattling from the vehemence of her shaking, I blurted out, "I wish I were a Bamarre."

Annet gave a strangled laugh.

Lady Mother's expression settled to stone. Through lips that barely moved, she said, "If you were a flea, you would disgrace your fellow fleas." She dropped me.

I landed hard and lost my balance and could no longer hold back my tears. From the floor, I bawled.

Lady Mother and Annet left. I heard a bolt driven home. I hurled myself against the door, willing to say anything to be freed. "I'm sorry! I didn't mean it. Please let me go. Please! Let me go. I don't want to be a Bamarre. Let me go. Let me go. Let me go."

CHAPTER FIVE

I FAINTED. When I awoke, I was still alone. I rammed my shoulder against the door. Again. Again.

Didn't Lady Mother know how I was suffering?

If only I didn't mind being in a small space. If only I could be calm. If only I could stop throwing myself against the door.

Didn't anyone love me enough to rescue me?

An hour later, Lady Mother found me, exhausted, pacing the periphery of the chamber. Blood stained both shoulders of my kirtle, and my forehead was sorely scraped. I would bear bruises for weeks.

I hugged her, as I couldn't remember doing before, and sobbed. "I'm sorry!"

She held me, which I also couldn't remember ever

happening. "Never mind. Your oratory will improve." After a minute she let me go and left the chamber.

My heart rose to my throat, but she didn't close the door behind her.

I didn't dare dash away again, so I waited a few dutiful minutes to see if Annet would come and considered where I might go if I were really on my own.

I knelt on the window seat to look outside. The castle dominated the tallest hill in the region, and the tower room rose high enough for me to see beyond the inner and outer ward walls. The town crowned the next hill.

In eastern Lakti the terrain was flat and grassy; in the west, where Father fought, flat and stony. The Eskern Mountains in the south diminished to high hills in the center of the kingdom and gentled further in our northland.

A blue sky turned the moat water into a pretty ribbon. Tiny April leaves dotted the bushes beyond the castle. The gray stone walls and rust-red slate roofs of the town guildhalls enticed me, as distant objects always did.

Closing my eyes, I leaned my forehead against the mullioned glass and wished for Lady Mother to approve of me no matter what I did and for me to want to do nothing but what she would approve of.

I caught a whiff of peonies, which wouldn't bloom for months. Behind me, I heard crackling, as if fat had been thrown on a fire—but the fireplace was empty. We Lakti lit no home fires after winter ended.

I jumped off the window seat. A twirl of rainbow-colored light sparkled from the floor to the ceiling, between me and the table. I pressed back against the window and shaded my eyes. My heart pounded in my ears. A fairy? Or something else?

Couldn't be a fairy.

Within the swirl I saw a figure, shaped like a person, the size of a grown-up.

The light faded around the figure, and there she was, even taller than Lady Mother, very slender, with white hair caught up in a silver net and the papery skin of the old. Her face calmed me. Maybe it was the smile lines around her mouth, although she wasn't smiling. She just watched me, appraising me, as Lady Mother did, her copper-brown eyes intent.

I gathered my courage. "Are you a fairy, or something terrible?" Perhaps a monster from Old Lakti, where we Lakti had lived before the creatures appeared there.

"I am the fairy Halina." Her ringing voice echoed off the stones. *Lina lina lina.*

"But fairies don't appear to the Lakti." They'd stopped when we conquered the Bamarre, who had taken us in after we'd fled our kingdom.

"This fairy is appearing to you."

"Why?"

Now she did smile. "Do *you* always have a reason for speaking?"

My bones thrummed with excitement. I grinned. A fairy!

Her smile widened.

I remembered she'd asked a question. I nodded. "But I don't always have anything to say." Sometimes I just told Father—not Lady Mother—whatever came into my mind. I had a reason, though: because he listened and thought about every word.

"This fairy has a reason today." She bent down so her face was inches from mine, and I noticed her long gray eyelashes. "It is to warn you against wishing to change yourself from what you most are, a person who despises a cage."

I found myself arguing. With a fairy! "It would be easier if I felt cozy in a cage."

She straightened again. "Nonetheless, that is your nature."

"If I have to stay the same, can you cast a spell and make Lady Mother always think well of me?"

She raised a hand, palm up. "Even fairies bungle that sort of thing . . . and no one else can do it in the slightest."

Too bad. A polite child, I said, "It's nice to meet you anyway." I added, "Can you hear my thoughts?" I formed a clear one, the wish to be able to turn into a blur of light, too.

"This fairy can hear—so long as I'm listening." She frowned. "Only *we* are creatures of light."

Had I offended her? "Sorry!" Might she turn me into a toad? "Did you make yourself look the way you do to talk to me?"

"I did."

"Do you often listen to my thoughts?" What had she heard?

"This fairy has other matters to attend to."

Whew!

"I know when to listen."

When? Which thoughts would catch her attention?

She went on. "For the most part, your thoughts are your own. You enjoy poetry, don't you?"

I hesitated. I'd learned that most of the Bamarre loved poems and most of the Lakti sneered at them. "Yes."

She placed her hand on my head, her touch so light I barely felt it through my blanket of hair. "Good. Fairies love poetry."

"Is that why you visited me?"

"It's one reason. And to tell you that you are marvelous as you are."

Not even Father had ever called me *marvelous*. I bounced on my toes in excitement. A fairy approved of me, even though I couldn't orate, even though I didn't always measure up.

She began to shimmer and glow again, but her voice remained round and ringing. "Look at the south wall."

The wall hanging vanished, and the stones behind it lit up as if the sun were shining on them. A mountain-scape appeared. I saw snowy summits above forested slopes. The air smelled fresh and sharp. My hair streamed behind me in a blowing wind, as if I stood on a summit, too. A bird, black against the bright sky, rose from behind a peak.

Not a bird! A dragon, belching fire!

CHAPTER SIX

AFTER A MOMENT, the dragon dived below the ridge, and the scene faded. I turned. Halina had disappeared.

Breathing hard, I sat in the window seat. The mountains must have been the Eskerns, which were in the south, dividing New Lakti, where we lived now, from Old Lakti, our former home. The dragon must have been one of the monsters in Old Lakti, where ogres, gryphons, and specters also lived. Were they coming here?

"Halina, come back!" I squeezed my eyes shut and thought, shouting in my mind, Tell me what this means! Why did you show it to me?

I opened my eyes. Dust motes slanted in from the windows. A crow cawed outside. Had I just imagined the fairy?

My back heated. I whipped around. The wall went bright again, then darkened. Clearly, in my mind, I heard her voice. *The monsters can't leave Old Lakti. Fairies made sure of that.*

Good. But why did she show me that scene? I decided that fairies were mysterious.

I looked down at myself to see if her touch had changed me. Nothing I could see. I considered my interior self, and decided my insides were the same as ever, too.

If the fairy thought well of me, she thought well of my peregrinating, so I left the chamber, intending to go to town, but there was Annet, who'd been sent to fetch me to supper. On the way to the great hall, I imagined telling Lady Mother about Halina. I would have done so if she'd asked me a single question. However, she didn't, and I had been taught to stay silent in the hall unless speech was requested.

She always came to me in the evening, my favorite time of day with her, because she was more at ease then. She'd tell me tales of Old Lakti or we'd play Nine Men's Morris.

That night it was to be Nine Men's Morris. When she came in, Annet opened the chest next to my bed, which held the game board and the black or gray stone "men."

"Lady Mother?" I hoped she'd believe me. "After you left me in the tower the second time, when you let the door stay open . . ."

"Yes?"

". . . a fairy appeared."

The lid of the chest clattered to the floor. Annet wasn't usually clumsy.

"Her name is Halina. She was a whirl of light until she took a human shape and looked like an old lady." I peeked at Lady Mother, and then stared.

She sat heavily on my bed, clasping her hands, knuckles jutting white. Her nose reddened, nostrils flaring. If she were anyone else, I would have thought she was about to cry.

For the second time that day, I hugged her. "Can't it be good? That the fairies visited a Lakti?"

She cupped my face in her hands. "You must never tell anyone you saw a fairy. If one comes to you again, let me know—me, and no one else." She released me, and I sat next to her on the bed. "Do you understand, Perry?"

I nodded. "Why can't I tell?"

"Because I am your mother."

I'd heard other castle parents say just these words to their children, but Lady Mother had never said them to me. I treasured the phrase, as if I were the child of Lady Mother's body.

I ventured another question. "Why are you sad?"

"Why would I be sad? What did the fairy say?"

"Can I tell?" Meaning that Annet would hear.

"Go ahead."

I told everything and finished with the mountain scene on the wall. "Then she vanished. When I thought I might have imagined her, the wall lit up again, not with mountains or monsters, just light."

Annet put the Nine Men's Morris game on the bed next to us.

"We won't play. Tonight I'll brush your hair, Perry."

Astonished, I sat at my vanity table. Lady Mother took up the brush. How gentle she was! She worked patiently at my tangles without pulling. Neither of us spoke, and Annet, who had to ask permission to address Lady Mother, was silent too. In the mirror, I saw the sadness fade from Lady Mother's face, replaced by a look of peace.

Later that night, Annet sat on the edge of my bed. I slid away uneasily.

But she smiled. Ordinarily, her smile was stiff, displayed only when called for. Tonight I saw humor in it and—could it be?—affection.

Not trusting her, I didn't smile back.

She stroked a handful of hair off my forehead. Then, to my amazement, she pushed her green tassel aside and kissed the scabs on my forehead.

"Because a fairy visited me?"

"It's a wonderful thing."

"Has one ever appeared to you?"

"No."

"Not yet." She was a Bamarre, so a fairy could visit her anytime. What was strange was that Halina had picked me.

"They don't come to many of us."

I understood this the only way I could. Fairies visited few of *them*—the Bamarre.

"And hardly ever come. I don't know if there's been a visitation in a hundred years."

"Why do you think Lady Mother said I can't tell anyone?"

"Lady Klausine doesn't confide in me."

True. "Why else did you kiss me?"

She didn't answer.

"Because I said I wanted to be a Bamarre?"

"No." Pause. "Maybe. It's good if you notice the differences between being a Lakti and being a Bamarre— if you notice in your own way. And I liked the vision the fairy showed you."

I quoted the Bamarre greeting: "Soon, across the Eskerns."

"Yes."

"Why do people say that?" I was enjoying this rare openness between us.

She took a long breath. "The saying means we want to live in Old Lakti."

"With monsters?" But the Bamarre were weak! And cowardly. After only a few battles, we'd wrested the kingdom from them, and they'd rebelled just once, more than a century ago.

She shrugged. "Free. It's just a saying."

I'd be free when I grew up, but Annet would still have to be a servant.

"Do you remember your history and ours?" she asked.

"I do." We'd left Old Lakti when the monsters arrived out of nothing. We'd crossed the Eskern Pass. The monsters hadn't pursued us, had seemed unable to, and the Bamarre had taken us in. "It's our nature to conquer," I said, as I'd been taught.

"Was letting the Lakti in weakness or kindness on our part? We could easily have kept them out."

The pass was narrow. They certainly could have turned my ancestors away. I'd also been taught that the Bamarre had been weak to give us a safe haven. They'd known we were warriors.

But they may have been both weak and kind. "Maybe they thought it would be their fault if everyone died."

"Exactly." The tartness returned to her voice. "Which may be why fairies don't visit the Lakti. Fairies prefer kindness to cruelty." She went to the small table where she often used my ink and my quill to write I didn't know what.

Tonight I was curious. "What are you writing?"

"A letter to our—my parents."

"Our?"

She was silent a moment. "I meant *my*."

"Where do they live?"

"In Gavrel."

I knew my geography. Gavrel was a village in the east.

"Go to sleep."

I didn't speak to anyone about Halina, but I thought about her often. Would she visit me again? When? Most of all, why had she picked me?

For a week I was spared further declaiming lessons, almost long enough to persuade me that bolting had been a good idea. But instruction resumed, although Lady Mother moved my lessons in every subject, not merely oration, from the tower to the library, a bright room with tall windows that looked out on the castle's inner courtyard. When Annet and I arrived there, Willem sat at a table, next to Lady Mother.

I smiled so widely my cheeks hurt. "Willem!"

He nodded at me. I dimmed my smile because he looked sad. I wondered if he could hear well enough to have heard his name.

My smile expanded again. I couldn't help it.

Lady Mother gestured for me to sit across from them and slid the boils speech to me. "Speak, Peregrine, loud enough for Willem to hear." To him, she shouted, "Raise your hand when you can hear. Can you hear me?"

He raised his hand.

Oh. I was supposed to satisfy Lady Mother and make Willem hear, and if I failed, I'd have failed them both.

In an ordinary voice, she said, "Begin."

I wished I had something more delightful to read. In a louder voice than I'd achieved the last time—because this was for Willem—I said, "A plague . . ."

His hand stayed down.

I tried again. "A plague of . . ."

His hand remained where it was.

I roared, "A plague of furuncles spread . . ."

His hand shot up. I feared that the boils might remind him of the bumps people got when they had the pox, but his expression brightened.

I continued to boom. ". . . across the male population of New Lakti, a dreadful scourge, affecting the elbow. No one"—it dawned on me that boils might be the subject Willem would enjoy most—"was spared. King Skurd contracted . . ."

Lady Mother leaned back in her chair and nodded.

I went on, now wishing that the details about the boils were bloodier, more pus-filled, but those details there were I emphasized with hand gestures and facial expressions of disgust.

47

When I finished, Willem declaimed a different piece, this one about a recent battle my father and his had fought. Though he couldn't hear well, his speaking style had energy and feeling. At the end, Lady Mother had him join me on my side of the table so I could declaim his piece along with him.

I had trouble reading aloud something I'd never read before, but I stumbled along, and his voice covered my errors. After a few sentences I caught the flow, like a pebble in a current. My pitch rose and fell with Willem's, and I felt his voice reverberate in my chest. When we reached the end, he bowed to me. I curtsied. What I cared most about was his glad face.

Lady Mother never brought Willem to another lesson, but I had cleared the oratory hurdle. Though I didn't excel, I could force my voice out and muster a degree of expression.

And Willem and I were friends again. Even better, his hearing gradually sharpened until at last it was almost as keen as before the pox.

Lady Mother noticed our attempts to be together and our longing looks. A week after we'd declaimed, in the corridor on the way to breakfast, she said, "Willem will never be a match for you, Perry. You'll do better."

"He's no match for me now. I best him in all our sports."

"Of course you do."

Her meaning exploded in my mind. "To marry?"

She smiled. "There's plenty of time to worry about that."

I pulled my hand out of hers and ran half the length of the corridor and back to dispel my embarrassment.

When I reached her again, she retied the bow that held my hair at the nape of my neck. More to herself than to me, she said, "You are pretty enough. We Lakti are too sensible to require an utter beauty. And your hair is an astonishment."

Later, in swordplay against Willem, loyalty caught up with me. Here on the field, I could defeat him, but in every other way he was at least my equal. If I had to marry someday, no one would be better than Willem.

Later in the spring, when the peonies bloomed, I was forever catching their scent and thinking Halina had come back. I'd wheel about and look for her rainbow light.

But after the flowers wilted, the reminders ceased. However, I did follow Annet's advice to study the Bamarre, especially Annet herself, since she was my closest exemplar.

I became confused. Were Annet's gestures neat and economical because she was a Bamarre or because she was Annet? Did she choose her dull embroidery colors for either of those reasons, or because she had been instructed to do so? She said the latter, which led me to wonder if these were the only threads she had leave to use.

I asked myself if, without her tassel, Annet would be just like any female Lakti.

Probably not. It wasn't that she was short, or anything physical. Both the Lakti and the Bamarre were short or tall, thin or stocky, pale or dark. Yes, we were brave and the Bamarre were cowards, but you couldn't tell that by looking at a person. Still, there was a difference, though I finally gave up trying to name it.

Certain she wouldn't be betrayed, Annet had revealed my origins to the castle's Bamarre servants, who treated me with a degree more warmth than they bestowed on the other Lakti: bows and curtsies a bit deeper, eye smiles as well as mouth smiles, a word or two when a nod would have sufficed. Lady Mother seemed unaware of their special regard, but Father saw.

He was home over the summer when I was ten, during an unusual outbreak of peace. On an August day, he and Lady Mother watched me race and, of course, win. Afterward, the three of us stood by the bleachers at the edge of the arena, with Annet hovering a yard away. I was wet with sweat, and a Bamarre manservant bustled to us, bearing a towel. This servant was one of Mistress Clarra's helpers. He brought our weapons and set up obstacles when we rode across the field. He was in middle age and portly. I didn't know his name and neither liked nor disliked him.

He must have acted without thinking. Rather than hold the towel out, he draped it around my bare shoulders, bare because girls raced in sleeveless shifts, boys in sleeveless tunics.

Father slapped him.

Annet yelped. I gasped.

The servant fell back onto the first and second rows of benches.

Father's lips disappeared into a thin, flat line, and his eyes glittered.

The breath felt trapped in my chest.

Lady Mother said, "Tove . . ."

"Not now, darling." He pulled the man up. "Did you believe I wouldn't object to your *Bamarre* hands on my daughter's skin?"

CHAPTER SEVEN

THE SERVANT MANAGED a wavering "Beg pardon, Lord."

Mistress Clarra arrived and sent the man into the castle. He limped away.

"I'll see he's punished."

"See he's dismissed, Clarra." Father saw my face. "Oh, love, I didn't mean to frighten you." He kissed my forehead, which was now icy as well as sweaty.

"Does he really have to leave?"

Father frowned. "Why shouldn't he?"

My fear increased. I shrugged, pretending I didn't care. "He's always been here. He was here the first time I won a race."

Father's face cleared. "You don't need a Bamarre for

good luck, sweet. You're a magnificent runner. But all right. Clarra, let him stay."

I hoped his punishment wouldn't be severe, either, but I was afraid to beg for anything else.

"Darling," Father said to Lady Mother, "our Bamarre servants seem fond of Perry. Why is that?"

"I hadn't noticed that they are."

Afterward, I mulled over Father's fury and began to observe him. He wiped his hands on his tunic whenever a Bamarre happened to touch him, the same gesture he'd made after King Einar's audience. The Bamarre touch would be innocent, occurring in the course of performing a task, and Father never issued a rebuke, just attempted to cleanse himself.

I decided his behavior was simply one more example of the strangeness of adults. Besides, I'd been taught that our Bamarre were lucky to be ruled by us. Otherwise, they would have been conquered by others, who would have killed them all. With us, they were safe and had duties and food.

My studies in the library progressed. Curiosity drew me to the books, which soon captivated me. While reading ever more easily and while continuing to train with Mistress Clarra, I turned eleven . . . thirteen . . . fifteen, and became educated. Willem remained my only friend, and we still had little time to be together.

Annet attended me in the library, where I let her read, too. We were almost friends there—she no longer the bossy servant who seemed to dislike her mistress, I no longer the mistress who sometimes made the maid obey, and who had given up trying for her affection. We both preferred poetry over anything else. She showed me poems she enjoyed, and I brought her my favorites.

My interest in verse was odd for a Lakti, so I didn't mention it even to Father, who encouraged all my enthusiasms.

I wondered if a young Bamarre noblewoman hundreds of years ago had sat by a window with her maid, with sunshine making her book almost too bright to read, as mine was now. She probably would have been reading poetry, as I was. Few of the volumes of poems had been penned by Lakti writers, and those that had were collections of battle songs. I liked them but preferred greater complexity.

More than any other, Annet and I both admired Lilli, a Bamarre poet who'd lived a hundred years before we were born.

The first time I read a Lilli poem, Annet was leaning over my shoulder, as she wouldn't have done if Lady Mother had been with us. I opened the volume to a poem about a family dinner, a meal of stewed hen. The bird, which had a name, Metti, had almost been a pet before she had been sacrificed.

> *Too old to lay,*
> *Too good to waste,*
> *Metti gave again.*

In the next stanza, the stew is salty because the mother wept while cooking it. Everyone is sad when the pot is brought to the table. But the mood changes when the mother tells of Metti's last escapade, an encounter with a cat. In the following stanza, each of the three children wants a drumstick.

> *"How many legs*
> *Does a chicken have?"*
> *Asked the children.*
> *"Two!" cried the father.*
> *"One, two. One too few!"*

Mother and Father take the drumsticks and share bites with their children. They all talk with their mouths full. The oldest girl almost knocks over the milk pitcher. The mother wags her finger. The poem ends with everyone full and sleepy.

Why did this poem raise a lump in my throat? A strangled sound came from Annet, whose eyes were brimming.

The explanation for my sadness arrived as if it had always lived in my mind: I wished I had the kind of family the poem depicted. I longed for the ease these poem people had with each other—not always striving to win a nod, to be the Lakti ideal.

And Annet, now a woman of twenty-three, had been in service more than half her life. We'd both been deprived.

A different Lilli poem haunted me, though. It was called "Departure" and was about the exodus from Old Lakti after the monsters came.

> *Living ghosts,*
> *King Josef's last subjects,*
> *All that still breathed,*
> *Laden with a Lakti load,*
>
> *Heavy, heavy, heavy,*
>
> *Climbed the Eskern path,*
> *King Josef, arms like iron,*
> *Clinging to a cliff*
> *Against a gale of swirling snow,*
>
> *Blowing, blowing, blowing.*

My ears felt cold. Frigid air stung my nose. The library was usually chilly, though not like this.

In the poem, two dragons and many gryphons circled above the pass. A boy stumbled. His father reached out to catch him, but not in time. The boy plummeted.

Even though King Josef shot arrows at them, a dozen gryphons descended on the boy's body and began feeding. Then a dragon spiraled down to the king, who tried to pierce its belly with an arrow, but the monster hid itself in smoke. The poem ended with the dragon bearing King Josef away in its claws.

> *Was not the king fortunate?*
> *To soar above his land—*
> *Golden grain, fat flocks,*
> *Lakes, meadows, purple Kilkets—*
>
> *Lucky, lucky, lucky,*
>
> *Spared exile, granted*
> *A last look, his kingdom*
> *Caught in his dying eyes,*
> *That was to his people denied,*
>
> *Lost, lost, lost.*

I wept. Over poetry! And I memorized the lines and recited them to myself when no one could hear. What was wrong with me?

Nothing, perhaps. Since the verses were about our great Lakti tragedy, it would have been unpatriotic not to cry. I didn't think she'd weep, but I thought even Lady Mother might be moved by "Departure."

That evening, with the moon and the stars in the casement window as my backdrop, I recited it for her.

She didn't yawn, an excellent sign. When I finished, she looked puzzled. "A Lakti poet?"

I grinned. "Bamarre! Her name was Lilli, and she imagined how leaving Old Lakti might have been. Isn't it beautiful?"

"I suppose. You memorized it?"

"I did."

She nodded. "We Lakti have prodigious memories."

The annual audience with the Bamarre royalty was approaching, and the poem gave me an idea. For the last two years, Prince Dahn and I had been deemed old enough to remain with the others. I'd sat in silence while digging my nails into my skin to stay awake. When the visit ended, I always felt I'd failed Lady Mother and Father by not being gracious. Perhaps this year could be different.

"Could I recite it for King Einar and Prince Dahn?"

"I'll see what your father says." Lady Mother expected him the next day, and she smiled the smile only he could call forth.

He wanted to hear the poem before consenting, so I recited it in his study. He sat in the same chair he'd been in when I'd toddled to him fourteen years before.

I perched on a stool near his knee.

He made a steeple of his hands. "Recite away. I'm not eager to hear a poem, but you're the right reader for me."

How I loved him.

"After you recite, I have news I think you'll be eager for."

What? But I shook off my curiosity and didn't beg him to tell me. I stood and began.

He didn't yawn, either, nor did his eyes moisten.

> *"A last look, his kingdom*
> *Caught in his dying eyes,*
> *That was to his people denied,*
>
> *Lost, lost, lost."*

He applauded. "Sweet, it's well imagined, but you can't march to it."

Why had I thought he'd love it? That he didn't made me feel uncomfortably different from him.

He saw my disappointment. "You recited beautifully, and I'll be grateful if you perform for Einar and Dahn. You can prove we Lakti aren't savages."

Father looked at me expectantly, and I remembered that he had a surprise for me.

I sat again. "What were you going to tell me?"

He took my hands. His were dry and warm and big, the best hands.

"When I return to battle, you are to come with me." He squeezed my hands.

"Really?"

"Really."

"I won't let anyone kill you," I promised.

He matched my smile. "I'm sure you wouldn't. But you're not yet old enough to fight." Dryly, "I hope to survive nonetheless. The surgeon will need your help if we have wounded."

I was hardly disappointed. I was going!

"Your mother will stay at home and run the castle."

"Will the others my age come?" Or had I been singled out?

"The best of them."

I knew myself to be best of the best. I wondered if Willem was coming. He was among the best only sometimes.

But he was chosen. Mistress Clarra drilled the

appointed relentlessly. We ran, threw quoits, exercised to exhaustion—everything to improve our endurance, though none of us were old enough to actually fight. Some would stay in camp, helping the cooks, pitching tents, unloading supplies as they arrived. Others, like me, would be just behind the battle line, grooming the horses, helping the armorer, carrying messages between the fighting and the camp, or assisting the surgeon.

We were to leave the morning after the audience with Einar.

Audience day arrived. My two satchels were packed, including, tucked between my hose and my spare shift, a book of poems by Lilli. My longbow, my quiver, my sword, and my shield leaned against the wall next to the door. Even though we wouldn't be fighting, we would ride to Father's camp equipped as soldiers.

Annet's satchel slumped next to mine. Lady Mother said Annet wouldn't attend me once we arrived, since she'd be needed to help the other Bamarre servants, and I'd be billeted in a tent with the Lakti young people.

After supper, the usual entourage of nobles left. The kitchen maids carried the trestle table and benches to be stacked behind the screen.

Annet moved her stool to a few yards' distance from my side. The steward announced the arrival of King Einar and his two sons, Prince Dahn and Prince Bruce, a child of five years, whom we hadn't expected.

The bland mask dulled Father's face. Lady Mother's stiff smile banished humor to another kingdom. My fingers tingled and my lips went numb. How could I recite if I couldn't feel my lips?

The royal trio entered. Prince Bruce, who was small for his age, clung to his father's hand. After their bows, which were tardy as usual, and after the insulting Bamarre greeting, I curtsied so deeply my knee cracked and echoed in the silent hall.

They sat, Prince Bruce at attention in his own chair. We sat. My stomach clenched.

"The Bamarre believe," Father began, "or so I've been told, that we Lakti can't appreciate artistry, especially poetry. To counter that notion, Peregrine picked a poem to recite to you."

King Einar arched his eyebrows.

Prince Dahn actually spoke. "Begging your pardon, Lord Tove, but the topics were arranged in advance. We weren't warned of a poem."

Warned?

He added, "Begging your pardon, I prefer not to hear it."

My stomach clenched tighter, now in fury.

Father's polite mask stayed in place, but his eyes sparkled. He and Lady Mother said nothing, waiting, I supposed, for King Einar to contradict his son.

Instead, the king said, "I agree. I do not wish to deviate from our schedule for a performance that will trouble my ears."

Finally, Father said in a velvet voice, "Your Highness, do you think it wise to insult my family?"

"Lord Tove," King Einar said, "we have a right—"

"Your Majesty . . ." My voice shook. I shouldn't have said anything, but I was too angry to think. "This is just the latest insult from your son."

I felt Father's attention shift to me.

In the quiet, I heard Annet murmur, "No. Don't."

Lady Mother said warningly, "Perry . . ."

But Father didn't let me retreat. "What did he do, Perry?"

"When we were younger, I brought games I thought he might enjoy. I always tried to have a conversation with him, but"—I addressed the prince—"you ignored me, or"—I searched for the right word—"sneered me away." That was it.

Father stood and delivered the slap to Prince Dahn's cheek that had itched my palm for years.

Annet cried, "Oh!"

Prince Bruce wailed.

Prince Dahn covered his cheek with his hand.

Father gestured to a guard, and Prince Bruce was

carried from the hall. King Einar stood to follow him.

Father said, "Sit, Einar. No one will hurt the boy."

The king sat.

Father continued. "You may complain to King Uriel, but if you do, I predict disappointment."

King Einar's eyes seemed to bulge. "Begging your pardon, this is barbarous behavior, and—"

"And now," Father went on, "Perry will recite. If you choose not to listen, you may leave and the audience will be over. I'll decide if it will take place next year."

They stayed.

"Begin, Perry." *Do not disgrace us* was in the set of Lady Mother's head.

My breathing slowed. I felt as I did at the start of a race. I had practiced. I was ready.

> *"Living ghosts,*
> *King Josef's last subjects,*
> *All that still breathed,*
> *Laden with a Lakti load,*
>
> *Heavy, heavy, heavy."*

I forgot my listeners. My voice became servant to the poem. If the king grimaced and his son covered his ears, I didn't see them.

"A last look, his kingdom
Caught in his dying eyes,
That was to his people denied,

Lost, lost, lost."

I finished.

King Einar was staring intently at me. "Your daughter has promise. Beg pardon, I wouldn't have thought her performance possible."

I blushed and grinned.

"You needn't beg pardon for that." Father smiled, his congenial mask reestablished.

Prince Dahn looked delightfully disappointed.

Lady Mother said, "We're glad to have provided entertainment you could enjoy." She didn't nod at me.

After the royals left, I wrapped my cloak around myself to return alone to my chamber. Lady Mother had recruited Annet to go with her to the kitchen to pack a hamper with victuals for tomorrow's journey. Father said he was going to his study to enjoy the shaming of the king and Prince Dahn.

Glad for my fleet feet, I raced across the inner ward in a cold, stinging rain. In my room, I stood at the window, though I could see only blackness and stripes of water slanting across the glass.

I noticed a floral scent. The air crackled. I whirled.

And shaded my eyes against the brightness, until the fairy—Halina again?—took a human shape.

It *was* Halina!

How thrilling that she would come tonight! I curtsied and dared ask, "Did you like my reciting? Do you like that poem?"

"Yes to both, Peregrine."

I had forgotten how her voice echoed.

"This fairy liked them very much." She frowned. "But you criticized your prince. He isn't worth much . . ."

Oh, no! Did she visit me because she thought I was a Bamarre?

". . . but he's the son of your king, who—"

"They aren't my monarchs. I'm a Lakti."

Her fingers touched my cap. "You are entirely a Bamarre, lacking only a tassel."

CHAPTER EIGHT

I BLINKED AT her, my thoughts lagging.

"Annet is your sister."

It seemed more possible that I be a Bamarre than that Annet be my relative. "We're nothing alike!"

"Nonetheless."

I didn't know which argument to make first, so they all poured out. "But Annet can't run fast. She sleeps with four blankets. Mistress Clarra says I'm the best she ever trained at . . . at *anything*. I have a Lakti memory. My birth father was a Lakti knight."

"A duckling can be raised to think it's a chick—"

"I'm not a duck or a Bamarre!"

"Look at the wall."

It glowed. Where last time there had been mountains

and a dragon now appeared the interior of a cottage.

I sank down on my bed and saw played out my abduction by Lady Mother. I heard her voice, her pitiless words, the lamentations of my parents. They loved me! They didn't want to lose me!

A corner of my *Lakti* mind noticed that my father's posture was poor. My mother's forehead was smudged. Was she a slattern?

How much younger Lady Mother looked! How smooth her face was then. She'd been almost pretty.

When she stared down at me and picked me up, her expression softened.

The face of the girl who followed me out—Annet's face—was stamped with sorrow and terror.

The vision followed Lady Mother to my nursery, where she dressed me in my Lakti finery and removed my tassel. When she left, Annet picked me up and held me stiffly.

The wall became itself again. My tears flowed, though I was hardly aware of them.

Halina patted my shoulder, with a touch that brought unwanted comfort. I twisted away, rushed to the opposite wall, and sobbed, however un-Lakti-like my tears were.

In the middle of my endless weeping, I wondered how much time had passed. Would Annet return soon? Would Lady Mother come with her? How could I behave cheerfully?

"You can invent anything and make it seem real." I hiccuped.

"Think, Perry, and you'll know everything happened as I revealed it."

If what she'd shown me was true, no wonder Annet had always hated me. Two lines of poetry erupted in my mind:

> *Sisters expelled from home*
> *Lived together yet alone.*

The other Bamarre servants liked me. And I loved poetry, which felt as much a part of me as my need to run.

Whenever I accomplished something that pleased Lady Mother, she proclaimed it as Lakti. But if I were a Lakti by birth, why would she say anything?

Was she hard to please because I was a Bamarre?

She'd never revealed who my birth family was, even after so many years had passed and their grief must have subsided. But there could be other explanations for that.

Most of all, however, the proof was her distress over a fairy appearing to me. She'd known that Halina hadn't broken the tradition of never visiting a Lakti.

Father hated the Bamarre! Would he hate me?

I pushed the idea away. "Are my"—I didn't know what to call them—"my first parents well?"

The fairy's eyes were soft with sympathy. "Very

well. You have a younger brother."

"Who else here knows?"

"Of the Lakti, just Lady Klausine and her maid. The guard who was there was sent away the next day."

"Not Father?" But I knew the answer to that.

"No. All the castle Bamarre know. King Einar and his sons don't. The castle Bamarre protect you and Annet."

The weak protecting the strong. "Why don't fairies visit Lakti people?"

"If the Lakti let the Bamarre live as equals, fairies would visit them. This fairy certainly would."

I made the Lakti argument. "We're kinder to our Bamarre than other conquerors would be."

Halina said nothing.

"Why did you pick me to visit? Annet says fairies hardly ever appear to anyone."

She shifted her weight to one hip, a resting pose. "This fairy is tired of the burden the Bamarre carry."

I was supposed to change that?

"Yes, you are. I've been waiting for someone in your circumstances. You may disappoint me, but you're particularly placed, as no one else is."

My voice rose. "Why do I have to be a Bamarre?" Why did Lady Mother have to meddle in my life? Why did Halina?

"You *are* a Bamarre. Still, if you like, you can tell no

one and live as a Lakti. But if you do, you won't see me again."

What would I lose? "What good have fairies done the Bamarre?"

"I'm doing good now." She vanished.

A few minutes later, which passed while I stood in the middle of the chamber, barely thinking, Annet came in.

"What?" she said. My expression must have been strange.

I shook my head and sat at my dressing table for her to brush my hair. Should I tell her I knew?

She brushed roughly, as usual. If I told her, would she be gentler?

I wondered how it felt to wear the tassel.

Annet had watched over me, just as our parents told her to, if lovelessly. "Are you angry at me for tattling on Dahn? I'm sorry." I realized I was. I'd caused the shaming.

In the mirror I saw her shake her head, the green tassel swaying. "No . . ." She met my eyes. "*Prince* Dahn is as stupid as a Lakti. He should want you to recite poetry."

"I could be the Lakti who civilized her people."

"Yes." She stopped brushing and moved her stool so she could face me. "What happened to you?"

I frowned, confused. What had I said?

Oh. *I'm sorry.* Had I never said that to her before?

I half wanted to tell her about the fairy. But the instant the words came out of my mouth—*I know I'm a Bamarre*—I wouldn't be able to take them back.

"Nothing happened. I should say 'I'm sorry' more often."

Her eyes widened.

I'd made it worse. Now I had to come up with an explanation. "Maybe I'm growing up."

Weak, but she seemed satisfied. Half an hour later, I was in bed, staring up at the shadows while Annet slept.

When Lady Mother made me promise to tell no one about the fairy's visit, was she protecting me? Or herself, because of the deception she'd carried out? What would happen to her if I told?

And Father! Would he really hate me?

If my first parents met me now, would they still feel affection, or would I be a Lakti, to be feared and hated?

What about Willem? I'd never met a Lakti who admired the cowardly and endlessly polite Bamarre.

Though the night was almost over before I fell asleep, I had decided only one thing: I wouldn't announce the truth about my birth until after I'd returned from the battlefield. If I confessed now, the campaign might be called off. The Lakti could even lose the campaign as a result, and the fault would lie with a Bamarre girl.

Father would be disappointed if there were no trip. He'd been looking forward to taking me along—because he loved me. *Loved* me. Loved *me*.

CHAPTER NINE

AT DAWN LADY Mother came to my chamber with her maid, who carried breakfast on a tray, although usually we broke our fast in the great hall. When they came in, I was standing in the middle of the room, tying my belt around my surcoat.

Lady Mother held a burlap sack and wore her usual stern expression. Somehow I had expected her to be different, though only I had changed. She put the satchel on the floor by my bed.

What would I say if I told her I knew? *You ripped me from my life!* Or, *You saved me from my life!*

The maid put the tray on my dressing table. Not enough food for Annet, who was facing the window, pinning up her hair—and who was probably as hungry as I was.

Lady Mother frowned. "Didn't you sleep?"

I shrugged. "Not much."

"I hope thoughts of that absurd prince didn't keep you awake."

I shook my head.

"Excitement, I suppose. Here. This is for you." From the purse at her waist she removed a small velvet sack and shook out the contents in her hand.

"Oh!"

In her palm was a silver chain from which dangled a pendant—a circle of worked gold crossed by a tiny silver sword. Along the center of the sword's blade ran a line of diamond chips.

I'd never had jewelry before. The Lakti didn't adorn their children at all and didn't adorn themselves very much. "Thank you." Tired as I was, I barely held back tears.

"Don't touch the sword." She gave me the pendant. "I used to take this into battle."

Careful to avoid the sword, I slipped the chain over my head. The pendant hung just below the neckline of my surcoat.

"Annet," Lady Mother said, "look at Perry's pendant."

Annet turned. "It's pretty, Lady Klausine." She took a step toward me.

"Don't come closer, but keep watching. Perry, run a

finger quickly and softly over the sword."

I did. A light blazed. I cried out in surprise and stopped rubbing.

"I can't see!" Annet covered her eyes and bent double.

I gasped. Had I blinded my sister? "Will she see again?"

"Of course."

The pendant light dimmed after about half a minute.

Lady Mother should have warned Annet, who was still bent over. We watched her. She moaned.

Lady Mother shouldn't have done it at all. Didn't she remember who Annet was?

She shouldn't have done it to any Bamarre.

Annet straightened.

"Can you see?" I cried.

"Everything is blurred."

"It lasts several minutes," Lady Mother said. "Soon her sight will be as keen as ever."

It had been casual cruelty. Had I failed to notice a thousand similar examples? Had I committed many myself?

Lady Mother added, "Keep the pendant safe, Perry. It's for use in battle, not as an ornament. In battle, don't touch it unless you must. Victory in a fair fight is best, but use it to save your life. Your fellow Lakti warriors need you."

Had she forgotten I was ever a Bamarre? Or did she

think of it constantly?

"Can it blind more than one person at once?" I asked.

"Two, if their heads are close together."

"Where did it come from?"

"From sorcerers!" Lady Mother sounded triumphant. "In Old Lakti an apprentice sorcerer always lived at court. But they stayed behind when we left. I don't suppose any survived." She sat on my bed and lifted the sack onto her lap, where she worked at the strings.

I had an impulse to shine the sword light on her and run from the room. I could blind my pursuers, race to the stable, gallop across the drawbridge, and never come back.

But I didn't move, held by feeling for Lady Mother and Annet, no matter what being a Bamarre might mean.

"Old Lakti had elves and dwarfs too, who never troubled us. There." Lady Mother pulled out two shabby black boots. "These were a fairy gift many generations ago." She held a boot out to me. "Don't put it on."

I took it. It looked big enough to accommodate both feet.

"One step in these will take you seven leagues."

"Really?" I hugged the boot to my chest, dirty as it was. Seven leagues—twenty-one miles—in a single step! She was giving me the means of escape.

Her face softened. "They may satisfy even your desire to peregrinate."

"Do I have to do anything to make them go? Say a spell?"

"Just step, but, like the pendant, don't use them unless you must. And be sure of your direction and distance or you may come to mischief."

"What mischief?"

She shrugged. "I've never used them. I don't know if they'd tunnel through a mountain or scale it. They might stop with you encased in stone or drowned at the bottom of a lake."

Oh!

She took back the boot. "Now, eat your breakfast."

A Lakti breakfast did not coddle: coarse brown bread, hard cheese, lumpy pottage, and lukewarm almond milk. Lady Mother stood over me and watched. I ate as I'd been taught, taking small bites, chewing carefully but quickly, sipping, not slurping.

Halfway through, I swallowed and asked, "Can Annet go to her breakfast?"

Lady Mother's eyebrows rose above their usual arch. "Annet, you have my permission to leave."

She went, glancing worriedly at me on her way out, which reassured me that she could see.

"Ragna, would you ask my lord when he needs Perry?"

Lady Mother's maid nodded and left, too.

"Is there something you want to say?"

I opened my mouth to say I just thought Annet would be hungry—and closed it. Lady Mother would find that suspicious. How much I had changed already!

What could I say instead? "Er . . . Is it safe to have Annet or any Bamarre with us at the camp?"

"Ah." She nodded.

I felt the usual happiness—and felt unusually odd about it.

"We believe so. Our Bamarre servants allow more of us to fight, and we don't let them near the battle. Any more questions?"

Taking myself by surprise, I asked, "Will you miss me?"

No nod. "What a question!" She went to my dressing table and opened the drawer where Annet kept the shears. "Your hair may get in your way. Sit." She gestured at my dressing table.

I did, reluctantly. My hair was my one beauty. As Lady Mother had once said, I was pretty enough: square face; large, square teeth; dark eyes under level eyebrows; small, squarish nose; clear complexion; lips that could have been fuller. It was a blunt Lakti face regardless of my birth, softened by my extravagant hair.

Lady Mother had once speculated about how long my hair would grow if left uncut. "You could sleep on a mound of hair and have enough left over for a blanket."

With unusual humor, she added, "You'd be the ideal of Lakti economy."

But when it reached my waist, she always told Annet to cut it to shoulder length, which I didn't mind. Shoulder length was still long.

Now, however, Lady Mother lopped off a hank of hair level with my cheekbones.

I put my hand over the spot. "Do you have to?"

In the mirror I saw her look down at the hair in her hand. "I won't have your hair endanger you." She added softly, "I wish I were going with you, but you'll be back in two months." Her voice strengthened. "If you need to come home—whatever the reason—use the boots."

I almost blurted out the truth then. Only caution held me back, but I had my answer. She'd miss me.

CHAPTER TEN

THE JOURNEY TO Father's headquarters lasted a week, starting with four days of easy riding on our widest road across meadows and over forested hills, which grew steeper the farther south we went. On the fifth morning we met the east-west road and turned west. The terrain began to flatten and the ground become stony. We had entered the New Lakti barrens. Woods of Maze cypress trees grew here, dense with the entwined branches that gave the tree its name.

I relate this geography from books, because I saw little. On the first day, I rode half-asleep. For the rest of the trip, I was more awake but barely alert to what passed around me.

Often, Willem maneuvered his horse to my side.

Before Halina's visit, I would have been delighted. Now I had to make myself smile. Always alert to feelings, he rarely spoke, but once he tilted his head at me in a silent question. I just shrugged.

My only comforts were the memory of Lady Mother's good-bye and thoughts of her gifts. I wondered if Father knew she'd given them to me, because he never mentioned them.

The Lakti in our company numbered fifty, including my fellow students and Mistress Clarra. They made merry, joking and calling to one another and often singing. If I knew the words, I made myself sing along. This chorus penetrated my haze:

> *"Brash, strong heroes on milky-white steeds,*
> *Fearless soldiers forging great deeds,*
> *Sure of fighting well, sure of being bold,*
> *Sure of striking hard, sure of killing foes,*
> *Laughing, roaring, pounding in the saddle,*
> *Castle-bred folk with minds on battle."*

"Father," I asked when the song ended, "do you think the long-ago Lakti sang this when they rode against the Bamarre?"

"We may have. These verses are very old, although the Bamarre never merited a lay."

I made myself not look back to where Annet rode with a dozen more Bamarre servants. Behind them, teams of oxen pulled carts loaded with food, blankets, and bandages. We traveled in order of rank, with the Bamarre between the exalted and the beasts. Why would I become a Bamarre?

My only other memory of the journey is of an oddity. By the end of the second day, my hair had grown long enough to graze my shoulders. Four days later, it reached my shoulder blades.

Bugles woke me from my reveries, blown by soldiers when we approached camp. It was November 2, late afternoon, chilly, no wind, lowering clouds, the camp wreathed in smoke from many bonfires. I formed an impression of a warren of brown leather tents, living quarters for Father's troops, a thousand strong, who had continued fighting in his absence.

Two towers rose above the barrens' flatness, one only a few yards to the north of the camp, the other a smudge on the horizon, perhaps half a mile to the south.

I guessed that lookouts were stationed in the near tower. Cypress stumps dotted the camp. A wood had been cleared for us.

We dismounted at the southeastern edge of the tents, about four miles from the battlefield, as I learned later. I lifted down my satchels, which held, along with a change of clothes, my precious pendant and seven-league boots, and the book of poems. Mistress Clarra led her charges, including me, to the tent that would house us all.

The tent hung too low for me to stand upright inside. The distance from flap to back was no more than fifteen feet—for the eight of us. I set my things down near the opening, because I still feared confinement.

Willem set his satchels next to mine. Mistress Clarra told us to follow her to the big mess table for our supper. We filed out, zigging and zagging between tents, Willem at my side when there was room. We hadn't gone far before I felt a tap on my shoulder.

A Bamarre kitchen maid from the castle smiled at me and tapped Willem, too. "Your fathers want you. You're to sup with them."

We followed her, a dark shape in deepening dusk.

Father's tent stood entirely across the camp. If the tents themselves were to march to battle, his would have led. A gap separated it from the others, providing room for horses and dashing messengers.

Smoke eddied out and curled around our knees. Inside, we came first to a coal brazier, which radiated welcome warmth. A scuttle of fresh coals and a pot of tapers stood next to the brazier.

Our fathers smiled at us, Sir Noll's smile as easy as his son's, Father's more brilliant, a natural leader's smile.

A soldier would keep that smile in mind as she rode at a wall of foes.

Father tilted his head at the stool next to his chair. "We're planning for tomorrow."

I sat. Willem took the stool next to Sir Noll's chair, his seat the same height as mine, as his father's chair was the same as my father's, no rank evident here.

A meal had been spread on a high table along one edge of the tent. My stomach rumbled, but neither father was eating, so I ignored my hunger, possible for one trained to be a Lakti.

Under the table were two chests, several satchels, and a covered basket. Father's drawn sword leaned against the arm of his chair.

Open on a low table between the two men was a map of western New Lakti and the southeastern edge of the Kyngoll kingdom. Our village of Erlo, marked by crosshatches for houses, lay fifty miles to the south. Across the border, east and north of our camp, crosshatching signified a town twice the size of Erlo.

"Where is their camp?" I asked.

"In their town," Father said.

"Do they outnumber us?" Willem asked. The Lakti didn't mind unfavorable odds.

Father stretched out his legs. "We're evenly matched, more or less."

"We intend to make them run," Sir Noll said.

"Will you go into Kyngoll?" I asked.

Father grinned. "We'll chase them. Noll"—he touched the map—"let's mix arrows with spears tomorrow."

Both Willem and I had been taught military tactics. Spear soldiers usually fended off an attack, while archers took the offensive. Ordinarily, the two were kept apart.

Sir Noll nodded. "Good. We haven't done that in a while."

I said, "We'll have more arrows." Archers risked running out of ammunition, unless opposing archers were shooting back at them, which would be more likely if they were with the spears.

"Exactly, Perry!" Father patted my shoulder.

He was proud of me. He loved me.

Willem said, "The archers will have the safety of the shield wall." Spear soldiers moved together, shields touching.

A hint of sharpness entered Father's voice. "There's no safety in battle."

I would have blushed in shame, but Willem, in his unchallenging way, challenged Father. "Still, I'd like to have a shield to duck behind. If not, I'd fight anyway."

"Good lad. You're seventeen, right?"

Willem nodded. "Yes, sir."

"Noll, let's put him in. He can wield a spear."

Willem clapped his hands and grinned. I felt both frightened for him and jealous.

His father frowned. "In the second or third row, Tove."

"Of course. We'll put him behind Ivar."

Sir Noll's face cleared.

Father explained, "Ivar is a butcher with his spear. No one gets past him. He's been in a hundred fights and never been scratched."

"Can I fight if he's blocking me?"

"You'll be able to fight enough," Sir Noll said. "Not much, I hope."

"The battle spell will fall over you." Father waved a hand at Willem.

We'd heard about the battle spell. Time slowed. Senses sharpened. Warriors felt stronger than ever before.

Father stood. "If you're going to fight tomorrow, you should dine well tonight. And Perry, if you're going to help the surgeon, you should eat, too."

"I'm almost as tall as Willem." I was nine inches above five feet. "Can't you put me behind someone like Ivar?" Battle, I thought, will make me forget about being a Bamarre—or whatever I really am.

Father bent down and kissed my forehead. "Your mother would assassinate me. When you're Willem's age, you'll ride at my side."

While we ate our hard cheese, harder bread, and brined

carrots, Father and Sir Noll talked more about tactics. I learned that the Kyngoll rarely attacked and never retreated, which accounted for the present stalemate. We charged, and they didn't budge.

"They're a worthy opponent, Perry." Father gestured at the map with a chunk of bread.

I heard *unlike the Bamarre* hang in the air, unspoken.

Sir Noll laughed grimly. "I'd rather have them unworthy, so we can win and be done with it."

If we succeeded, I supposed that we—the Lakti— would treat them as we did the Bamarre. If we lost, they'd do worse to us. I'd heard about their cruelty.

Sir Noll stood. "Willem should sleep."

"I'll keep my daughter a little longer." Father followed them to the tent flap. With his back to me, he gestured for me to join him outside.

My heart hopped. I'd never felt uneasy with Father before. What if he somehow sniffed out my Bamarre nature? What if I blurted out the truth?

A soldier gave Sir Noll a torch. We watched the flame bob away.

"Father"—I managed to keep a waver out of my voice—"would you still care about me if I was"—Don't tell!—"going to be short?"

"What?"

"Would you still—"

"Perry, sweet, I'd love you if you were three inches tall, although I'd be surprised. You'd still be the fastest Lakti ever."

Determined to go on, I asked, "What if I could hardly run at all? What if I was as slow as mud?"

"I'd love you. As long as you were you, I'd love you."

If you knew I was born a Bamarre, would you think I was still me?

He would. He loved me entirely, better than Lady Mother did.

Or would he? The Bamarre disgusted him.

I was afraid to speak.

"Come." Father led me behind the tent, where he put an arm around my shoulder. He chuckled. "There's no danger that you'll be short. Soon you'll be gazing down at your mother while she frowns up at you."

I smiled. "Can we creep up on the Kyngoll at night?"

"We've tried. They post sentries, just as we do."

As my eyes grew accustomed to the dark, I saw a black shape resolve itself into a cypress's twisting branches.

"Sometimes I send scouts to see if they can bring in a sentry or a straggler. We caught one a month ago."

"Is he dead?"

The Lakti never traded prisoners. Captured soldiers were killed. First, if we could, we persuaded them (not gently) to tell us what they knew. The Kyngoll did the same, we believed. We joked that if they let a Lakti live, he or she would soon be ruling the kingdom.

"She. Yes, she's dead. Perry, you'll fight soon enough. Have you studied why we go to war? I don't mean this war. War itself."

I quoted the deepest belief of Lakti philosophy. "'The purpose of war is to create eternal peace.'" Meaning that when we were finally one kingdom, killing would cease. "'Whoever wins the final contest will deserve to rule.'"

"That's the deep truth, but I'm glad I won't live in eternal peace. I can't imagine anything more boring. Yes, I can—an entire day in the company of King Einar."

I forced a laugh.

"Perry, fighting is fun. I don't know if anyone ever told you that. When you see your foe trembling before you, you expand. You feel as if you could uproot trees."

I wondered if killing people was fun. It was fun to win a fencing match, and it might be even better if your opponent were vanquished forever.

"But there's one rule you must follow." Father turned me and held both my shoulders. "Do not look into the eyes of your enemy. Watch his hands and feet, to know what he's likely to do next. Never meet his eyes. Will you remember, darling?"

I treasured the *darling*. "Why not look?"

"Because it will be harder to kill him. And the joy will

go out of it. Now, come." He led me back into the tent, where he pulled the basket out from under the high table and raised the lid. "Don't tell your mother."

I saw a package wrapped in canvas and tied with brown string. He lifted the bundle out carefully, sat in his chair, and undid the knots. "Occasionally on the ride here, my thoughts traveled to this, one of the pleasures of being away from home." He peeled off the cloth.

Nestled in the canvas were at least two dozen figs, handfuls of almonds and walnuts, four marchpane candies, and a stack of honey wafers. We had a treat like this only when King Einar and his sons came.

He grinned wolfishly. "Save some for me."

Shortly before dawn I woke from a dream of running across country in my seven-league boots, dragging Lady Mother behind me.

Banishing the dream, I raised my head. Willem's blanket lay flat. Had he been called to battle already?

When I sat up, I discovered that my rump was on my hair. This had to be Halina's work. What was she doing?

Tucking the mass under my cap, where I was sure it made odd bumps, I slung on my cloak and pulled up my hood.

Outside, following a guess, I circled to the back of the tent and saw Willem a few yards away, facing cypress woods. I smelled the piny scent of the trees. Pink brightened the sky just above the branches. Last night's clouds had been swept away by a sharp wind that still blew.

A sentry, one of the patrol guarding the camp, marched by and paid no attention to us.

How I envied Willem! To go to battle, to have an undivided nature—and to have hair that grew at the usual pace!

"Power comes from the back leg," I said.

Mistress Clarra had told him this dozens of times. A weak spear thrust could cost him his life.

He turned and grinned. "More advice."

I blushed. "Unasked for."

His smile sweetened. "But welcome. Thank you." He gestured for me to join him. "The squirrels like the cypress cones."

Under the nearest tree, two gray squirrels were chewing busily, oblivious to us.

He added, "Lakti squirrels. They'd enjoy our bread."

I chuckled. "Even the Lakti don't enjoy the Lakti bread." I realized I hadn't said, *Even* we *don't enjoy* our *bread.* "Are you excited?"

"I could hardly sleep. If your father hadn't questioned my courage, I'd just be running errands or chopping vegetables with everyone else."

Few died in battle unless there was a rout. Still, we'd lost three of our company since September. Willem could kill someone—or be killed himself.

"Keep your shield up." His shield arm tended to droop. "And stay behind Ivar."

He frowned. "Do you think I'll be a terrible soldier?"

"No. I think you forget that your power is in your back leg. You use your shoulders too much, and you let—"

He was laughing. "You're the most honest person I know."

I recognized that as a compliment and blushed again. Honest about everything except being a Bamarre. I continued the truth telling. "You're the best person I know, aside from Father, and you're my only friend."

"I doubt I'll always be your only friend, but I'm your friend forever."

I wondered.

CHAPTER ELEVEN

A MESSENGER CAME for Willem, and the two left together. I found Annet at the mess, where trestle tables
had been set up outside the cook tent. She was serving
soldiers, struggling to carry a tray loaded with bowls and
two tureens of pottage. A lady's maid wasn't used to heavy
work, but I was, because of Mistress Clarra's training.

Without thinking, I took the tray. Annet let me, too
surprised to do anything else.

"Where does it go?"

"Don't!" She reached for it.

"Where?"

She led me to a table. I set the tray down between two
men.

One said, "Where's your tassel?"

The other shook his head at him.

Annet started for the cook tent, and I followed. They'd probably all be Bamarre in there. Good. Safe.

Good?

Inside, she turned to me. "What's the trouble, young mistress?"

The tent was warm and bustling. I saw a lot of tassels, but Annet's speech suggested the presence of a few Lakti.

"Did you bring your shears?"

She looked confused. "Yes?"

I leaned down and whispered. "My hair won't stop growing. It's below my waist."

Loudly, she announced, "I'll take care of you, Lady Perry."

Her small tent lay at the southern edge of the camp. It was blessedly empty, though there were four bedrolls. I knelt and whipped off my hood and cap. My hair tumbled down to the middle of my thighs.

"Perry!" She lopped my hair off at the middle of my ears. When she finished, she came around to face me. "Don't do my work for me. People will wonder. What happened to your hair?"

You're the most honest person I know.

"Halina came again. I think she made my hair grow, but I don't know why. She told me I'm a Bamarre and we're sisters."

Annet sank down on her haunches.

I hoped for an embrace that didn't come.

She said nothing for what seemed a week, so I said, "What are our parents' names?"

"Adeer and Shoni."

Not Lakti names, but pretty. Annet added, "What will you do?"

I shook my head, which felt light without the weight of hair. "I'm not sure. Halina said I can pretend to be a Lakti forever and she won't come again."

"Why don't you do that?"

Did she want me to? "I may."

"Lord Tove will disown you if you tell." She pressed her hands together. "He might do worse."

A voice called from outside the tent. "Perry!" Mistress Clarra.

Annet moved her bedroll over the mound of my hair cuttings. "Don't admit you're a Bamarre unless you're ready to *be* a Bamarre."

I replaced my cap and covered it again with my hood. I should have taken the shears.

Mistress Clarra berated me all the way back to our tent, where I removed my cloak and surcoat and pulled on my hauberk—the chain-mail shirt—and my chain-mail hood. Then I slipped the pendant necklace over my head.

"No adornment!"

"Lady Mother wants me to wear it." I covered the mail with my cape, my cap, and my hood. The sheath at my waist held my thrusting dagger. I had killed dozens of straw soldiers with it.

The others had gone ahead to the battlefield. Mistress Clarra had stayed for me. "Where's Father?"

"Lord Tove rode out at dawn."

At the edge of camp, horses waited, already saddled. I felt chilled to the bone. In summer, chain mail was unbearably hot. On a raw day, it drew in the cold.

"Where is Father fighting?" I asked.

"He's everywhere, but he commands the western flank, and Sir Noll has the eastern."

Near our destination, we passed through a copse of cypress trees. I heard a dull roar. Beyond the trees, the battle line came into view, twitching with energy. I saw the backs of horses and their riders and the backs of pike soldiers on foot. The sounds clarified to shouts, pounding hoofs, stones flying from underfoot, and horses neighing and squealing. I smelled sweat and a sour odor I learned to recognize as fear. Even the Lakti could feel fear.

A woman lay on her cloak outside the physician's tent. When she saw me approach, she tried to sit up.

Could I do something for her? Was I supposed to know what? I ran to her. "Can I help you?"

"I'm just bruised." She collapsed, coughing.

I saw no blood to stanch. How useless I was.

Not far from her, a fire smoldered. Suspended from a wooden frame over the logs, a cauldron hung.

The surgeon, Master Hakon, emerged from the tent and sent me to collect fuel for the fire, which I was to tend. "Keep it hot." He handed me an ax. "Hurry. Bring live wood, too, and don't strip the needles off the branches."

After a backward glance at the woman, I took the wheelbarrow that waited by the fire and ran the quarter mile to the cypress copse. Battlefield medics needed a fire. A heated poker would be applied to wounds to cauterize them. Boiling water would make herbal infusions and compresses. The smoke from cypress needles eased pain.

When I reached the woods, I collected dead branches until the wheelbarrow was half full. Then I picked a small tree and attacked it awkwardly with the ax until it fell. I lopped off the branches, saved them, split the wood, and finished loading the wheelbarrow.

In all, I was gone about an hour. When I got back, the woman seemed not to have moved. Master Hakon and his two apprentices bent over a figure who was blocked from my view.

The surgeon said, "Bite down, Ivar."

Ivar? Let there be more than one Ivar! Let this not be the Ivar who never got a scratch, who was shielding Willem from harm, who was keeping him from being killed.

CHAPTER TWELVE

I WORRIED WHILE I tended the fire, running twice more to the copse for wood. First the pox, then this battle—I wished Willem didn't keep frightening me. I imagined him on the ground, bleeding, while the battle raged around him. Again and again, I banished the image, only to have it reappear.

A few wounded came in, and Master Hakon said even more might arrive when the day's fighting ended.

Ivar lost his leg below the knee and wouldn't fight again. No one died except the wounded woman, who had been hit in the chest by a horse's hooves. I wished I knew something about her: if she had children, if she'd fought many battles, if anyone had avenged her injury when she was struck.

Soldier—steadfast, stalwart—
By death defeated.

At dusk, Father, leading half a dozen wounded, approached the physicians' tent. I ran to him, and he said Willem was fine.

Exuberantly, I juggled twigs before tossing them in the flames.

"Ivar," Father said, "young Willem gored the soldier who slashed you."

"Did the villain die?" Ivar said.

"Yes."

I felt jealous again. Willem had killed a Kyngoll.

As evening darkened to night, Master Hakon, his apprentices, and I lifted the wounded into an oxcart and made them as warm and comfortable as we could for the journey back to camp. Master Hakon drove the cart, while the apprentices and I rode alongside on horseback. An apprentice held a torch to light our way. When we neared the cypress woods, another flame flickered at us, which turned out to be Willem waiting on his horse and holding his own torch, whose flame stretched and wavered in the wind.

"Perry!" His voice sounded strained.

Master Hakon gave me permission to go to him. "But if you tarry returning to camp, your father will dine on my liver."

We walked our horses behind the cart until Willem reached out to touch my arm. Ignoring Master Hakon's warning, I reined in my mare and let the cart gain ground ahead of us. "Congratulations!" I couldn't help adding, "You remembered the power in your back leg, and you kept your shield up." Admit I helped you.

"I don't know what I did."

We entered the copse.

"What?" I shouted. I couldn't hear him over the wind.

"I don't know what I did."

I wanted him to be happier than he sounded. "I wish I could have seen you kill the Kyngoll."

His horse's hoof unloosed a stone, which skittered off to the side.

"Ivar will live," I added.

"I'm glad." He didn't sound glad.

"What's wrong?"

"It was just a lucky thrust that pierced his neck."

"Whose neck?"

"The soldier I killed. I was furious when Ivar went down. Everybody was shouting. I think I was, too."

The battle spell.

"I struck, and I've never felt so strong."

Willem turned to me in the saddle. I saw a tightness around his mouth that hadn't been there before. "There was only a little spot where the soldier had no armor. I got it by accident. He spouted a fountain of blood and I stopped being angry. I said *him*, but it could have been a woman. Doesn't matter which it was."

The apprentice's torch disappeared in the trees ahead.

"Did you look in the soldier's eyes?"

"All I saw was blood, and then the line closed in front of me. I didn't use my spear again. I just moved with the line. I don't think I even kept my shield up."

How lucky he hadn't been gored, too!

I didn't know what to say. Why was he telling me?

"As soon as I killed him, I seemed to wake up from a dream. I felt like I was the only person in a pack of barking dogs, and a moment before I'd been a dog, too."

In his place, I'd have stayed a dog. Willem was the true Bamarre and I the true Lakti, no matter who our parents were.

I wanted to comfort him. "Father told me not to look in the eyes of our foes because it takes the joy away and you still have to fight them. Seeing the blood was like looking in—"

"I almost fainted. If I had, I would have been trampled. Then I almost threw up."

"Vomiting in your helmet would be horrible!"

"I don't want to fight again. Do you think I'm a coward?"

I didn't know.

"Am I?"

I searched for words that wouldn't wound him. "It took courage to tell me." That was true. "Maybe other people are like you, but they pretend not to be because *they're* cowards." But I thought he might really not be brave, not in battle anyway.

A few more trees ahead and we'd be through the copse.

"What will your father say when I refuse to go back?"

Was this why he told me?

"Will he even let me not fight?"

"I'd go in your place." I regretted the words instantly. I didn't mean I was better than he was.

He spurred his horse. In an instant he was out of the trees.

"Willem!" I had to apologize. To explain.

I kicked my mount, too. As she gathered herself to sprint, a rope snare dropped over my head. I fell out of the saddle and landed hard. The mare rode on. Willem must have heard something, or my riderless horse may have passed him. The coward turned his horse to come back to me and was captured, too.

CHAPTER THIRTEEN

STUPID! STUPID! STUPID! The Kyngoll must have made some noise that I could have heard, even in the wind if I'd been paying attention. Or I should have smelled them—they wore rose perfume to battle!

Stupid again, I forgot Lady Mother's pendant until after my hands were bound behind my back. Every bit of me ached from my fall. In the night, our captors were just three shadows. Without gagging us, they slung us across Willem's steed's back. If we shouted, we were too far by now from the surgeon's cart for anyone to hear.

The Lakti regarded captives as deserving their fate. Lady Mother and Father would have to live with the shame of a daughter foolish enough to be caught.

But not with a Bamarre in the family.

Father would be beside himself. The thought of his distress almost made me weep.

And Lady Mother! But the thought of her banished tears. She'd taught me not to cry.

I turned my head and found Willem regarding me.

"I'm sorry for what I said," I whispered.

"It doesn't matter."

Not exactly forgiveness.

"Now you won't be able to go in my place."

Not forgiveness at all.

My head kept bumping into the horse's flank. Our captors were silent. My eyes had adjusted to the dark.

"Perry—"

"Sh!" Who could guess what names they knew?

He nodded. "Your father wasn't the reason I told you." He paused. "No. I don't mean that. He was, but I'd have told you anyway, because you tell the truth."

"You're very brave. You came back for me."

After a moment, he smiled. "Truth."

But it might have been better if he'd really been a coward and had galloped ahead and raised an alarm.

"I still don't want to fight again."

He might never have to admit that to anyone else.

Halina, I thought, what should I do?

Her ringing voice echoed in my mind: *Be a Lakti for now. Escape.*

Was that her or my imagination? Still, I asked for more aid. Help me escape!

Actual voice or not, her tone was resentful: *I just did*.

After perhaps a quarter hour of travel at a walk, a Kyngoll slapped our horse's rear, and he broke into a trot. I thought my bones were going to fly apart. If they planned to cook us, we'd be tender by the time we reached their town.

My voice vibrated as I recited a ditty Mistress Clarra taught us years ago, Lakti poetry.

> *"We Lakti don't mind pain.*
> *Torture is in vain.*
> *My body obeys my brain."*

Willem joined in, and we continued for the rest of the miserable journey, even as we entered the Kyngoll town and clattered down a cobblestone street.

A moment after our steed stopped, I was lifted off. My heart hammered. I shook my shoulders so that my cloak covered the magic pendant.

Our captors were three women, one tall, one short, one in the middle, who held a torch. The short woman had the horses' reins. The tall one drew my hood away from my face, although my hair—whatever length it had grown to—was still concealed by my cap.

"They're children!" Her accent softened the *ch* to *sh*. "Are they sending *shildren* into battle?"

The short one said, "The girl is younger than my Marla. Don't be afraid, *shild*."

"Probably not afraid," the tall one said. "They beat fear out of them."

I'd never been beaten! And I doubted Willem had been, either.

The tall one grabbed my arm, and the medium-sized one took Willem's.

On one side of the street rose a large stone edifice, the baker's guildhall, judging by the iron rolling pin nailed to the wooden door. On the other side were prosperous half-timbered houses, seemingly untouched by war. A few hurrying figures rushed by, leaning into the wind. Voices raised in song emanated from a tavern, the Quilted Pig.

We were marched down three houses to a door guarded by two Kyngoll men. Our captors pushed us inside and prodded us up a narrow flight of stairs.

Another guard let us through a low door into a solar—the great hall of a house—with an arched ceiling. A fire blazed in the fireplace, and no fewer than five coal braziers smoked the air. My eyes smarted. I smelled sage in the rushes that covered the floor tiles. All un-Lakti-like luxuries.

A clean-shaven man watched us from a bench placed

to the side of the fire. He wasn't as lean as Father or truly fat, but I thought he liked his meals.

Embroidered linen panels hung on every wall, each depicting a garden. Between two large glazed windows, an open cupboard displayed stacks of bowls, platters, and table linens. On the wall across from the fireplace stood a buffet. Pride of place in the middle of the buffet was taken by an oaken carving of a cat, perhaps a foot tall, sitting on its haunches.

Cushions were scattered across the floor and spread along the bench where the plump man sat. "Come in." His voice was full and deep. "Sit."

I was pushed down and sank into a floor cushion. Comfortable.

Soft.

The women removed their cloaks. They were well fed, too.

"I am Sir Lerrin. How old are you, lad?"

Willem hesitated. "Seventeen."

No harm in telling. Our youth was obvious.

"Fascinating. I expect you're both hungry, though I suppose you'll deny it." He grinned. "Are you hungry?"

We each shook our heads.

"Well, I'm hungry."

The short woman said, "You always are."

I was surprised she'd speak that way to her superior.

"Yes, Zasha, I am."

The women smiled.

Sir Lerrin continued. "Then we should eat."

Did the Kyngoll poison their captives? Would they unbind our hands so we could eat? Or would they feed us?

The women assembled a table from the board and trestles that leaned against the wall next to the buffet. Sir Lerrin stood with the litheness of a cat and was revealed to be no taller than Willem. He padded to the cupboard and lifted an embroidered tablecloth from the top of the pile of linens. Holding it, folded, over the table, he announced, "Good tablecloth, please set thyself."

When he let go, the tablecloth hung in the air and unfolded itself. It settled crisply over the tabletop. And then—

I yelped. Food, on fine platters and in tureens and bowls, popped out of nothing above the table and descended gently, in more variety than I'd ever seen at a castle feast: quail, honey-glazed by the skin's glisten; sliced roast boar; a whole golden carp; leek-in-cream soup; pickled onions; boiled beets; rolls studded with raisins; almond-milk frumenty; and a wheel of soft cheese.

My open mouth watered, and my stomach rumbled, perhaps loud enough for everyone to hear. "Is it fairy-made?"

No one answered.

The shower of food ended, but six silver spoons and six empty bowls in a stack arrived, the top bowl almost falling and then righting itself. The tablecloth expected Willem and me to eat.

The Kyngoll filled their bowls to brimming. I marked what they served themselves. If our hands were untied and we agreed that we should eat, I'd take only what they had.

No. I wouldn't eat at all. I'd use the pendant and draw my thrusting dagger, and Willem would draw his. With the pendant, we had a chance of defeating them all.

But Willem didn't want to fight again. I didn't know if he'd make an exception to escape.

Sir Lerrin himself freed us, after removing the daggers from our waists. He went to the door and handed them to the guard.

We each still had a little knife in our purses, but they were for eating with—capable of killing nothing bigger than a mouse. I flexed my wrists.

Willem took his cloak off, but I kept mine on to hide the pendant.

The tall soldier said, "Wouldn't you like to take your cloak off, young mistress?"

"I was chilled today, and I can't seem to get warm."

"Strange chill," Sir Lerrin said, "with beads of sweat collecting on your forehead."

Hastily I wiped the wet away.

Zasha chuckled. "When my Marla keeps her cloak on, it's because her kirtle somehow doesn't please her."

Let them think me as vain as a Kyngoll.

"At least," said the tall soldier, "take off your hood."

I pulled the hood back, lifted off my cap, and then tugged off the hood of mail. My hair tumbled out. The locks that didn't pool in my hood descended to my shoulder blades.

"Marla will be green with envy."

I was expected to meet Zasha's daughter?

Willem's eyes met mine. "Should we eat?" we asked each other at the same time.

"You should," the short woman—Zasha—and Sir Lerrin said in unison, too.

Willem and I probably shared a thought, too. If they killed us here, we'd die after a full meal.

CHAPTER FOURTEEN

"THE TABLECLOTH ISN'T fairy-made," Sir Lerrin said.

We filled our bowls, both of us choosing only dishes that the others were eating. I wished someone had taken the cheese puffs, a treat I'd tasted just once and relished.

Could I overturn the groaning board and create chaos that would let us escape?

They'd catch us, or the guards would.

"You Lakti!" Sir Lerrin helped himself to several cheese puffs.

I took a few, too. What did he mean?

He explained without being asked. "Cautious. Self-denying."

Self-denying, yes, but not at this moment. I pointed at the cheese puffs with my spoon. "They're delicious, Wi—"

I stopped myself before his name came out and changed the *Wi* to *why*. "Why don't you try them?" Everything was delectable, the flavors purer than anything I'd ever tasted.

Willem helped himself to cheese puffs. "How are we cautious, Sir Lerrin, when we're renowned for courage?"

I wondered if he was thinking of his doubts about his own bravery.

The tall woman said, "Neither of you is eating anything we didn't taste first."

Sir Lerrin sat and leaned back against his ridiculous cushions. "Little mistress, you eyed those cheese puffs as if they were family you hadn't seen in years."

I blushed. "You said the tablecloth wasn't fairy-made, but you didn't say who did make it."

"We purchased it before the war. The Lakti merchant said it was a sorcerer's creation from Old Lakti."

Like my pendant!

The tablecloth had come from a pile of linens. I gestured at it. "Are they all magical?"

He shook his head. "None are, but we were told that others like ours exist."

Were there were other magic pendants, too? Might Sir Lerrin or any of the others be concealing one right now?

"What other differences are there between the Lakti and the Kyngoll?" Willem scooped up a dollop of frumenty.

A perfect question. We might get information Father could use—if we escaped.

"That's easy," Sir Lerrin said. "We're deep thinkers."

Meaning the Lakti weren't.

The others chimed in.

"The Lakti are cruel."

"Relentless."

A good quality in war.

"You worship war."

"For the peace that will follow," Willem said. "And we don't *worship* it."

Yet Father had confessed that he'd find endless peace dull.

"Lacking sympathy."

Sir Lerrin stroked his chin. "The Lakti live in cities that the Bamarre built. What have you added to culture? To cookery?"

Zasha added, "You have no poetry."

I burst out, "I love poetry!"

Willem stared at me.

I pulled back my shoulders to recite a poem that Lilli wrote near the end of her life:

> *"Heavy with hope denied,*
> *Leaden with the lid*
> *Slammed on tomorrow . . ."*

I gulped.

> *"What eases my heart?*
> *A scent of sea, music,*
> *A speckled stone,*
> *Parchment under my pen.*
> *Writing my horizons away."*

Outside, a bell rang the hour. Eight o'clock. Father would be frantic.

Sir Lerrin coughed. "Fascinating. A poem by a Lakti master, young mistress?"

I admitted that the poet had been a Bamarre.

The mood shifted back to scorn. I wondered what Kyngoll poetry was like.

"A difference you'll both care about," said Sir Lerrin, "is that we Kyngoll don't kill our prisoners."

Would we be imprisoned forever?

Zasha said vehemently, "We'd never kill a child. Never!"

Sir Lerrin served himself a big wedge of cheese. "Tonight, we'll hold you. Zasha, take the boy to the guildhall. I want to talk to the girl alone."

Don't separate us!

The tall soldier said, "She's just a youngster. She's probably tired."

Sounding annoyed, Sir Lerrin said, "I know. Go!"

Willem's hands were bound again. They left. Three fewer people to stop me if I used the pendant. Then I'd go for Willem.

"What do they call you, young mistress?"

He might know Father had a daughter named Peregrine—Perry.

Sir Lerrin cocked his head. "You think I might recognize your name."

"We're told to give no information if we're captured."

"Might you be Lady Peregrine, Lord Tove's daughter?"

I succeeded in not changing my face and giving the truth away.

"An unusual name. Is there a tale behind it?"

I didn't answer.

He continued. "Another quality that we Kyngoll have and you Lakti don't is intuition. Lady Peregrine, there is around you an air of destiny. I believe you'll be a queen. Of New Lakti or perhaps of Kyngoll."

I laughed. A Bamarre queen of New Lakti! I could hardly catch my breath. I prayed my wild laughter wouldn't dissolve into tears.

Sir Lerrin stared.

My laughter finally died. "I hope your last prisoner didn't give secrets away when you told her about her future crown."

What were the women saying to Willem?

I trusted him! He wouldn't be deceived, either.

"I've never . . ." Sir Lerrin shrugged. "You won't believe me." He set his bowl on the table. "Good tablecloth, I thank thee for a fine meal."

The remaining food vanished, along with the bowls, tureens, platters, and silver. The cloth folded itself and settled softly on the table.

"Everything shrank!" Or so it had seemed.

"Yes. I sometimes wonder if the air is full of dots of food so small we can't see them."

Might there be other sorcerer-made items? A magic loom? Carpenter's tools? Cobbler's? Might miniature cloth and houses and shoes be drifting about us, too?

"You don't distribute the tablecloth's bounty to your soldiers? The Lakti would."

"Our soldiers eat well."

"This well?"

He looked discomfited. "Perhaps not this well." He changed the subject. "You truly love poetry?"

I nodded.

He stood. "Here's one by a Kyngoll poet:

> *"Kingdom—*
> *Yours, mine—*
> *Enduring, ennobling,*
> *Above petty purpose,*
> *By virtue victorious,*
> *Kyngoll."*

I wished he'd recite more. What would it be like to live in a kingdom where everyone revered poetry, where I wouldn't have to choose between being a Lakti or a Bamarre?

"You surprise me. The boy, too. I'll remember you both. You have a friend in Sir Lerrin, Peregrine." He seemed to startle. "Turn your head, if you please."

Feeling uneasy, I didn't.

He began to step around me. I moved to keep facing him.

He saw anyway. "I'd swear your hair has grown while you've been here!" He shook his head. "Fascinating. We're showing off our magical tablecloth when you yourself are made of magic."

I wondered if I might use my hair. Halina, is this why you made it grow?

He approached me. I made myself stay still. He touched a length of hair, rubbed the strands between two fingers. How dare he?

"It feels like hair. I don't suppose you'll explain?"

Controlling myself, I smiled a secretive smile.

He shrugged. "We'll figure it out. Your hands, please."

Don't bind them!

Surprise was on my side. I shook my head and lowered my chin to my chest. Behind a cascade of hair, I opened my cloak.

"Hair, hair," I chanted, "make your magic." The battle spell fell over me. Time seemed to slow. With an exquisitely sensitive finger, I rubbed the pendant's diamond sword.

He staggered back, throwing his arm across his eyes and bending double. Feeling the muscles in my arm, the power in my fingers, I pulled his thrusting dagger from the sheath at his waist. He sensed me and tried to catch my hand. I jumped away.

I might have stabbed him—but he'd recited poetry!

I slid the knife into my sheath. If I just left him, he'd come after me in a few minutes. "Hair, hair, blindness everywhere." A rhyme for him. I ran to the buffet and picked up the wooden cat. Heavy—five pounds at least. I swung it hard against his head.

The crack sounded deafening. He fell, moaning. I hit him against his ribs, and this time he made no noise.

Don't die, Sir Lerrin! But don't wake up soon!

I backed away. As I passed the table, I scooped up the tablecloth and held on to the cat sculpture.

Now for the guard outside the door. I opened it.

Still shaking my hair around my chest and shoulders, I rubbed the pendant. The guard shielded his eyes and cried out. I reached for Sir Lerrin's dagger, then raised the cat instead. Why was I sparing him? This one hadn't recited anything.

Kyngoll-foolish, he wore no helmet. I brought the cat down twice on his head.

Footsteps.

"Hair, hair, make your magic."

The figure lurched. As he tumbled backward down the stairs, his hood fell away and I saw his face.

I dropped the wooden cat.

Father!

CHAPTER FIFTEEN

HE LANDED IN a heap.

I rushed to him, taking two steps at a time. "Father!"

"Peregrine?" He groaned, then tugged me down and hugged me. I felt his tears on my forehead.

"You came for me!"

"You're my daughter," he said into the top of my head, "though you may not have needed me, though you've blinded me." He released me.

"Is it terrible? It will clear."

"I'm beginning to see again. I'll try to stand."

I jumped up and held out my hands, but he managed on his own. He seemed to have appeared, like Halina, like the meal from the tablecloth, out of thin air. He'd risked his life and the whole Kyngoll campaign for me.

I heard muffled shouts.

"Come!" Father opened the door, and the voices became strident. "Hurry!"

I picked the tablecloth up from where I'd let it fall.

Outside, Willem sat on a horse behind a Lakti soldier. With my senses still heightened, I noted the strain in his smile and the misery in his eyes.

Two other soldiers on horseback and one riderless steed waited in the middle of the street. Father mounted, and I leaped up behind him, settling the tablecloth in my lap. He spurred his horse.

Zasha sprawled across the steps to the guildhall, her throat open and blood pooling around her shoulder and neck.

The battle spell flew out of me. I swallowed again and again to keep down my meal. Marla had lost her mother.

But Zasha would have killed Father if we hadn't killed her.

We clattered down the street. Beyond the town our horses reached full gallop. I wondered why I hadn't stabbed the guard. Had my Bamarre side reared up? Had it been cowardice?

When we slowed to an amble to give the horses a brief rest, Father said, "Your mother didn't say she'd given you the pendant. You made excellent use of it."

I smiled. "Thank you."

The first to meet us outside the camp was Sir Noll. Willem jumped off his horse, and the two shook hands awkwardly.

But then Sir Noll grasped his son's shoulders. "Are you hurt?"

"I'm as well as I was at battle's end."

I took that to mean not very well.

But Sir Noll seemed satisfied. "I'd have come for you, too, but Tove swore he'd do as well without me, and I could run the war if any—"

"Perry had already escaped." Father dismounted, too. "My soldier girl."

How I loved pleasing Father, being the daughter he and Lady Mother admired, being a Lakti.

We marched triumphantly through the camp, where no one seemed to be asleep.

"Noll, my daughter will stay with me tonight. I have to keep looking at her to persuade myself she's safe."

Sir Noll said he planned to do the same. They left.

Father guided me by my elbow, as if I were an invalid, to his tent. Inside, he sat me in his own chair and went to the coal brazier, where he added fresh coals from the scuttle.

Then he took the stool next to me. "Don't spare me, Perry. What did they do to you?"

I grinned. "They made us endure an endless recitation of our Lakti faults."

Father squinted at me. "I want the truth."

I put the tablecloth on the low table in front of me. Then I stood, removed my cloak, and held out my arms, turning slowly so he could inspect me.

"Wasn't your hair shorter last night?"

I'd forgotten! My hair now touched my waist. What to say? I was dreadful at lying. "Was it? I don't think so."

"Weren't you saying something about your hair when you blinded me?"

I forced a laugh. "Lady Mother says it's my one beauty."

"It's not!"

I really laughed.

He realized his mistake and laughed, too. "I mean, you have many beauties."

"The Kyngoll were surprised at how thick it is." I sat again. "I pretended it's magical. When I used the pendant, I shined it through my hair."

"I suggest you take it off now in case your *beautiful* hair rubs it."

I put it in its velvet case in the purse at my waist.

"You used it admirably. Cleverly."

"Sir Lerrin accused the Lakti of being clever but not deep thinkers."

"Sir Lerrin himself?"

"Is he their commander?"

"He is. What else did he accuse us of?"

I told him what I remembered. He asked a host of questions about Sir Lerrin. When I told him that the knight could recite poetry, he snorted.

"That, Perry, is why we'll defeat them." He added, "They were trying to learn our secrets." He chuckled. "Clever, but not deeply thought through. Perry, love, were you frightened? They were going to kill you in the morning, I suppose."

"They told me they don't kill their prisoners. The woman who died outside the guild—"

"Say that again."

"The woman—"

"Before that. They told you they don't kill their prisoners?"

"Yes, Father."

He stood and paced.

"What's wrong?"

He sat again. "Never mind." After a minute, he shrugged. "It's nothing you can't hear. They captured two soldiers last year. Suppose their allegiance changed . . ."

"Did they know any secrets?"

"No, but our soldiers can teach them our way of fighting, our refusal to give up. Even soldiers foolish enough to be captured are superb fighters."

"Do you think I was foolish?"

He hesitated. "A little."

"Did I disappoint you?"

"No. Definitely not. You're still a child, and Willem is just out of childhood. I expect he was lost in describing his triumph and you were listening raptly."

Something like that, except for the triumph.

"I'm proud of you. I've been proud of you since you toddled toward me the first day I saw you." His smile widened with the recollection. "You fell and picked your own self up, tiny as you were." He showed me with his thumb and forefinger, as if I had ever been an inch tall. "You're the best child I can imagine."

My eyes brimmed. Joy filled me, and the first peace I'd felt since before Halina showed me the vision. But, wanting more, I just said, "I'm forever disappointing Lady Mother."

"You can't possibly disappoint me."

There. Nothing to worry about. I could be both a Lakti and a Bamarre. I smiled while tears streamed. Lakti smile, Bamarre tears.

Father stood me up and hugged me. "You've had a hard day. You can cry." He chuckled. "I won't tell your mother."

I sobbed against him, and he held me until my tears stopped. He let me go then and went to the high table, where he crouched to pull the basket out. "I have more figs tucked away."

"You said you'd love me if I were short—" My chest felt tight.

"And there are—" He looked up at me. "Darling, why short? You're not short."

"Or anything." I swallowed. "Like, what if my parents were Bamarre?"

He exploded in laughter. "You're a paragon of a Lakti! Love, you're not a Bamarre."

I said nothing.

He stood and took my hands. "You want to know if anything—anything!—could make me not love you."

"Yes!"

He sighed. "Perry, I've never pretended to be perfect."

"You never give yourself airs!"

"A kind interpretation." He put the basket on the table and sat in his chair. "Doubtless there are worthy people among the Bamarre, but I couldn't love one of them. You've seen how they disgust me."

There it was.

"Can you accept that in me?" he asked.

"Of course. I love you."

But he didn't love me, not all of me. The ground seemed to shift and the tent to revolve. I spread my legs for balance. The world righted—or wronged—itself into a new arrangement.

"Are you well?" He was at my elbow.

I nodded. "I think it's . . . everything." One thing,

really. I couldn't go on as his pretend child.

"You had a thrilling evening, darling. Sometimes, after a hard battle, I think I'm fine, but then my knees buckle and I have to sit. Luckily, I found the cure." He waited.

I tried to sound curious. "What is it?"

"Figs!" He held them out, looking eager.

How charming he was—to a Lakti.

CHAPTER SIXTEEN

I TOOK A fig. My mouth was so dry I could hardly chew. "Delicious."

We shared the treats in what would once have been a companionable silence.

The seven-league boots! Which were in my tent.

After Father fell asleep I'd slip out, get the boots, don them, and go—somewhere.

Eventually, he said, "Your mother would be furious that I kept you up so late." He smoothed the linen across his pallet. "Take it. I've slept on the ground before. I'm going out. I want to plan tomorrow's battle, but I'll be right outside the tent."

I lay down in all my clothes. He'd expect that. The brazier coal was spent, and the air had chilled.

He knelt next to me. "My brave child." He stood and left.

I'd always believed he loved me more than Lady Mother did. I squeezed my eyes tight to hold back the tears. They came anyway, but I kept myself from sobbing. I didn't want him to hear, to comfort me. A river seeped out of me until I was finally empty.

Raising myself, I tied the tablecloth around my waist under my cloak, although I couldn't leave yet, not with him right outside. How long could he stay in the cold?

Long. He was a Lakti, born and trained.

Despite myself, I slept—

—and woke when I heard movement. Groggily, I raised myself on my elbow. "Father?"

Two guards hauled me up. The tent flap had been pulled back. Father stood in the opening, and behind him, a gray predawn.

His face! The polite mask. He wiped his hands on the front of his cloak, again, again.

He knew!

"Your questions about loving you made me curious, so your maid and I had a conversation, and she told me the truth. Now give me the pendant."

With icy fingers, I slid its pouch off my belt and dropped it into his hand. Had he hurt Annet?

He told the guards, "Regrettably, Peregrine has displeased me."

How much had Annet told him?

I held myself in a vise of control. If he hoped to see Bamarre weakness, he would not.

"Take her to the south tower and make sure she can't get out."

Imprisonment! My control broke. I tried to squirm away. "Father! Don't shut me in!"

As they bore me out, I cried, "I can't bear it! Father, you know I can't stand it! Please!"

For the second time, I was slung over a horse, this time by my own countrymen. The horses trotted, and too soon we reached the south tower, half a mile from camp.

I was lifted from the horse—lifted carefully, handled gently. Father hadn't told the guards I was a Bamarre. They didn't know if his displeasure would end and I'd be his beloved daughter again.

The tower loomed as we approached. I saw fist-sized stones cemented in place with daub; a crenellated roof with uneven, crumbling teeth; small windows near the top and nowhere else; and an iron-banded wooden door.

Terrible!

A guard unlocked the door with a huge bronze key. The hinge creaked. I smelled stone and mold.

They had to drag me in.

A guard spoke absurdly polite words. "We bid you good day, young mistress."

They turned to leave, but I grabbed the arm of one of them. I would remember his face forever. Gray mustache, watery brown eyes, jowly cheeks like a bulldog's.

"Take me with you, I beg of you. Father doesn't mean it. It will save you the return trip. Don't—"

He put me aside. The door thudded shut. No light. No food. No blanket.

I crumpled into a heap.

When I returned to myself, my mind divided into a sensible self and a frenzied self, and the two began to jabber at each other.

I can escape. I should look around.

I'm trapped!

The darkness was complete.

I should pretend there are no walls. If I can't see them, they may not be there.

If I can't see them, they could be closing in!

Both halves shouted out loud, "Halina! Help me!" My cry echoed around and around.

I took shaky steps until I reached the wall. Moist, cold stone.

Was Father thinking of me? Changing his mind? How could he do this to someone he loved?

What had he done to Annet? Could he have killed her?

Had she given me up easily to save herself, whether that had spared her or not? How much had she told him?

I felt along the wall, reasoning, with what reason I had left, that there must be a stairway. Spider strands covered my face. At last I came, not to stairs, but to a ladder, which I didn't have the sense to test before climbing. I went up like a crab, clinging to the rungs and the sides. Luckily, they held my weight.

Finally I reached the next story. The opening for the ladder, which continued upward, let in faint light from the story above, where the windows must be. I climbed again.

Eight windows, all barred, the bars too close together to squeeze between.

The windows weren't glazed or even covered with oiled parchment to block the cold. Through the first window I went to, the sun was the tip of a fingernail above the horizon. A hawk flew black against the pale sky.

I ran from one window to another, leaping over gaps in the floorboards. The windows were no higher than my chest; the wooden ceiling hung only a few inches above my head. The window bars didn't budge when I shook them.

At the last window, I beat on the bars with my fists, then banged my head on the sill. I huffed, "Be a Lakti. Be unafraid."

Halina!

Eventually I gave up and collapsed. The light grew gradually. I lay in a pool of hair. Dust and spider threads and perhaps spiders themselves spangled the strands.

My stomach grumbled. The tablecloth!

I untied it from around my waist and expected it to feed me.

Nothing happened.

I heard hooves. I ran to the north window. Four riders. None of them Father—I knew how he sat a horse. I practically threw myself down the ladder. Father must have remembered he loved me. I was a Bamarre but not loathsome. They were going to take me back to camp!

At the bottom I raised my hood to cover my hair as well as it might.

The lock turned. The door opened just wide enough to admit one guard, and he came in sideways. They hadn't come to release me. In the moment of light before the door closed behind him, I saw that this one was clean-shaven, with thin lips and a sharp nose.

"Let me out, please. I'll never forget you if you do."

"No, young mistress." He set down two satchels and a jug. I had a silver coin in my purse. I offered it to him to let me go, but he ignored it and left in the same sideways fashion.

Fa—Lord Tove—still hadn't revealed that I was a Bamarre, or the guard wouldn't have called me *young mistress*.

The tower pressed in on me again. My frenzied self

gibbered that I would die here.

Still, I hauled the satchels and the jug up the ladders. In one satchel, I found, wrapped in burlap, an entire wheel of cheese and two loaves of hard bread. The jug contained water mixed with vinegar, which made the water safe to drink.

The second satchel held a mat and a blanket. At least Lord Tove didn't want me to freeze to death. Did that mean he still loved me? That he merely needed time to get used to the truth?

Under the blanket, I found my book of poems, the seven-league boots that Lady Mother had given me, and the other sundries I'd brought from home. He must not have recognized the boots, or he may have just told the guards to bring me my things except for my weapons.

Funny. Jailed with boots that could take me anywhere.

What if I put them on and took a step? Might I tear through the walls and be free?

Or be battered to death?

Better to die than remain imprisoned.

The prospect of escape calmed me. Food first. With my little knife, which no one had taken from me, I cut a wedge of cheese and a chunk of bread and imagined where I'd go.

Funny again. Eating hard bread and cheese when I had a tablecloth that could produce a feast.

This tower rose in western New Lakti; Kyngoll lay

to the west and northwest; home, or my former home, beckoned from the northeast; my first parents lived in the eastern village of Gavrel, where I'd been taught two Lakti families also lived, and an unknown number of the Bamarre.

For a minute I considered going to Kyngoll in the boots, but I doubted I'd be welcome. I stuffed the food and my things into a single, bulging sack.

No large lakes lay to the east. I wouldn't drown. If I was unlucky enough to arrive in a village, I'd simply take another step—if the enormous boots hadn't fallen off in transit.

As soon as I pulled the first one on, it shrank to fit my foot! It was still filthy and worn, but it fit perfectly. I held out my foot to admire this wonder. Then I donned the other marvel, which also molded itself to my foot.

I stood, faced the southeast window, lifted my sack, and stepped—

—and was forced to the floor by a swirl of light. Halina took shape.

I hadn't seen her angry before and wished I weren't seeing it now.

The light illuminated her in an orange glow. She pulled me up and jabbed a finger into my chest. "Fool, thoughtless . . ."

My chain mail dug into me with each poke.

". . . caring only for yourself." Her finger stopped, but her jaw still jutted forward, and her eyebrows still slanted alarmingly upward.

"What?" I choked out.

"Did you think—if you thought at all—that magic boots are toys? Stepping into a wall! This fairy would be standing over a corpse." A smile replaced the anger. "This fairy doesn't think you're usually a fool." She touched my cheek. "You've done well, except for almost destroying yourself. Your hair is growing beautifully. I was proud when you decided you couldn't continue as Tove's daughter."

I blurted out, "Why do I matter to you? Why do the Bamarre?"

Her gaze shifted away from me. "We—fairies—lost a battle. Not here." She waved her hands around the tower. "In our realm. I was there, part of our failure. The result was that monsters came to Old Lakti, though they can't go anywhere else. If the Lakti hadn't crossed the Eskerns, the Bamarre would be free. Who knows what your life would have been? Your sister's life? The life of every Bamarre subject of New Lakti? That's why this fairy cares." She vanished.

Into the air I said, "How can I free anyone if I can't free myself?"

"Perry?"

Halina must have kept me from hearing hoofbeats. I tripped on my hair as I rushed to the north window.

Willem gazed up at me. No horse. He'd come on foot. "Perry?"

Did he know? Had Lord Tove told the truth about me?

"Why are you here?" he said, revealing he didn't know.

I wasn't ready to tell him and lose my only friend. "Hello, Willem." Yesterday's wind had died to nothing. I didn't have to shout. "You're not fighting today?"

Kindhearted as ever, he didn't press me. "No, but Lord Tove is."

Of course.

"I told Father I didn't want to, and he said I'm too young anyway." He shrugged. "I didn't admit I never want to fight again. Tomorrow I'm to help the armorer."

Probably to give me time, he told me about camp doings. A tent had caught fire and, accompanied by great hilarity, the blaze had been extinguished with slop buckets. But then he came back to his question. "Why are you shut up here? And why was your maid sent home in chains?"

"She was?" Poor Annet!

At least she was alive.

He nodded and waited.

What could I say?

The truth. He liked that in me, and what difference

would it make? "Lord Tove put me here because he found out I'm a Bamarre." Would I disgust Willem, too?

"What? Am I going deaf again?"

I repeated myself, fairly shouting the words, and felt my face redden. "My birth parents were Bamarre." Everyone knew I'd been adopted.

He stared up at me. "You're not a Bamarre."

"I am. Lord Tove despises me."

"You can't be."

I waited.

"If you are, everything we were taught is wrong. You're not weak, for one thing."

"I might be weak if I'd been raised a Bamarre."

"But the Bamarre are supposed to be naturally weak."

"I can't bear being penned up in here. That's weak." Why was I arguing?

"But you are bearing it."

True, even though gusts of terror kept whipping through me. I asked, despite a different fear, "Are you still my friend?"

He didn't hesitate. "Why wouldn't I be? You haven't changed."

CHAPTER SEVENTEEN

MY NEXT BREATH filled my lungs, unobstructed by swallowed tears. I was bathed in gratitude for having such a friend.

"Who told you you're a Bamarre?"

"A fairy."

"A *fairy*?"

"Halina. She made my hair grow." I pushed a lock between the bars and fed it out. The ends dangled a few feet above his head. Soon, they'd reach the ground.

He shook his head in surprise. "Why?"

"I wish I knew." I began my story, starting with Lady Mother in my parents' cottage.

He took a step backward. "She stole you?"

"And Annet." I went on, and it was a relief to tell,

because I saw Willem's sympathy—and no disgust. I omitted only that Halina expected me to free the Bamarre, *us* Bamarre.

At the end he said, "I know why the fairy picked you."

"Why?"

"If I had a purpose, I'd choose you to carry it out. I don't know what her goal is, but you're strong-willed and—"

"Even though I'm a Bamarre?"

He just continued. "And determined. Unafraid."

Except of confinement.

"Thank you." I did have those qualities. "Why do people think I'm here?"

"It's rumored that Lord Tove now blames you for getting us captured."

"Me, not you?"

"They think I'm excused because I killed a Kyngoll. They all want to talk about that." His face turned a darker shade. "I'm getting credit for modesty."

"If you enjoyed the killing, you still wouldn't want to talk about it. You *are* modest."

"You don't boast, either."

"But I'm happy to explain how I run fast or how I fence well. Even if no one asks, I've been known to tell anyway."

He grinned, and I felt pleased. I'd never before said

something amusing on purpose.

"Perry . . . I have to leave. If I'm not there for the noon meal, Mistress Clarra will search for me. I'll try to come tonight."

I doubt I'd ever smiled so widely.

He blinked up at me, almost as if I'd shined the pendant at him. "I'll find a way."

"Can you bring shears? I can hardly walk with all this hair."

He frowned. "How would I get them to you?"

"You can tie them to my hair. I'll pull them up."

He ran off, arms close to his sides, knees high, as I'd taught him.

Cheered beyond anything I could have expected, I went on smiling.

Perhaps I would read some poems. I turned from the window and saw my hair eddying across the floor, dunes of hair, a landscape of hair.

If I braided it, at least it would be a little shorter.

The task filled most of the afternoon. Just keeping the strands separate was job enough, and pulling the whole length of each across the other took time. I picked out spiders, spiderweb strings, clumps of dust, and pebbles. When I couldn't untangle the knots, I braided them in.

While I labored, I pushed away my fear and banished thoughts of Lord Tove and Lady Mother. However, I couldn't help thinking of Annet. In my mind's eye I saw her stony face. Did she think I'd betrayed her?

What had she told Lord Tove? Had she mentioned Halina?

She'd be in a cart, wouldn't she? They wouldn't make her walk, would they?

How had she thought of me, these years? As a Lakti or a Bamarre? Had she ever loved me?

Had I loved her?

Yes. She was my companion always, there for my victories and my defeats, as difficult as Lady Mother. I loved them both. The difference was, I'd struggled to please Lady Mother. I hadn't tried to please Annet.

Finished, the braid snaked back and forth across the floor. I wrapped it around my waist to get it out of the way and returned to watching the beautiful free countryside outside the window. Between the tower and the Maze cypress woods that grew to the south, about forty feet away, was a fountain, which no longer spouted. Around the fountain, a mosaic of tiles had been laid.

The tiles showed white birds against a background of black. Doves, I thought idly.

But as I stared, the white dove tiles receded, and black tiles pushed forward against a field of white. The black tiles were cats! I clapped my hands and smiled.

I continued to stare. After a minute, the birds returned.

Then the images shifted back and forth.

Oh! The bird was the Bamarre, the cat the Lakti, one the prey of the other.

Eventually I tired of looking. Hungry, I tried again to use the magic tablecloth. I shook it out. Nothing happened, except the part that dragged on the floor got dirty. Were the words Sir Lerrin had spoken a magic spell?

The tablecloth had been folded, and Sir Lerrin had held it. I did as he had.

"Tablecloth, set . . ." No. "*Good* tablecloth, set . . ." No. "Good tablecloth, *please* set thyself."

It pulled away from me, hung in the air a moment, then opened. It hesitated, as if seeking a table, before spreading itself over an invisible one, the cloth falling crisply from edges that weren't there. Cautiously, with my jaw probably flapping, I pressed down several inches in from a corner. Hard, like an actual table. And there was no longer a speck of dirt on the cloth.

Food arrived, not the largesse of last night, but more than I could eat: half a stewed capon; two enormous poached goose eggs; asparagus, which, without magic, could be had only in spring; slices of roast mutton; a half-moon loaf of bread; raisin pudding; dried dates and figs; and walnuts already shelled.

Daylight dwindled while I ate. I noticed that my hair continued to grow. I had begun the braid at the nape of my neck, but now loose hair descended to my waist.

When I could barely see what I was eating, three candles appeared in silver candlesticks and lit themselves. Beeswax candles! A pure light, little smoke, and no stink of rancid meat that tallow candles gave out.

I finished eating, but I didn't make the food disappear because the candles would vanish too.

"Perry?"

I ran to the window.

Willem, who had a torch, asked about my light. "I saw the flickering halfway from the camp."

He crowed in triumph when he heard that I'd stolen Sir Lerrin's tablecloth.

I explained about the candles.

"Oh." He paused. "I don't think you should use the tablecloth at night unless I'm here with the torch."

Ah. If guards came after dark they'd see the light and discover how I happened to have it, and they'd take the tablecloth. "Thank you."

He grinned. "You *should* thank me. This is the kind of advice you give me."

"Which you receive with ill humor." Had I ever teased anyone before?

"But after an hour of thinking, I'm always grateful."

I liked banter!

"What does the tablecloth bring a prisoner? Not just hard cheese?"

I told him. "It's not fair I can't share."

"It's not fair you're in there. I have the shears."

I had an idea. "You can bring them up."

"How?"

I told him.

He laughed. "Peregrine, Peregrine, let down your hair!"

I pushed my braid out the window until it reached Willem's head, which was tilted back, his mouth open in astonishment. I doubled the cord of hair I still held and tied it around a window bar, so that Willem's weight wouldn't pull on my scalp. "Ascend!"

He planted his torch in the ground and tucked the shears into his belt.

My view of his climb was blocked by the windowsill. Don't fall!

Remembering Sir Lerrin's words—*Good tablecloth, I thank thee for a fine meal*—I dismissed it.

When Willem's face appeared above the windowsill, I summoned food again. Cleverly, the tablecloth created a table right at my elbow, and it delivered more food and four candles.

The windowsill projected far enough from the tower for Willem to sit. Before I could offer him food, he passed the shears between the bars. "I have something else for you." He loosened the drawstrings of the purse at his waist.

My heart raced. The Lakti rarely gave gifts.

He extracted a snail shell and passed it to me.

I loved it. "It's beautiful! I've never seen one with so many colors." It was striped blue, brown, ruby, and white.

"It never held a snail. It's made of resin and clay."

I couldn't tell.

"When something troubles me, I hold it in my hand. The feel of it is soothing."

"It is!" Smooth, and I could trace its shape as it curved in on itself. "Might it break easily?"

"I don't think so. I've dropped it many times." He lowered his voice, as if anyone could hear us. "It has magic."

"If you hold it to your ear, you can hear the sea, right? Even though it isn't real?"

He smiled. "Try it."

I put it to my ear.

"Surprised? I'm—"

His voice was uncomfortably loud. I took the shell away.

"—not sure how far you can hear with it, maybe half a mile."

"Where did you get it? Is it fairy- or sorcerer-made?"

"I don't know. My father's mother gave it to me for my last birthday. She said I shouldn't use it to eavesdrop." He puffed out his cheeks on a long exhale. "But you should. It could save you."

It might! "Thank you!"

"Do I smell lamprey?"

There was lamprey in a green sauce, a roast duck, fat mushrooms stuffed with cheese, buttered carrots, braided bread (had the tablecloth noticed my braid?), and pear-and-custard pie.

But the bowls, even tilted sideways, didn't fit between the bars. I passed Willem a duck drumstick and a folded-over slice of bread. Our hands touched. My breath caught.

He mumbled thanks and looked as surprised as I felt.

To cover my discomfort, I said, "I'll have to feed you the rest."

When he smiled, his mouth tilted up more on the right. No one else had such a smile.

I speared a slice of lamprey with my little knife and poked it between the bars. He brought his face close to eat.

I dropped my knife, luckily inside the tower. "Sorry!" I put the dirty bit on the tablecloth and wiped off my knife. The fallen food and the grease stain shrank and vanished.

"Oh!" Willem cried.

"When you send the food away, everything shrinks." It was easier to talk than to think about the nearness of his mouth.

He may have felt the same, because, between bites, he asked about my escape from Sir Lerrin.

"I feared I was a coward by not killing the guard, but

now I'm glad." The Kyngoll had been nothing but kind. I added, feeding Willem half a mushroom, "I wouldn't have left without you."

"I didn't think you would." He paused. "If not for you and Father, I wouldn't have gone back with Lord Tove. I liked the Kyngoll. They wouldn't have made me fight."

If not for you. I'd hold that to think about later. I said, "It's possible they're pleasant only so prisoners don't resist."

"You sound exactly like a Lakti." He shook his head, seeming bewildered. "Since I left you, I've been noticing the way we treat our Bamarre servants but not the Lakti ones and what we say about the Bamarre while they're standing right there."

I told him about Lady Mother shining the pendant in Annet's eyes, and also about her failing to think that Annet might want breakfast. "I wonder how it will feel to live as a Bamarre." If I wasn't imprisoned here forever.

"It would make me furious, but we don't know what it would be like to grow up as a Bamarre. They don't seem to be constantly angry."

Annet did.

He added, "Anger could be dangerous. Try not to be angry, Perry."

How could a person not be angry if she was angry?

"I mean, try not to show anger."

"Lakti self-control."

He quoted Mistress Clarra, "'Lakti training prepares one for anything.'"

Ironic. We smiled at each other.

He rapped the windowbars with his knuckles. "I wish these weren't between us."

"Then I'd be fr—" Something in his expression stopped me. "Why do you wish it?"

"Because I'd kiss you."

I blushed. "Oh." What else could I say? "Oh."

He drew back, possibly embarrassed, too. "I hope . . ."

"What?"

He raised one hand and let it fall. "I don't know what to hope. Yes, I do—that our friendship continues."

I nodded along with his words.

"And that I can kiss you."

I blushed again.

"I forgot! Lady Klausine has come."

CHAPTER EIGHTEEN

MY HEART SKIPPED a beat, then galloped. "Really?"

"Really. This afternoon. I saw her. Father said she set out on a fast horse and changed horses all the way. He said she left four days after we did. She'd hoped to be here for your first battle."

What would Fa— Lord Tove say to her? And she to him?

"Maybe she'll persuade him to free you."

As a Bamarre or a Lakti? Might his heart be changed?

Maybe he'd imprison her, too. He wouldn't execute us, would he?

Willem and I said little for the rest of the meal. I made myself silence my worries and enjoy his presence.

After he shook his head at an offer of more pie, he

yawned. "I should go. If you're still here, I'll come tomorrow or tomorrow night."

"Not if it's dangerous!"

"I won't. I promise. Put the shell to your ear."

As he descended, I heard his breathing, the rub of his hands against my braid, the swish of his cloak, and the thump when he reached the ground. As he walked away, I heard the crunch of his feet. He should step more softly for safety!

Then I heard him sing, not very tunefully, "I will kiss my lady Peregrine!"

I watched his torch diminish until it winked out.

If not for you. And he wanted to kiss me. And I wanted to kiss him.

I might never see him again. Now that Lady Mother had come, something would change, for good or ill.

By candlelight I pulled in my braid and wrapped myself in my blanket. "Good tablecloth, I thank thee for a fine meal." The tower darkened, but my fears didn't crowd back. I searched my mind and my peacefully beating heart. Confinement no longer troubled me. I gave Willem the credit and fell asleep.

As soon as I awoke, I listened in the magic shell, hoping for hoofbeats and Lady Mother.

Outside, the breeze streamed a sigh, squirrels chattered,

and the branches complained in dry voices. A woodpecker drummed in its tree—and on my skull. No hooves. I lowered the snail shell.

What had Lord Tove told Lady Mother? What did she think? Was she furious with me?

I used Willem's scissors to shear my hair to shoulder-length, cutting as neatly as I could. When I finished, I coiled the braid as one would sailor's rope. The result was a roll that stood as tall as my thighs. Outside, light snow had begun to fall, probably not enough to end the day's fighting.

Nervous energy wouldn't let me be still, so I dusted the tower, using the tablecloth, because the filth would vanish when it brought me food. Spiders and insects I couldn't name succumbed to me. As I worked, I dreamed up this gloomy verse:

> *I did what I believed*
> *Daughters do. Spiderlike,*
> *I spun a pattern*
> *To please my parents,*
> *Only to learn my thread*
> *Was wrong in length,*
> *Wrong in strength,*
> *Wrong all along.*

Sad. But poetry always comforted me. I felt cheerier.

When I finished dusting, I nodded approvingly and noticed that my hair wasn't any longer than when I started.

Near the end of the day I gave up hope of Lady Mother coming and stopped taking out the magic shell every few minutes.

But half an hour later, I heard hoofbeats. I ran to the north window. Lord Tove and Lady Mother trotted toward my tower. I flew down the ladders and stood at the door, breathing hard, trembling, my heart pulsing in my ears.

My ears! I fumbled in my purse and drew out the snail shell.

The hooves half deafened me. I heard Lady Mother's and Lord Tove's breath and their bodies pounding in their saddles, but no words.

When Lady Mother finally spoke, her words made my eyes fill. "This is where you put our daughter, Tove?"

He didn't answer.

"Don't think you can stop me from taking her home."

Hastily, with the shell still to my ear, I climbed the ladder for my things.

"I seem unable to stop you from doing anything, my dear."

She planned to take me. What did he intend?

154

"As I keep saying, she's a Lakti. I saw to that."

Seemingly, this argument had gone on since she arrived.

"She's *not* a Lakti!" In a kinder voice, he added, "I know how much you wanted a child, sweet."

They were silent for a few minutes. I lugged down my satchel with the tablecloth inside and stood at the door, ready.

Lady Mother burst out, "You agreed to see her."

"I promised nothing more than that. I'll see her. You'll make sure she hasn't died."

How cold he was. And unchanged. I would not weep!

He continued. "You'll embrace her. But you won't take her to our home."

The battle spell took me. With fingers that didn't tremble, I dropped the shell back in my purse, knelt, untied the satchel strings, and exchanged my ordinary boots for the magical ones. That done, I slung the satchel over my shoulder and put the shell back to my ear, but Lady Mother and Lord Tove weren't speaking. I'd missed whatever else might have been said.

The hoofbeats stopped. Two thuds when my parents' feet touched the ground. I put the shell away. The key scraped in the lock.

Willem wouldn't know what happened to me.

The door creaked as it opened. Lord Tove held it. A

crow cawed. Lady Mother stood just to the side, less than an arm's length from me.

I reached out and touched her cheek. "Farewell." I stepped.

Lord Tove cried out.

Did Lady Mother nod? I thought so, but I was moving too fast to be sure.

Impossible speed! Speed beyond anything I'd dreamed of. As much freedom as I could imagine.

My foot was stuck ahead of me in a single, magical step. All the world's winds seemed to push me forward. My back foot glided a little above the ground. The lazy snow became needles, exhilarating me!

The barrens thrust toward me. Thank you, boots!

I tried to go faster by leaning forward and tightening my leg muscles but felt no difference.

Maze cypress woods ahead.

Ouch! Oof! I scraped by trees and through branches, heard cracks and groans, and kept a vise-like grip on my satchel.

The forest retreated into the past.

River!

I splashed in and out, my legs soaked. Another woods. More pain. More barrens.

The boots slowed. It took me half a minute to realize, the change was so gradual. As their speed diminished, they lowered themselves and skimmed along the ground. When they stopped I might stumble into another step, just as a racer continues beyond the finish line.

I prepared.

The boots, which had rushed along with no heed for their wearer, now treated me as if I were made of glass, slowing gently, gently. Stopping.

I dropped to my knees, then lay flat.

How long had I been dashing? Five minutes? Ten? One?

Lord Tove would organize a pursuit. But whatever he did would take time, and he was far behind me, seven leagues—twenty-one *miles*—behind. I clapped my hands gleefully. I had escaped—

—from everyone I loved.

The snow that had slanted at me now drifted down. I sat up.

The tower door had faced east. I was still in the barrens. Remembering, I took Willem's gift out of my purse and held the snail shell to my ear.

No human sounds, but a cacophony of tiny scrapes and squeaks. What could they be? Oh! They came from me! Mites, fleas, lice.

I started to jump up but remembered the boots in time, so, in a frenzy, still sitting, I shook myself and brushed myself off. The noises continued. We all had the creatures, but we didn't all have to hear them. I returned the snail shell to my purse.

Behind me, my passage left a clear path in the snow that Lord Tove might discover. I should step again before night. The sky was already darkening.

Two more steps took me to the edge of the barrens, where more grass grew than stones and where little snow had fallen. I came to rest on a gentle slope, which was as deserted as the last places I'd stopped.

I removed the magic boots. No hope of shelter, no means of making a fire, but I was Lakti-trained. I could endure.

"Good tablecloth, please set thyself."

As before, the tablecloth created an invisible table, but this time, when I approached it, the cloth billowed out. Oof! I stumbled back as something hard slammed against my calves. My knees folded. I would have fallen, but instead found myself seated—

—in an invisible chair, wooden, because I felt grain, and with arms that curled down at the ends.

The thoughtful tablecloth sent steaming soup, stew still bubbling, and cheese puffs (which appeared in every meal), seemingly just out of the oven. I grew toasty warm.

But as I ate, I worried and wondered. What would happen to Lady Mother? Would Lord Tove do anything to her? Would she try to help me? How?

Would she tell him about the boots? (I thought not. She hadn't when she gave them to me.)

How was Annet faring?

And Willem, who would be frightened for me?

I didn't want to leave forever without saying good-bye. He'd return to the tower when I didn't come to camp.

Tomorrow morning I'd double back and hide in the woods near the tower. Perhaps when we said good-bye, I'd receive my kiss—our first and last kiss.

I slept under the table. In the morning, a weak November sun glowed just above the horizon. I breakfasted quickly and donned the magic boots. If I faced the way I came, would they follow yesterday's path?

Holding my satchel, I stood so that the sun was behind me and to my left (for a late fall sunrise), and stepped.

The boots stopped a few yards to the left of the flattened snow that marked my last arrival. I went to the spot and stepped again. And again.

The tower rose ahead. I raised my arms to protect my face, but the boots stopped a few inches away.

I poised myself to step again if anyone was there, but the area seemed empty. When I finished changing into my ordinary boots, I looked up and noticed that the tower door was ajar.

Lady Mother and Lord Tove may have left it that way,

or someone might be inside. Willem! I put out my hand to open the door fully but restrained myself. It could be someone else, and whoever was in there would come out eventually.

Praying I wasn't observed, I fled to the Maze cypress woods south of the tower, where I stood in tree shadow and held my magic shell to my ear.

The ladder inside the tower groaned with strain. Someone was climbing.

"Oh, Perry!" Lady Mother sounded distressed. She may have discovered my coil of hair.

Was Lord Tove with her?

I put the magic boots on again.

Hoofbeats, coming from the north, the direction of the camp, growing louder.

The horse and its rider rounded the tower. The rider dismounted, his or her face hidden by a hood, not tall enough to be Lord Tove. Calling out, the figure approached the tower door. "Peregrine, Peregrine, let down your hair."

Willem!

Hands at the third-story window pushed out my braid and played it out.

Lady Mother's hands tied the braid to a window bar, as I had done. He began to climb.

She called to him, "Did she tell you she was a Bamarre?"

"Lady Klausine? Where's Perry?" He'd almost reached the window. "Yes, she told me."

"She told *you* she knew she was a Bamarre and not her mother!"

Either her hands trembled with fury and jogged the braid or her tone startled him. He lost his grip and fell.

CHAPTER NINETEEN

FOR A FEW moments I stared in shock. The door opened. Lady Mother emerged. I saw her face—red, streaming tears.

"Willem!" I started toward his crumpled form.

The boots! I forgot! I hurtled by, too quickly to see if Willem moved or even lived.

I careered through the Lakti camp, then the battle, glimpsing quarter-second images of a woman dropping a basket of onions, a barking dog, a rearing horse, a foot soldier thrusting a pike.

I howled, "*Willem!*"

Into the Kyngoll town, caroming along a street. Into countryside, across stony fields, through another cypress forest.

Willem, be alive! Don't be badly hurt!

The boots slowed and stopped.

I spun on my heel, stepped again. But I hadn't faced precisely the right way. I arrived west of the tower, which barely showed on the horizon. Quickly, I changed boots and ran and listened in the magic shell. Hooves.

Even if Lord Tove was there, I'd reveal myself.

But by the time I reached the tower, panting, Willem and Lady Mother were gone.

I stood over the depression in the snow where he'd landed. No blood. He must have been injured, though. Broken bones or much worse.

Please, not worse.

I retreated to deep in the woods and finished the day there, hardly thinking, sunk in misery and fear. At night, I wrapped myself in my cloak and dozed.

The next day, heavy snow fell, which would end fighting for the year. Willem would certainly be moved, if he hadn't been already, when the soldiers broke camp.

I stayed in those woods, waiting, worrying, and thinking.

Thinking about Lady Mother's jealousy and grief.

About Annet, who was Lady Klausine's victim more than I was.

About my birth parents, who were strangers to me.

About me, who couldn't be a Lakti and didn't feel myself a Bamarre.

What tormented me most was not knowing how badly

hurt Willem had been. If he was taken to Lord Tove's castle, I'd never get close enough to find out, but if he was carried to Sir Noll's manor, I might be able to. I would go there. But I had to wait. If he was badly wounded, he'd be conveyed in an oxcart, which moved slowly.

After a week of cold weather that tested my Lakti training, I set out. I knew where the manor was, and I doubted there would be any mistaking it, a rich man's house among farm cottages.

I saw it as I sailed by in my boots and had to hike back, up and down steep, forested hills and across streams, because the boots hadn't followed any road.

The house, which topped a tall hill, had a castle's dignity without its size: ivy grown halfway up the stone walls; five chimneys belching smoke; a crenellated roof but no moat, drawbridge, or guardhouse. At the bottom of the hill, a tree-lined walk met a north-south highway— dirt lined with round stones, wide enough for a wagon. I arrived as day was ending and climbed the opposing hill, which, unlike Sir Noll's, was wooded. At the summit, I clambered up a spear pine for a view.

Silly, but I waved at the house. *Greetings, Willem's home. Willem, are you there now?*

No one walked on the path. A few goats, minuscule from here, grazed between patches of snow. Despite the distance, I believed I could see well enough to know

Willem if he stepped outside.

I put the magic shell to my ear. Voices, yes, but too distant for me to make out words.

At mealtimes, the magic tablecloth fed me. I was cold, but I endured. Almost daily, in the course of the next week, Sir Noll with companions (never Willem) left the manor at dawn and returned in the evening, bearing the deer, hare, or boar they'd brought down. They never entered the woods I occupied, which, I reasoned, must have been thoroughly hunted long ago.

Was Willem inside and too sick to go out? Was he dead?

Hope of seeing him dwindled, and yet I lingered, unable to leave the place where he might be. But finally, when winter began in earnest, I decided to go. The only destination that offered a speck of hope was Gavrel, where my birth parents lived.

As soon as I made up my mind, my stomach fluttered. Maybe they'd welcome me.

Not that I could stay with them. Lord Tove would discover me there sooner or later. But perhaps they could suggest a permanent refuge.

Having decided, I wasted no time. Crossing half the kingdom—thirteen steps, I calculated—would bring me close to Gavrel.

Again, I donned the magic boots, then realized a single

boot was plenty, so I removed the left and replaced it with an ordinary one. I'd be less likely to hie off by accident if my other foot gave me time to think.

It was midafternoon, bright and bitter cold, with a light wind. As I barreled along, I wondered if I could influence my direction. I leaned right, and the boot veered a little. I leaned harder, and the shift increased. Left, and the boot swung back. The turns were wide, of course, because of my speed.

How beautiful New Lakti was! I crossed snowy fields, crashed through ancient forests, bypassed (or splashed through) lakes and streams, and rushed past villages and a town.

On my right the Eskerns rose, looking on this crystal day close enough to run my fingers along their peaks.

A black dot rocketed up from behind a ridge. A fleck in my eye? I blinked but the dot expanded, grew big as a thundercloud, and took the form of—a gryphon!

I gasped and almost choked on the stench of spoiled meat. In its beak, the monster carried a bone that still held bloody flesh. Its greedy eyes bulged. Scars crisscrossed its lion's hide; bald patches mottled its eagle wings.

The gryphon shrank to a dot again, its proper size at this distance. Halina! Why show me this?

For my next several steps I saw little. When I came back to myself, the ground had flattened into grasslands.

I'd reached eastern New Lakti, but I'd lost track of my steps. I could be leagues to the west of Gavrel, leagues to the east. Or I could be close.

Dried grasses poked through a few inches of snow. The magic shell revealed no human sounds. I changed out of my magic boot. A wide stream on my right flowed serenely east-west and might lead me to a village where I could ask directions. A road might even accompany the stream on the other side, but I couldn't see because of the steep bank. Travelers might come along and tell me where I was. I waded in. Cold!

On the other side there *was* a road. I continued eastward, because I had to go one way or the other. After running for half an hour, I caught up with an elderly Bamarre, who directed me. Eleven miles to Gavrel.

Now, at last, here I was. In this flat countryside there were no real hills, but I stood at the crest of a knoll under a spreading oak, the only big tree nearby, looking at the village by the light of a full moon. Seven small Bamarre cottages and two modest Lakti houses in a line faced the road and, beyond it, the stream. A wisp of smoke drifted from each chimney. People had banked their fires and had probably gone to bed. No one was outdoors in the chilly dark.

Inside one of these homes were my parents, my true parents. My stomach tightened.

A copse of pine trees grew north of the village. Bushes rimmed the south side of the road but gave out at the village edge.

When I reached the village, I walked its short length and halfway back. No one would be looking out. Why would they?

The Lakti houses lay in the middle of the line. Between them, across the road, stood a whipping post. The sight quickened my breathing until I noticed that the wood was old and cracked and stained moss green. Lashings were probably rare.

The wind changed direction. Barks erupted from every house.

·

CHAPTER TWENTY

I RAN. In a minute—before anyone had time to leave a bed and look out a window—I was past the houses.

Let the villagers be slow to open their doors. Let the dogs be old or lame or fat. After another minute, they were released, no longer barking but panting behind me. I kept running. Soon, the dogs fell back a little. Another minute and I dared to turn. The pack of hounds bunched together. They'd stopped chasing and resumed barking. I had crossed a boundary that only they knew. I ran on a while, hoping to convince them the threat was over. The barking diminished to silence.

I stopped on the knoll, under the oak. How was I going to get back into Gavrel?

From the sound of their footfalls in my magic shell, the dogs were loping home. Still listening, I started slowly back. After a few minutes, I heard doors open.

"Get in, you cur. It's cold!" Woman's voice.

"What could Baka have heard, do you think?" Man's deep voice.

"Dimwit dog will chase anything!" Man's voice, not as deep.

Doors thudded shut.

"Baka, you're brave." A child's light tones. "I'm brave, too." Laughter. "You can lick me!"

"Poppi . . . Mama . . . that could be Perry. I told you she might come."

Annet!

"Will we be blamed for the noise?" Female. Must be a Bamarre.

I saw the black shape of the first cottage and began to circle behind the buildings, hoping to stay beyond the range of the dogs' noses.

"Begging your pardon, she'd endanger you again?" My father?

I stopped circling.

"Poppi, pardon me, but if she's running away, where else can she go?"

It *had* been my father.

"I have no idea." My mother? "She's a Lakti."

My chest hurt.

"In the morning we'll see if the dogs brought anything

down." An unfamiliar voice, probably from another cottage.

Annet said, "A Lakti most of the time, Mama. Not always."

That *had* been my mother.

Silence fell.

"Wouldn't the dogs have warned her away, Annet, love?"

She called Annet *love*?

I wondered where else I could go.

"The dogs might not catch her," Annet said.

I smiled.

"Perry can outrun dogs?" The child's voice. Oh! The brother Halina said I had.

"The dogs were probably after a wolf anyway," my father said.

They didn't speak again, and the other cottages quieted, too. I guessed people were returning to their beds.

My parents didn't want me. I'd sleep under the oak tree and set off again tomorrow.

In her annoyed tone, Annet said, "I should see if it *is* Perry."

"A wolf will eat you!" My mother's voice.

The boy said, "I'll go! Please!"

My father sounded resigned. "If she's there, we can't leave her."

My ears drummed and the sound in the shell vibrated. I should put on a boot and leave if they were so reluctant to venture out for me.

But I didn't.

He continued. "I'll take Baka. Drualt, you can come. Between us and Baka, we're the equal of a pack of wolves."

Annet said, "I'll go with you, if you please. She knows me."

My mother said, "I'll come, too, but we should let everybody else fall back to sleep first, don't you think?"

Sensible.

My father said, "You're right, Shoni."

Shoni was my mother's name.

I headed—slowly, softly—back to the road beyond the village so they'd find me. The snail gave me no more conversation. Two village snorers formed a duet, one with a rattle, the other long and smooth.

Maybe my family would like me. Maybe they'd feel our kinship and would be sad I couldn't stay.

What seemed like hours passed.

A door creaked. A dot of light appeared. They'd lit a torch—dangerous if anyone was awake, but the snores didn't change nor did the dogs bark.

I thought I might explode by the time they reached me.

A few minutes passed, and there they were. My father

lumbered, leaning on a staff. My mother walked easily, her hand on the shoulder of my young brother, enacting a repeated pantomime of him trying to escape her grip, of her pulling him back. And Annet, shorter than my mother, stamped along, closest to my father, the dog moving with her as if on a chain. She wasn't limping. If Lord Tove had hurt her, she could still walk.

Drualt cried, "Look! A person, not—"

"Sh!"

I dropped the snail shell into my purse.

He freed himself and broke into a run. Baka the dog went after him.

I took a step forward, then back.

He stopped a foot away. The dog jumped up on my cloak.

"Sit, Baka," Drualt said. "Are you Perry, begging your pardon? I'm your brother." He yanked off his glove and held out his hand. His grip was strong, though not quite Lakti firm. He smelled of garlic. "Can you really outrun dogs?"

"I just did. I have more stamina than they do." I was trembling.

Annet and the others reached us. I was a head taller than my mother—Mama—and almost as tall as my father—Poppi. They all reeked of garlic. No one else shook my hand. No one hugged me.

"Annet . . . did Lord Tove beat you? Did he make you walk in chains?"

"Hello, Perry. He slapped me. That seems to be his preference. I rode in a cart. Lady Klausine sent me here."

Poppi told me he was my father. "Greetings." He bowed stiffly.

I curtsied, and Mama did, too.

Drualt asked, "Did you really see a fairy?"

"Yes."

"You can't come home with us, begging your pardon," Mama said.

Poppi said, "Please forgive us. Annet says Lord Tove will look for you here."

I was surprised he hadn't come already, but he might be with the king, as he often had to be when he wasn't fighting.

Poppi continued. "We must think of our children, Mistress Peregrine."

Mistress. I was one of their children! "Thank you for coming to tell me."

Mama begged my pardon again. "Where will you sleep tonight?"

"I can stand the cold. I didn't come to stay. I just wanted advice about where I might go." And I wanted to meet you and for you to love me.

"Can't she come home long enough to tell us about the

fairy?" Drualt put a wheedle in his voice. "Please, Poppi."

Poppi sighed. "I shouldn't have stolen food. We're here now because of me."

"That was years ago!" Mama said.

I followed a thread of blame beginning with my fault for coming here, going on to mine for dropping a hint to Lord Tove, Halina's for revealing my birth to me, Lady Mother's for taking me in the first place and lying to everyone about me, and Poppi's for stealing, as he'd just said. Centuries ago, the Lakti's for bringing the Bamarre to their knees, our knees. Even before then, the Bamarre's for taking the warlike Lakti in.

I reached in my sack for a boot.

Light whipped in a spiral between us and Gavrel village. The scent of peonies sweetened the air. I heard three gasps and a happy shout from Drualt.

The light dissolved, leaving the fairy in her human form. Her voice rang out. "I am Halina."

They'd hear her in the village!

"Put your boot away, Perry," she said.

I did.

"I'm Drualt, Perry's brother. Pleased to make your acquaintance." He swept an elegant bow. "Please let my sister stay."

The rest of my family curtsied and said in trembling tones that they were glad to meet her.

Halina put a hand on Drualt's head. Her long sleeves draped over his cap and curls. "I have high hopes of you. First, you must help Perry." She turned to my parents and Annet. "I have high hopes of Perry, too. I want her to free you Bamarre." She turned and reached toward me.

I backed away uneasily, but—without seeming to move—she followed me and ran her hands over my cap, along my neck, my arms, and down to my feet.

A fire leaped up inside me.

CHAPTER TWENTY-ONE

OH, WOE! I closed my eyes, fearing they'd boil over. My skin, my stomach, even my bones, seemed to blaze. I would have screamed, but I didn't want to belch flame and burn the world.

In the distance I heard my parents and Annet cry out in dismay. Drualt crowed, "Fairy magic!"

Halina snapped, "Don't go near her!"

Drualt sounded indignant. "Let go of me! Begging your pardon. Why not, begging your pardon?"

"You'd die."

"Oh."

At last, I felt the chill air again.

Poppi stared at me and gasped. "Aunt Nadira?"

"Where's Perry?" Mama added, "Beg pardon."

I swallowed and tried to speak. No sound came out.

Poppi told Halina, "Aunt Nadira's dead. I had a letter a month ago. Who's this, begging your pardon?"

"I'm Perry." My voice sounded scratchy. Poppi, a yard away, stood taller than I did, and my eyes were level with Annet's. "I shrank!" But I felt just like myself.

"Fairies haven't done this in centuries, and we never used to do it often." Halina touched my arm, and her peace infected me again. "I've given you the form of your father's late aunt. It's convenient she died. . . ."

Had the fairy killed her?

"Certainly I had no hand in her death. A thoroughly unpleasant woman, however. She lived far from here. It's perfect." She smiled her glowing smile.

I looked down at myself. My clothes seemed to have shrunk to fit me. The skin on my hands was looser and my knuckles more prominent. I felt for my hair, but I had to reach higher before finding a lock. When I held it out, only a few strands of black threaded through the gray.

If I found him, Willem wouldn't recognize me!

Halina added, "Now you can stay with your family." She addressed them. "Don't forget to call her Nadira."

"Why does she have to save us Bamarre?" I heard pity in Mama's voice. "I'm sorry, but she deserves an ordinary life."

"She does." Halina sounded sad. "She's never had one."

"Can't *you* free us?" Poppi said.

Halina moved to Poppi, her chin an inch from his nose. He backed away a step.

She followed. "I suppose fairies should make sure nothing bad ever happens. No tragedy. No injustice. No misfortune."

Poppi bobbed his head. "That would be a kindness."

"Fairies will not free the Bamarre."

I felt as if I were hovering apart from everyone. "How long will I continue to look this way?" I wondered how my mouth appeared when I spoke.

"Since she looks just like Nadira, she can stay with us," Poppi said. Once, he'd been heartbroken to lose me.

"Excellent!" Halina beamed at him.

"How long will I look this way?"

"Fairies are proud of you, Aunt Nadira."

Answer me!

"You've struck fear into Lord Tove."

I couldn't have.

"Nonetheless, you have. You're trained and talented. You escaped from your prison, and you blinded him. Certainly he's frightened."

Drualt stared at me, wide-eyed.

"Is Willem alive?"

"He is."

I smiled and couldn't stop. "Is he well? Where?"

She didn't answer. Did that mean he wasn't well?

Poppi said, "Who's Willem?"

"A young Lakti. They're in love." Annet drew out *l-o-o-o-ve*, mocking me.

Halina wheeled on her. "Nothing that has happened to you has been your sister's fault. I'll thank you for remembering that truth."

Annet raised her arm to protect herself.

I felt glad, but I defended her. "She did her best."

Halina sighed, and her peony scent grew stronger. "Nothing was Annet's fault, either." She turned to my parents. "Aunt Nadira must grow up a little more and learn to feel that she's a Bamarre. I expect all of you to teach her." She smiled. "You're a fine family."

"How long will I look this way?"

Halina tipped up my chin. "Don't begin your task before you're ready, but don't miss your opportunities."

"If we teach Aunt Nadira," Poppi said, "will you stop the Lakti cruelty?"

Halina pursed her mouth as if she'd eaten something spoiled. "Goodman Adeer, if you help your daughter, there will be consequences, and if you don't help her, there will be, too." Her expression softened. "You may be inspired to greatness." She vanished.

Poppi stared at the space where she'd been. Finally, he said, "Come." He drew Mama's arm in his and started off.

Annet hurried and clasped Poppi's other arm.

I was alone until Drualt took my hand in his firm grip. I asked him how old he was. From his height and his determined stride, I guessed eleven, but he said he was nine, which meant he'd been born five years after Lady Mother took me.

He said, "I want to save us Bamarre with you."

I sang a battle verse, changing *Lakti* to *Bamarre*:

> "*Let arrows fly,*
> *Let spears thrust,*
> *Let swords slice*
> *The shattered air.*
> *Courage will not crumble,*
> *Resolve will not fade.*
> *Bamarre will triumph.*
> *Bamarre will prevail.*"

When I finished, he sang,

> "*Daring Drualt beside*
> *Proud Peregrine,*
> *Riding to victory.*"

I smiled. How unexpected, this brother.

***

I'd never lived anywhere as humble as my parents' cottage, only one room with their sleeping loft above. A spinning wheel stood in one corner and a square table in another. Bolts of fabric lay under this table. Was Poppi or Mama a tailor?

A leather-bound book rested atop a long table, the one we'd eat on. I estimated the cottage's length to be twenty paces, a little less in width. Under the loft, the ceiling grazed Poppi's head. The cottage stank of mildew, smoke, and garlic.

On the first night, despite my protests, Drualt gave me his pallet and slept, wrapped in blankets, on the rushes by the fireplace.

I kept my eyes open in the dark. The dying fire glowed. Annet and Drualt were dark shapes. Baka lay at my sister's feet.

Except for Drualt, my birth family considered me a chore, as I had been to Annet. A lump rose in my throat.

I swallowed against it and then made myself sadder. Where was my second family now? Was Lady Mother preparing to fight in the spring campaign, now that I was gone? I knew she must be sad. And probably disappointed in me for giving myself away.

Annet and I both thought Lord Tove would come here, and I believed he'd arrive soon. Not knowing my whereabouts would gnaw at him. He'd suppose me here or with the Kyngoll—because what other choices did I have?—and he couldn't go to *them* for information.

Fear gripped me. I imagined him riding through the night, coming ever closer. He could have overtaken me earlier today!

I fumbled for my purse, which I hadn't removed for sleep, and pulled out the magic shell.

Only peaceful sounds. Snores, people turning over, dogs rumbling in their sleep.

If not on his way, was Lord Tove lying in his bed as I was on this pallet? Might he be thinking of the child he'd loved? Did his loathing ever subside enough for him to miss me?

A tear slid out, but I squeezed my eyes shut against it. Using my Lakti training, I imagined the peaceful village, the blinking stars, a rabbit crossing a snowy field—and slept.

When I awoke, I was surprised all over again to be Nadira.

Everyone else was already awake. The table was spread with a breakfast of bread, cheese, and sweet onions, but I pulled the magic tablecloth out of my sack anyway. I might be a more welcome guest if I could provide wonderful food.

"Good tablecloth, please set thyself."

The tablecloth opened next to the real table.

"Pe— Aunt Nadira!" Annet cried.

"Magic!" Drualt shouted.

Mama and Poppi yelped, one high, one low.

We received two loaves of bread, a green-onion omelet, shrimp piled four inches thick, and a bowl of blueberries. Five white bowls were stacked next to five silver spoons.

Drualt fairly leaped to the table, took a bowl, and began to help himself to shrimp.

"Don't eat that!" Poppi knocked the bowl out of his hand. It fell without breaking, but the shrimp scattered on the rushes that covered the dirt floor. "You don't know if it's safe."

More shrimp appeared on the platter. And another bowl replaced the dirty one.

I cut myself a slice of the white bread. "It won't hurt you. It's delicious."

"See?" Drualt reached again, but our mother pulled him away.

"What if someone came in?" Poppi said. "A Lakti?"

Did they come uninvited?

"Will it stay here forever?" Mama asked.

"Please make it go away, Aunt Nadira," Annet said.

"Good tablecloth, I thank thee for a fine meal."

Everyone gasped as the meal shrank and vanished, including the shrimp on the floor, but what was left of my slice of bread stayed in my hand. I finished it, swallowing my unhappiness along with the bread.

Drualt looked as disappointed as I felt.

Lady Mother had been hard to please, too. I just had to discover how to earn my family's nod. Love was conditional here, too.

CHAPTER TWENTY-TWO

WE BROKE OUR fast on my parents' plain fare. I'd never shared a meal with any Bamarre before. Just as we did, they picked up their food with their fingertips and speared the common cheese with their little knives.

Just as *we* did? I was a Bamarre! And why was I surprised?

I asked Annet, "How much did you tell Lord Tove?"

"He said he already knew you were a Bamarre!"

"He didn't, but I'd made him suspect." My great mistake.

She went on, "I told him we were sisters and how Lady Klausine took us."

"Not about Halina?"

"No."

"What did you say about how I found out I'm a Bamarre?"

"He didn't ask."

Once he knew what I was, he didn't care about anything else.

"Did he keep questioning you?"

"Aunt Nadira," Poppi said, "begging your pardon, don't badger your sis— niece."

I ignored him. "You didn't mention the magic boots, did you?"

She shook her head. "He had no more questions."

"Magic boots?" Drualt cried.

I grinned and explained. Mama and Poppi had to restrain him from trying them.

When he'd settled down, Poppi said, "Shoni, Annet looks like you used to."

"I was never as pretty as Annet."

Annet blushed, a new sight for me.

"You are a lovely woman, Shoni."

Mama touched her hair.

"Do I look like anybody?" Drualt asked.

Poppi hugged his shoulder. "You resemble an Eskern Mountain puppy."

Drualt barked and laughed.

I saw what Poppi meant in my brother's big eyes, enormous half-circle smile, and shaggy eyebrows, especially on a child.

"Did Aunt Nadira look like any of us before she was changed?" Drualt said.

Mama said, "It was too dark to see."

After breakfast, while Poppi built a pallet frame for my mattress, the rest of us stuffed a canvas sack with straw from a shed behind the cottage. Black specks dotted the straw—fleas, too numerous to pick out.

When we finished, I pronounced my new bed excellent.

Annet said, "Begging your pardon, Pe— Aunt Nad—" She stopped herself. "Poppi, do I really have to call her that?"

I answered for him. "You should."

Annet's eyebrows rose.

"Ooh!" Drualt sounded surprised.

My parents frowned.

"*Nadira* is safer," I said. Wasn't that obvious? "We all have to get used to it." And I had to get used to looking like an old woman.

"Aunt Nadira," Annet said, "if Poppi were Lord Tove and someone asked him a question, would you answer for him?"

I started to say I would, if I knew the answer, but that wasn't true.

They waited, watching me.

If the person Annet had asked were a Lakti and my own age, I would have answered, but not someone older or higher in rank. If the person were a Bamarre, no matter how old, I would speak. That I was being disrespectful wouldn't occur to me. I blushed. "I shouldn't have spoken for you, er, Nephew."

He squinted, which I had learned meant he was thinking.

Everyone waited.

He said, "If we're going to win our freedom, we also have to learn what it's like to be a Lakti. We'll watch you, too."

Annet swept the breakfast crumbs into her hands and flung them into the fire. "We know what the Lakti are like, and Aunt Nadira should have thanked us for making her a bed."

Mama wrapped the remaining cheese in burlap. "Sweet"—she touched my unsweet sister's nose—"living in that castle, some of you is a Lakti, too. Both of you need to become completely Bamarre."

Poppi squinted. "Shoni, take Aunt Nadira with you."

I jumped up from the table bench. "Where?"

"With me, Adeer?"

Poppi nodded. "The best way to learn to be a Bamarre is by serving the Lakti. Aunt Nadira, Shoni cooks for one of the families."

My chest tightened. Why was I afraid of my own people? "I'm ready."

"Begging her pardon," Annet said, "she doesn't even know how to scrub a carrot."

No one answered. Poppi stirred up the fire. I realized they didn't want to argue.

"Please show her, Annet. Now Her Mistress-ship will have not two but three servants for the wages of one." Mama did a gliding dance step to the hooks by the door. "I've been lucky to have you with me."

She meant Annet.

We donned our cloaks.

"Aunt Nadira . . ." Mama faced me. "We call them the Ships because they think they're so grand. His Master-ship glares, as if a snake was squeezing his liver. Her Mistress-ship fancies herself a wit. Laugh if you can, but be sure to smile. Her twins, the two little Ships, are six, old enough to know they can order us about." She put on her cap with its dangling green tassel.

I realized—probably we all did—but Annet said it: "Aunt Nadira needs a tassel."

My stomach twisted.

"We have many, Aunt Nadira," Mama said. "Adeer makes them and sells them. Sometimes they fall off. People often need one."

Poppi left for the shed. Mama rummaged in a basket and

lifted out a plain brass brooch. Poppi returned with a tassel.

I hugged my cap to my chest, unwilling to hand it over.

Drualt put on his own cap and tilted his head from side to side so that the tassel swung back and forth. He made his eyes cross following it.

I couldn't help smiling. I gave the cap to Mama, who pinned the tassel to the band and returned the cap, an ordinary cap, nothing to reveal that I'd been a lord's daughter—just loose, unbleached linen sewn to a starched band that circled my brow, ran under my ears and around the back of my head.

I remembered a couplet from a poem called "Circle":

> *Nothing waxes but to wane.*
> *In the start, the end awaits.*

I put on the cap and felt no different. Still a Lakti on the inside, I followed Mama and my sister out of the cottage.

Outside, a light rain greeted us.

"Annet, please be pleasant. Aunt Nadira, please don't talk." Mama added, surprising me, "They have their troubles, too."

The walls of the two Lakti houses were made of stone and daub, as the Bamarre cottages were, too, but these houses had slate roofs, rather than thatched, and were four times the size of a cottage, with a complete second story and small glazed windows on the first floor. The upper windows were covered with greased parchment, as all my parents' windows were.

Mama stopped at the first Lakti door, which was freshly painted a bright orange. She turned and brushed the drops that beaded on her shoulders and told us to do the same. "Her Mistress-ship doesn't like drips." She straightened my cap, tucked Annet's hair into her cap, and smoothed her own cloak in front.

Did we have to be perfect for these Lakti?

Mama added, "She lets us use the front door when the widow isn't watching."

The widow, I later learned, headed the other Lakti household.

We entered a small vestibule, stairs straight ahead, closed doors left and right. A child's cry, another child's triumphant shout, and a woman's harried tones came through the door on the left. We entered the one on the right, and Mama closed it behind us. Blessedly unpopulated—except for a cat sitting on the long worktable—the kitchen was as big as our cottage but a quarter the size of the castle kitchen.

Across from us, the logs in the fireplace glowed, barely alive.

"We're late!" Mama cried. "Breakfast in half an hour."

What would happen if we weren't ready?

Hastily, we took off our cloaks and hung them on hooks next to the door. I started to remove my cap, but Annet shook her head at me. The tassel had to stay on.

Pots and pans hung from the ceiling. Cupboards lined the walls. Under a window in the back wall stood an iron sink and a pump, which would deliver water from the village well. A hose ran from the pump to the sink. We had several pumps in the castle, none in my parents' cottage.

The door opened a crack, and a Bamarre woman Mama's age squeezed through despite her plumpness.

"Across the Eskerns." The Bamarre greeting. Then, "Oh!" at the sight of me. She curtsied to me first, then to Mama, then to Annet. I wondered why I'd come first.

Ah. My seeming age.

Annet curtsied back. I nodded, as would a Lakti to a Bamarre. Mama coughed. Annet made a strangled sound in her throat.

What?

Aaah! I curtsied, too. I wasn't supposed to talk, but I ventured my first "Beg pardon."

The woman curtsied again. "No matter. To apologize makes you good." She waited.

Not knowing how to answer, I said, "Thank you."

Mama and Annet said in unison, "To forgive makes you wise."

This little poem proverb—that's what I was supposed to say?

"Yes, of course," I said. "Exactly."

To cover my awkwardness, Mama introduced me to Goodwife Dyrin, who cleaned for the Ships. "Aunt Nadira arrived last night. She is kind enough to help us."

Annet stirred up the fire and fed it with kindling from a basket on the hearth. A covered pot rested on a trivet above the flame.

I had to do something, too! I gazed about stupidly.

Annet began, "Pe— Nad— Aunt Nad—"

Mama began, "Poor Aunt Nadira . . ."

Goodwife Dyrin's eyes traveled from one of us to the other.

Annet subsided and Mama finished, ". . . is recovering from phlegm fever."

Phlegm fever had the effect of making its sufferers dull and slow.

Mama continued. "It's a wonder she arrived safely. She came alone!" She chuckled. "Fairies watch over the fool."

That's how I discovered Mama's cleverness. In a stroke she accounted for my behavior and my solo arrival.

In unison, Goodwife Dyrin and Annet answered, "If only they'd punish the cruel."

Another poetic adage, this one aimed at the Lakti. How many proverbs were there?

Annet took my elbow and led me to an open cupboard stacked with pottery. "Aunt, we need four bowls, two platters, and two pitchers. Can you count them out and put them on the table?" Facing away from Goodwife Dyrin, she grinned at me.

I didn't think she was being mean. Instead, she was making this a game. Surprisingly, she reminded me of Drualt.

In my new, gravelly voice, I said slowly, "I think so, Niece." I carried the bowls to the table one at a time and made a show of counting when I got there.

Goodwife Dyrin asked, "Any news about your other daughter? Is she still a danger?"

I dropped a bowl.

Mama and the goodwife gasped, but, cushioned by the rushes spread across the wooden floor, it didn't break. What would be the punishment for shattering a bowl?

"Beg pardon," I remembered to say as I picked it up.

"No word of her, thank you. We hope she won't bring trouble down on us." Mama's eyes touched me and moved on.

I blushed hotly.

Goodwife Dyrin stroked Mama's arm. Her tone became matter-of-fact. "Shoni, can your aunt sweep out the rushes here and put new ones down? I'm racing like a donkey with spurs in its side. I just wanted to warn you that the Rest are coming for dinner, and Her Mistress-ship is in a Mood."

The Rest, I deduced, meant the other Lakti family. I'd soon learn what a Mood meant.

Goodwife Dyrin squeezed out again.

A broom leaned against the wall between two cabinets. I began to sweep, a task I'd never tried before. A tempest of dust and rushes ensued until Annet told me to wield the broom less energetically.

Using tongs, Mama lifted the lid on the pot and stirred its contents, the morning's pottage, which, it turned out, she'd prepared the afternoon before and left to cook over the smoldering fire. Annet chopped onions and scattered them on top.

When the used rushes were piled near the door, Mama had me sweep them into a dustpan and then into a pail, which I filled to brimming.

"Before you take them out, spread fresh ones. Her Mistress-ship doesn't like a bare floor." Mama showed me a basket under the table that held unspoiled rushes.

When I finished, she told me to toss the dirty rushes into the road.

I opened the door to the vestibule without putting on my cloak because cold didn't trouble me. But then I decided it would trouble Nadira. Congratulating myself on thinking like a Bamarre, I returned to the kitchen and wrapped myself up. Back in the vestibule, a sprinkling of rushes fell out when I picked up the pail. Now I'd have to fetch the dustpan. For slowness, I might as well have had phlegm fever.

A door opened. "What are you doing?" A woman's voice, and sharp.

Startled, I let the pail sway. More rushes cascaded.

"Put that down!"

I did and straightened up.

A tall woman slapped me.

CHAPTER TWENTY-THREE

"WHO ARE YOU?"

My cheek stung. *I* was Lord Tove's daughter! Who was *she*?

The woman leaned toward me, her chin jutting out, too. She matched my fury until her eyes began to show surprise.

Realization dawned. I should cower and apologize.

But I wouldn't.

Still, I mustn't strike her back. I pulled in my chin and relaxed my shoulders. Words! I needed words. Which words?

Remembering my supposed illness, I forced myself to speak slowly. "My name is Nadira, Mistress." What else?

I felt a frightened stillness from the kitchen behind me.

"I've been ill with phlegm fever. It's made me clumsy.

I'm Goodman Adeer's aunt, if you please. I came to help Goodwife Shoni."

"How lucky we both are. I hope to be elsewhere when you're *not* being helpful."

I remembered she thought herself a wit. My smile was probably a grimace.

"Clean up your mess." She went into the kitchen.

Halina, what must I do to free us?

I slipped back into the kitchen. Her Mistress-ship was telling Mama what she wanted served for dinner. Mama stood in front of her, nodding, but her eyes shifted to me. Annet was chopping onions again. I got the dustpan and brush, returned to the vestibule, and left the door a few inches ajar.

Her Mistress-ship said, "Chicken brewet, then milk soup with leeks . . . Our guests are a trifle piggy, so give them roast pork next." She waited, I supposed, for Mama and my sister to laugh.

Mama chuckled. I heard nothing from Annet.

"Pudding, almonds, and dates at the end. Bread, certainly."

I swept up the spilled rushes.

Her Mistress-ship continued. "It's a good menu. I will not be criticized for it." Her voice rose in volume and pitch. "I will not!"

That was a Mood? To shriek? To hit an old woman?

I heard Her Mistress-ship start for the door. Hastily,

with my real speed, I left the house and emptied the pail as directed. When I returned to the kitchen, Mama was alone, because Annet was setting the table in the solar, where, as in a castle's great hall, a family dined and entertained guests.

"Why was your cheek red before, Nad— Aunt Nadira?"

I explained, though I wouldn't have mentioned the slap if she hadn't asked.

"I see." She changed the subject. "Can you catch and kill a chicken, if you don't mind?"

I said I could. I was a warrior.

Mama pointed me to a door in the back wall, which led to a wooden pantry that held barrels of apples and winter vegetables, sides of beef and pork on hooks, and crocks of spices. The pantry opened into a yard with a stable and a chicken coop.

I caught a chicken easily, wrung its neck, and enjoyed the feeling of success when the bird hung limp in my hand.

"Thank you. You were quick about it." Mama was fast, too, chopping currants and walnuts. "If only the pudding could be made that readily."

"Will you have it in time?" Dinner would be served early in the afternoon.

She shrugged. "We'll delay. They'll laugh at the Bamarre sluggards. Her Mistress-ship will be criticized for our slowness."

"Who will criticize her?"

"His Master-ship will, in front of everyone."

"Will she hit you if he does?"

Mama smiled grimly. "She'd pay dearly if she did. She's already going to suffer for striking you. She'd think it strange if I didn't do something."

Really? "What will you do?"

"This morning's pottage will be much too salty."

"She won't hit you for that?"

"I can add worse things than salt." Mama's smile widened. "It isn't easy to find a new cook in a tiny village."

A mosquito's revenge.

An idea began to form but dissolved before I could grasp it.

Mama continued. "His Master-ship will blame her. His tongue is venomous. I'm a fool, but I pity her."

Mama could be kind. I was glad to learn that about her.

"A double fool," she added, "because I pity him, too."

"The magic tablecloth makes pudding."

She put down her knife. "It will taste good?"

"Delicious."

Annet came back in, and Mama asked her what she thought.

"Mama," I said, "I've eaten many tablecloth meals. They're wonderful."

"Beg pardon. I asked Annet."

I'd been a Lakti again. "I'm sorry."

The two of them said, "To apologize makes you good."

What came next? "To forgive makes you wise."

Mama nodded, not Lady Mother's slow, important nod, but a nod nonetheless.

I waited for my sister to give her opinion.

"Let her. We don't have to eat it, and it will save time."

I'd use the tablecloth in our cottage, because her Mistress-ship's kitchen would be too risky. Since there wouldn't be as many people in the cottage as at the feast I'd have to start and stop the tablecloth several times to get enough pudding, but I didn't mention this, because I expected it to still take only a few minutes.

After Annet showed me how (nothing to it), Mama set me to scrubbing beets, carrots, parsnips, and onions in the sink while she and Annet served breakfast—and came back laughing over the salty pottage.

Annet wrung her hands in fake distress and imitated Mama. "'Perhaps I confused the measuring cup with the measuring spoon. Silly me.'"

I forced a smile. The castle Bamarre must have laughed at us exactly this way.

The idea that had chimed before rang again and then faded.

Mama set me cutting the vegetables I'd washed into chunks to be roasted with the pork. Using my soldier training with a knife, I got the knack quickly and enjoyed making each bit exactly the same size as every other bit.

Shortly before noon, I left for the cottage. Inside, Poppi hunched over his worktable, sewing by dim light through a parchment-covered window. Drualt sat across from him, stitching too. Both jumped up when I came in. Baka welcomed me as if I'd lived there her whole life. Drualt also looked happy to see me.

I loved him already.

"Are your mother and sister all right?"

Poppi shouldn't be afraid whenever his family left the house—another reason to free the Bamarre.

But was he a coward?

"They're fine."

"Then why did you come back?"

"My niece said I could use the tablecloth to make pudding because otherwise it will take too long."

What if he told me not to? It would be too late now to start the pudding. Maybe I was acting like a headstrong Lakti, but I didn't wait for him to say anything, just picked up my satchel from the floor by the stack of our three pallet beds.

Baka growled. I froze.

We heard hoofbeats. I dropped the satchel as if it were on fire.

A fist hammered on the door. "Open! Or we'll break it down!"

CHAPTER TWENTY-FOUR

POPPI STOOD UP.

They might notice if I was near the sack when they came in. I ran to the fireplace bench and sat.

Drualt faced the door, looking eager. Poppi crossed the cottage, moving deliberately, not rushing, which made me proud. No coward, but he must have been regretting taking me in. He raised the latch.

The door swung open. A soldier stepped aside.

Lord Tove and Lady Mother, wet but regal-looking, entered. I couldn't see from here, but they must have traveled with soldiers. Might Willem be among them?

At the sight of my former parents, I felt both chilled and fevered. I gripped the bench to keep from fainting.

The last time I'd seen Lady Mother, she'd been

weeping at the bottom of the tower, with Willem in a heap at her feet.

"I apologize for the intrusion." Lord Tove's benign mask smiled. "We seek a young woman named Perry."

"Welcome." Poppi bowed.

I had to curtsy, but I wasn't sure my legs would support me. Using my hands, probably looking more ancient than the real Nadira before she died, I stood and performed a wobbly curtsy.

Drualt bowed with a flourish.

Lady Mother shut the door behind them, leaving their escort outside. She peered about, unaccustomed to the dimness. "You are Goodman Adeer?"

He admitted he was and introduced me and Drualt.

Lord Tove nodded. He took off his coat and laid it across our dining table, and with that seemed to take ownership of the cottage.

Lady Mother added her cloak to his. As always, she was more direct. "Where is Peregrine?"

Poppi said, "Begging your pardon, we haven't seen her in fourteen years."

Drualt, thinking quicker than either of us, said, "Is my sister safe?" He added, "I'd like to meet her."

He could joke at a time like this?

"In truth, I'm worried about her." Lord Tove sat on the fireplace bench next to where I stood. I smelled the ambergris in his beard. I used to love that smell.

Lady Mother stood by Poppi's worktable, feet spread, hands behind her back in her surveying-the-troops pose.

"We had a disagreement," Lord Tove said.

Poppi nodded. "Such things happen, begging your pardon."

If I laughed, I'd give way to hysteria.

Lord Tove nodded, too. "Lady Klausine and I raised her to be brave and, I fear, not to consider the feelings of others, including her parents. In short, she ran off before I could assure her of my love. We don't want harm to come to her."

Poppi sounded genuinely indignant. "We'd never hurt her!"

"You haven't seen her, either, Grandmother?"

More humor—I was the only one who could say with truth that I hadn't, since the cottage had no mirror. I opened my mouth, but nothing came out. I shook my head.

Lord Tove extended his long legs. "People—the Bamarre especially, though I mean no disrespect—lie in gestures more easily than in words. Speak! Have you seen her?"

Poppi began, "Aunt Nadira—"

He didn't know I was supposed to be getting over being sick! He might say something that Mama would contradict, because Lord Tove would certainly talk to her, too.

Fear created my voice. "Beg pardon. I'm dull from phlegm fever. I haven't seen my great-niece."

Mentioning the fever made me remember the pudding. What would happen if it didn't appear?

"Then you should sit." Courteously, Lord Tove made room for me on the bench.

I placed myself at the end, as far from him as could be.

"Goodman Adeer," Lady Mother said, "where are your goodwife and your other daughter?"

Annet and Mama were fetched, which, I hoped, saved them from having to produce the pudding. His Mastership and Her Mistress-ship, as well as the other Lakti family—the widow and her grown daughter—came as well. I stood again when they came in.

How much space each Lakti took up! I'd never noticed before. No one stood close to anyone else, except the five of us crowded in the middle of the cottage, as if we were prisoners. The newcomers dripped on the floor, and the air reeked of wet wool.

Lady Mother let the other Lakti stay only long enough to satisfy their curiosity. She announced that any information they might have about me, Peregrine, would be rewarded and ordered them to leave.

Always gracious, Lord Tove added, "We'll be quicker on our own. We don't want to disturb the village or the goodman and his family any longer than need be."

"The wife and girl were serving us our dinner. Are we meant to go hungry?" His Master-ship's glare was prodigious. If his eyes had popped farther out, they'd have tumbled to the floor.

"Alas, you may have to get your own dinners this once." I recognized the dangerous brightness in Lord Tove's eyes.

When they left, my family moved apart a little, and I returned to the bench, as I thought a sick old woman would.

Lord Tove let in two soldiers, both male, neither known to me, and instructed them to search the cottage. If Willem were among the company, I was sure he would have managed to come in.

While Lord Tove and Lady Mother stood on either side of the fireplace, one soldier went to the pallets, where he cut apart the mattresses, including mine, which we had just stuffed a few hours before. I hoped the fleas would migrate to him. The other soldier went to the cupboard.

My parents and Annet had dulled their expressions, but Drualt looked about to erupt. He couldn't! I was sure Lord Tove seethed with rage, too, and Drualt might not survive setting him off.

What could I do?

Not *do*! Words! Was there something I could say?

"Drualt?"

He whipped his head around to me. "What?" Furious. A challenge.

My parents heard the fury and turned to him.

A good Bamarre and a sweet boy, he added, "If you please."

"Er . . . Can you recite a ditty to keep our spirits up? I can't think of any. My brain must still be fogged."

He shook his head so hard his tassel flicked back and forth, then said, "Beg pardon."

Mama started reciting,

> *"Five in a hut crammed together*
> *While the winter weather . . ."*

Poppi and Annet joined in.

> *"Made a mule turn to leather*
> *At the end of her tether . . ."*

Drualt's face relaxed, and he recited, too.

> *"And the folks didn't know whether*
> *To laugh or cry alone or together . . ."*

I nodded, since I didn't know the words.

"Till their noses tickled a red feather
And they all sneezed together."

Ah! Something to do. I tickled my brother, who let out a shout of laughter.

Meanwhile, a soldier picked up my sack from the floor next to my pallet and spilled the contents on the floor, including the tablecloth and the magic boots Lady Mother had given me.

CHAPTER TWENTY-FIVE

MY HEART STOPPED. The tablecloth seemed mere linen, but the boots!

Lady Mother picked one up and held it out. "I wonder that you keep such worn-out footwear, Goodman Adeer." She smiled at the absurdity of the Bamarre. "Look, Tove. The sole is flapping."

She'd protected us! And squelched any interest Lord Tove might have had in my sack.

Poppi said, "Poor people don't discard anything that may be patched, Lady." His eyes flicked to me.

He'd given me away!

Lady Mother's eyes found mine, too. I didn't know how to look, so I smiled at her.

Her face froze in horror. She'd recognized my smile—I'd given myself away!

Then she frowned, seeming puzzled. I could almost hear her thoughts: Perry could have the same smile as the great-aunt. They're related. She couldn't be her own great-aunt.

Had Lady Mother told Lord Tove about Halina?

She wouldn't have if she hoped to protect me.

The ransacking of our small cottage didn't take long. When the soldiers finished, Lord Tove told them to search Poppi's and Drualt's clothing. Then he opened the door and called in a female soldier.

"Search the women."

Oh, no! When my purse was emptied, both Lord Tove and Lady Mother would recognize my little knife, which he himself had given me when I was eight. The brass handle was a representation of a hawk's feather.

The female soldier, also a stranger to me, began with Mama.

Lady Mother said, "I tire of waiting. I'll search the aunt."

Lord Tove raised his eyebrows, revealing that he didn't entirely trust his wife. I tried to look old, sick, and as defenseless as he thought all us Bamarre.

"Stand, Goodwife." Lady Mother faced me with her back to Lord Tove, which also blocked him from my view.

I stood. She had me take off my cap, as if I might have hidden I-don't-know-what atop my scalp.

"Your hair is thin, Grandmother." She returned the cap to me, patted lightly around my waist, the small of my back, up and down my legs, wherever I might have concealed anything worth noting.

As she bent down, I was able to see that Lord Tove had lost interest in me. A dog lover, he was engaged in petting Baka.

"Your purse." Lady Mother untied it from my belt and unknotted the drawstring. I heard a tiny intake of breath. "Look at me!"

My chest seemed to close in. I met her eyes. She was going to reveal my little knife!

"How do you come to have a silver coin?" Her voice was harsh, but her eyes were as soft as I'd ever seen them.

I felt Lord Tove's attention.

Why might Nadira have such a big sum? Few Bamarre were rich, and I doubted any of my relatives were. What could I say?

My family seemed to cease breathing.

"Er . . . I . . . Begging your pardon. Er . . . I found it in the road."

In two steps, Lord Tove stood before me. "You lie to my wife?"

"Er . . . begging your pardon . . . it's true."

"And you took it? When it didn't belong to you?" He drew back his arm and punched me, catching the side of my face and my ear. The tassel dug into my skin. My neck jerked.

Someone gasped.

Poppi said warningly, "Drualt . . ."

My ear felt on fire. I fought tears.

And rage. I could punch him back. My attack would be unexpected. My muscles tensed. Freedom for the Bamarre!

Lady Mother said, "Grandmother, the truth is safer than a lie."

Her voice calmed me. I unclenched my fists.

"How did you come by it?" she asked.

Let me cry rather than attack, since I'm a Bamarre. I sobbed into my hands. Mistress Clarra taught her students to live to fight again. Dignity didn't matter.

"Let me see the purse, Klausine."

My little knife! In a minute he'd know me. I looked up, tears still streaming.

Lady Mother gave him the purse. I glanced at her face but couldn't read anything there.

Lord Tove undid the drawstring, which Lady Mother had retied, and emptied the contents into his hand: three copper coins, the silver, and my snail shell. Lady Mother must have taken the knife and saved me.

"Where is your little knife?" he asked. Everyone, whether a Lakti or a Bamarre, carried one.

I swallowed. My face hurt so I could hardly think. I sensed Lord Tove's impatience. If he hit me again, I didn't know what I'd do.

"I lost it?" I wailed. "I don't know"—Nadira might not know to call him *Lord*—"er, Master? Er, Sire? Er, Sir?"

Lady Mother asked me when I'd noticed the knife was gone.

I decided to answer everything in a questioning tone. "Just now, Mistress . . . Lady? Yesterday?"

"When did you find the coin?" Lord Tove softened his voice, as if his victim could be won over. "Nothing bad will come of telling me."

I knew how to shrug as a Bamarre, having watched Annet for years. "The day before yesterday? Tomorrow?"

"Near here?" Lady Mother said.

"Not far? Very far? Tell me what to say, if you please." I felt a spark of pleasure in my playacting.

They asked me more questions before giving up. Lord Tove took the coins and returned my purse, with the snail shell back inside.

The soldiers went on searching. I sat with my head bent. The tears dried as if they'd never been, but the rage smoldered. I recited *Freedom for the Bamarre* again and again in my mind.

Finally, the soldiers finished and were sent out. Lady Mother told us that she and Lord Tove would be camped

215

along the road west of the village.

He said, "Perry may still be on her way to you, or she may send a letter." Then, to my astonishment, he knelt! "She is as dear to me as the breath in my lungs. We've trained her in arms—"

Lady Mother broke in, "—and to be hardy and *cautious.*"

It was a message. *Take care.* The pain in my ear would remind me.

Lord Tove stood again. "But she's young and may not always be able to tell an enemy from an ally. Please, if you can lead us to her, do not hang back. You'll be returning her to those who love her most. You'll be relieving yourself of danger as well."

The threat inside the sweetness. My family wouldn't miss it.

They'd been right not to want me.

I'd been selfish to stay.

Lord Tove hadn't finished. "I doubt this will matter, because I see how worthy you are, but I will reward you with a purse of gold coins merely for information, if it leads to her recovery."

Would my family get rid of me and become rich?

"And, Grandmother, counsel your relatives. Everyone will benefit if Perry returns to us. You've discovered the foolhardiness of defiance."

I licked my lips. "Master, I've never been defiant in my life."

"Good." He flung on his cloak. "I'll rely on you."

They left.

Without them, the tiny cottage seemed large and empty—and a wreck, with mattress straw everywhere, crockery out of the cupboard, pots and pans scattered, Poppi's thread in a jumble, bolts of cloth unspooled on the floor.

Drualt ran to me and touched my face softly, but his touch still hurt. I called on my Lakti endurance.

We began to put things to rights.

At first, no one spoke. I'm sure we all suspected we'd be overheard.

Mama whispered explosively, "Why didn't you say you had a silver coin?"

"I forgot I had it." I remembered to add an apology.

After everyone recited the proverb, Annet raised one eyebrow. "Still a rich Lakti, begging your pardon."

"We should have told the fairy we couldn't keep her, no matter whose body she was given." Mama rolled up a length of brown linen. "Too late now."

I said, "They would have come anyway."

Annet said it was Lakti-like and rude to contradict people.

As if unaware of the anger flying about, Drualt said,

"Aunt Nadira, you should rest. Phlegm fever is tiring!" He laughed, as if he'd told a marvelous joke.

I gathered my courage. "I'll tell them who I am. They'll take me and go."

Drualt shook his head violently.

Annet whispered, spitting in her vehemence, "You stupid Lakti! Begging your pardon!"

"How am I stupid, begging *your* pardon?"

Mama explained. "If you admit who you are, we still sheltered you."

"You thought I was Nadira."

Everyone laughed, not just Drualt.

"They'll see through that," Poppi said. "We'd be punished."

Apparently, they didn't believe the promise of gold coins.

Mama whispered, "Why did Lady Klausine hold up the boots?"

"She gave them to me. She kept my little knife, because Lord Tove would have recognized it. That's why I didn't have it. I think she knows who I really am."

"Magic boots, a magic tablecloth," Poppi said. "Dangerous—"

"The pudding!" Mama cried.

I took out the tablecloth.

The meal arrived soundlessly. Drualt lunged and,

before Poppi had time to stop him, crammed a cheese puff in his mouth. As soon as he swallowed, he whispered, "I've never tasted anything so good."

Mama frowned. The tablecloth had delivered a peach tart and a small bowl of marchpane but no pudding. Each dessert was enough to serve us, but not the Ships and their guests. Even I knew Mama couldn't bring the tart when peaches were out of season, and she said the marchpane was too rich for His Master-ship's pantry.

I made the feast disappear. On the next try, we got sugarplums and fried apples drizzled with honey. No pudding.

Mama set the apples aside, because they could be served.

I kept calling forth fresh meals. Mother saved whatever might be used: a goat-cheese cake, gingerbread cookies, a walnut tart. And Drualt removed a platter or two as well. By then, no one stopped him.

Finally, we received a small raisin pudding. Mama decided she couldn't wait for more and began to arrange the food in a basket until Annet said, "We can't bring those dishes."

The pottery was rimmed with gold or silver. They exchanged the fine platters and bowls for plain.

Mama told me to stay home. "You've had enough Bamarre education for one day, and we've had enough of

the Lakti." She really meant she'd had enough of me.
    I thought,

> If I were a flea
> Another flea
> Would love me.
> Many bugs,
> Many hugs.

CHAPTER TWENTY-SIX

POPPI, DRUALT, AND I continued putting the cottage to
rights.

What were Lord Tove and Lady Mother saying to
each other right now?

The snail shell!

I opened my purse. When I put the shell to my ear,
I heard people in the village and soldiers in Lord Tove's
camp (Willem's voice not among them), but I didn't hear
Lord Tove or Lady Mother, who either were silent or had
moved too far away for the shell to hear.

Annet began to say something in the Ships' house,
but I pulled the shell away without listening. On top
of my other offenses, I didn't want to spy. I handed the
shell to Drualt, whose face lit up when he put it to his

ear, although Poppi frowned.

After listening for a few minutes, he announced that His Master-ship had pronounced the tablecloth's desserts excellent. "His Master-ship said to Her Mistress-ship, 'If only you could please me more often.'"

I understood Mama's pity.

Poppi took a turn listening. Finally, he lowered the shell and said that one of Lord Tove's soldiers had stopped at every door to promise the gold purse for information about me. "The Lakti will want it, and the others will be tempted."

"Dyrin!" I cried.

"What about *Goodwife* Dyrin, begging your pardon?" Poppi said.

I described my mistakes. "That's when my niece said I had phlegm fever."

Drualt laughed. "Mama is quick!"

Poppi grinned. "She is." He squinted. "I doubt Goodwife Dyrin would ever imagine that Aunt Nadira is you, but your arrival just when Perry might have come is a difficulty. And you misspeak almost every time you speak, begging your pardon." He put the shell on his table, obviously taking possession of it.

I didn't argue, though it was Willem's gift and all I still had of him.

When Annet and Mama came back, Mama began my instruction in being a Bamarre. The lesson continued late into the night. Finally, when we stopped and I stretched out on my pallet, even that was wrong. The Bamarre didn't sleep on their backs as if they were safe anywhere.

In the morning, she woke me before dawn to begin again.

"Begging your pardon," she said, "you'll have to stay indoors until you can do better than you did yesterday."

My walk was wrong. "Aunt Nadira's person is soft, but you make her angular. Think curves! And you move too fast!"

I crossed yet again from the cottage hearth to the door.

"Not so fast, if you please!" Mama said, again and again.

My posture was too stiff, my gaze too direct.

After Mama left, I practiced, because we Lakti persevered.

That evening, during our meal, Baka barked sharply.

An envelope was slid under the door, and I recognized Lady Mother's seal. Poppi and I stood, but, realizing I should, I let him get it.

He opened it and read for only a moment. "It's to you, Aunt Nadira." He passed it to me.

The first word was *Dearest*. I couldn't read further because I was sobbing. The parchment rattled in my shaking hand.

What sort of Lakti had I ever been if one word could undo me?

Dearest Perry,

Lord Tove no longer trusts me when it comes to you. I am convinced that if you make yourself known to him, he will imprison you forever or worse.

Behead me? Hang me?

He will accord the same treatment to your Bamarre family, as I expect they realize.

You needn't fear he will reveal you to be a Bamarre, which would shame him, perhaps the only hazard you do not face.

If I had been a softer sort of mother, you might have come to me rather than to Willem.

She didn't realize Lord Tove already knew when I told Willem. She thought I had gone to my friend for advice rather than to her. If I had told her as soon as Halina told me, would I still be a pretend Lakti? I didn't know.

However, I am the sort of parent who would never thrust you from my heart. Once lodged there (which happened the first moment I saw you), you remain forever. Know that I will do everything in my power to save you.

But I understood now, as I hadn't then, that she would have protected me, no matter my choice. I had misjudged her.

Now you must be a Bamarre, which I'd wished to spare you. I hope the family of your birth will appreciate the sterling you are made of.

Your Lady Mother

I wept again. I was made of water, not sterling!

When I finally recovered, I gave the letter to Mama and Poppi so they wouldn't suspect me of keeping secrets.

Mama said, "Lady Klausine cooked her own pudding, and now everyone is choking on it."

"We're in an adventure! Thank you, Aunt Nadira."

My darling brother!

Lady Mother and Lord Tove camped near the village for three more days. When I heard they'd rode off, I wondered if I'd ever see either of them again.

They left behind two soldiers, a young man named Joram and an older woman named Kassia, whose charge was certainly to spy on the village and especially on us.

At home we continued to whisper. I struggled to

remake myself a believable Bamarre, but with scant success. I failed to apologize; I forgot to be grateful; I said straight out what I thought; I didn't even call colors by their correct names. To my eyes, cobalt, indigo, and navy were the same dark blue.

After squinting longer than I'd ever seen, Poppi declared the effort hopeless. "Begging your pardon, Aunt Nadira, you'll be a decade trying and still not learn."

"You can't give up!"

Drualt whispered, "Begging your pardon, we Bamarre don't order each other about."

I reminded them that Halina said I had to learn to be a Bamarre before I could free them.

Poppi said, "If we defeated the Lakti, however that might happen, we'd be the new overlords. What if we enjoyed being cruel? We'd hate that."

They all smiled at the irony, and Drualt laughed.

But it was no better to be tyrannized than to be tyrants.

Drualt said, "Begging your pardon, Poppi, I don't want to be a tailor when I grow up. I'd rather be free."

Mama snapped, "You'd get yourself killed to avoid sewing a cloak?" Her voice softened. "I'm sorry, Dru."

If most Bamarre were like my family, Halina was mad to think anyone could save them—us.

Then Mama shrugged. "Begging your pardon, Adeer.

I'll keep trying. Aunt Nadira can't stay in the cottage forever."

Instruction resumed. When Mama wasn't teaching me, I observed.

She and Poppi weaved around each other as if in a courteous dance, and she often touched the shoulder or cheek of Annet and Drualt. Poppi often drew one or the other into a hug.

Only Drualt seemed troubled that I was left out. He'd come to me after a loving display and ask about swordplay, which fascinated him. Or he'd tell me a joke and laugh and laugh. I had never encountered a merrier person. Out of all that beset me, he was the one great good.

Once, he whispered, "It's just the real Aunt Nadira they didn't love."

I was at the spinning wheel, the only Bamarre skill I'd mastered. It was the evening of my birthday, which no one remembered. I had turned sixteen.

He continued. "I never met her, but they say she didn't admire anyone and nothing pleased her."

Did I love or even like my family?

I loved Drualt without reservation.

But my parents' constant fear grated. Annet's resentment of me made me resentful in return. Often I longed for Willem so much I could hardly keep myself here.

Evenings were my favorite time, when I appreciated the best aspects of being a Bamarre. After Mama had given up on me for the night, Poppi and Drualt read poems aloud. The only thing I'd brought with me that pleased everyone was my book of poems.

This happy-sad verse stayed with me:

> *Lantern-shine, dim but kind—*
> *No starkness in darkness—*
> *Even I please the eye.*
> *Outside, wind and rain,*
> *Weather's fitful wax and wane.*
> *Tomorrow's sun will reveal*
> *What night conceals.*
> *All we lack, regret, know,*
> *Forgotten in lamp-oil glow.*

***

During my restriction to the cottage, a peddler named Goodman Marko, a Bamarre, came to the village. Peddlers, in addition to selling their wares, delivered mail and carried parcels. And they provided the Bamarre villagers a rare glimpse of the wider kingdom.

I wasn't allowed to attend the gathering in Goodwife Dyrin's cottage to hear the news, but Drualt told me what he remembered. A blizzard had struck the north; a three-headed piglet had been born in the far east; and

King Einar had survived a cold. Goodman Marko didn't mention my disappearance.

***

Gradually I improved, interrupted less often, remembered the polite phrases more often, refrained (usually) from insisting I was right—even though I was.

After a month, Poppi and Mama deemed me reformed enough to leave the cottage. Mama put the word out that I'd finally recovered from phlegm fever.

Annet added, "We've reminded people how odd and unpleasant Aunt Nadira often was, begging your pardon." As long as pardon was sought, Annet believed she could never be rude.

Drualt was jubilant. "Now we can free ourselves." He saw I didn't understand. "Us—the Bamarre."

The evening they announced my release, Mama told Drualt and me to pick through an enormous sack of speckled beans and discard the stones and rotten beans. As we sorted, I asked Drualt if he thought himself alone in wanting to be free of Lakti rule.

He whispered promptly, "Goodwife Dyrin made straw mannequins of His Master-ship and Her Mistress-ship. Often, when she comes home, she punches them. I know from Vanz." Vanz was Dyrin's son.

A coward's revenge.

Still, perhaps the goodwife's anger could be turned

into something useful. In an uprising, servants could murder their masters; tailors, like Poppi, could kill their customers.

But Mama pitied her masters. And I hadn't killed Sir Lerrin or the Kyngoll guard. Maybe too much sympathy—not cowardice—was the Bamarre fault.

"What are you thinking, Aunt Nadira?"

"We have no weapons. No horses. No one is trained to fight but me." I dropped my whisper even lower. "And I don't want to kill anyone." I was like Willem in this, after all.

"Everybody says, 'Bamarre's future; Bamarre's freedom,' and we greet each other with 'Across the Eskerns.' Besides, there are more of us than there are of them."

"Here. In Gavrel. But not everywhere."

"A good commander knows her troops."

I was startled. "How do you know that?"

"Common sense." He laughed. "Look, if you please! This is a funny bean. The speckles make a face." He showed me.

Knowing my troops . . . Mama was livelier and probably cleverer than Poppi. He was more of a deliberator.

"My niece and nephew would be good at strategy," I said. Annet would keep everybody angry, so we wouldn't lose our purpose.

Drualt declared, "I'd lead a charge. I'd be the left flank, and you could be the right."

I smiled. "Thank you."

He *could* lead troops—in a few years.

"I'll be the laughing general; they'll call me the Laugher."

I imagined Lord Tove killing him, beheading him, hanging him, running him through with his sword.

Halina, I won't try to save the Bamarre until Drualt is old enough to protect himself in battle.

I expected her to appear or argue with me in my mind, but nothing happened.

He was watching my face. "Begging your pardon, what?"

"A wily commander bides her time."

He nodded sagely. "I agree."

But he didn't drop the subject and often offered ideas. We should win over the few wealthy Bamarre, take small villages first, progress to castles of lesser nobility.

"Begging your pardon," I'd say, "but we're not ready."

He set me thinking, however, and the thinking became an exercise in war craft, such as I used to work through in fun with Lord Tove.

How might a rebellion be won by untrained soldiers whose habit was submission? Our single weapon was slyness, but the Bamarre couldn't triumph with guile alone.

231

Might crossing the Eskerns be more possible than overcoming the Lakti? On this side, tyrants; on that, monsters. I'd choose monsters and freedom. But the pass was guarded to keep us from leaving.

And neither could be accomplished without the will to win—and boldness. What might give them that?

Not I, who had no gift for persuasion, who could convince no one even to like me.

CHAPTER TWENTY-SEVEN

THE NEXT MORNING, Mama took me with her and Annet to the Ships' kitchen.

"In case the Bamarre aren't freed," she said, her tone
ironic, "you'll know how to cook."

To my surprise, I became interested. When Mama
allowed me to prepare a dish, I used the pantry's spices
daringly, remembering the tastes that the tablecloth had
sent.

I was more attentive to food than Mama was, begging
her pardon. My roasts were cooked through but not
overcooked; stews bubbled gently; fried bread never
burned. The result was less criticism from His Master-
ship and less trouble from her Mistress-ship. And a little
freedom for Mama, which enabled her to bring Dyrin into

the kitchen more often, supposedly to help us, but really so they could enjoy each other's company.

No one nodded, but I nodded at myself. I loved being useful.

My parents and Annet didn't come to love me, but their chill thawed. Sometimes it felt as if I'd never lived anywhere else, and both my castle years and Willem were a dream.

Strangely, I came to enjoy inhabiting Nadira's form. My age commanded respect; my spryness earned me compliments (Drualt could hardly hold back guffaws); my occasional rudeness was borne with forbearance. And my quietness persuaded some to consider me wise!

Meanwhile, I continued to think of freeing us, and the idea of crossing into Old Lakti kept growing.

On Wednesday nights, the village Bamarre gathered in one cottage or another for conversation and poetry. After Goodwife Dyrin praised my cooking, my parents' cottage became the preferred meeting place. My cheese puffs, which I never prepared for the Ships, were always requested.

Some of the villagers delighted me. Goodwife Dyrin, for example, could make the most dour among us laugh. Walde, her goodman, knew how to tell an anecdote so that his listeners practically lived his experience. Young Goodman Meerol, who spent each get-together following

Annet with his eyes, balanced her grumpiness with sweetness.

The left-behind soldiers also adapted to being here, and their watchfulness slackened. Joram, the young soldier, began courting the widow's daughter, and Soldier Kassia, the older woman, took to training His Mastership's children in Lakti athletic arts.

They needed instruction. I was astonished at the laxity of the village Lakti. Though the two families practiced swordplay weekly with wooden swords, that was the end of it. No one raced or played games of strength.

I wished I could have joined Soldier Kassia's exercises. One night in mid-March, I dreamed of running around the outer ward of Lord Tove's castle, chasing Willem. He looked back and smiled at me, his full lips tight as a drawn bow. My feet fused to the ground while he ran on, until he became no bigger than a grain of rice in the distance.

I awoke. A boulder seemed to press on me. The windows glowed, signifying a bright night. If I stayed here another moment, I'd feel as rooted as I had in the dream. I had to escape for a few hours if I could.

My family were all sound sleepers. The village dogs knew my scent by now and wouldn't bark.

I rose. First, I collected my magic shell from Poppi's table and listened in it. No one stirred near our cottage. I dropped the shell into my purse. Then I borrowed Mama's long kitchen knife in its sheath from the mantelpiece and slid it into my belt. I picked my sack off the floor next to the fireplace.

Annet said, enunciating clearly, "Boiling oil, losing heart."

I froze, but nothing followed. After a few long minutes, she rolled onto her other side. I glided to the door, cracked it open, and slipped out.

Outside, a three-quarter moon presided over a starry sky, where the Lakti queen constellation held three enemy warriors at bay. I smiled at the siege-engine constellation rolling up from the eastern horizon, as good for telling time as a sundial. Only the tip of the catapult showed, so the hour was no later than eleven.

Each stone that lined the road cast a sharp shadow. A piebald mouse skittered an inch from my feet, the moonlight bright enough to reveal its patches.

The west pulled at me. If he hadn't been badly hurt, Willem might have returned—willingly or not—to the battlefield. I could seek him there.

But I didn't dare. I feared Lord Tove, who would recognize Nadira.

With one magic boot on and with Lakti self-control, I pointed my toes southward. A peak in the Eskerns would provide the best view of Old Lakti.

I stepped. The mountains appeared, looking at first

like no more than a notched frill, but as I advanced, they surged and overwhelmed the sky.

The plains ended in foothills. Thank you, boot, for the effortless ascent. I had come to trust it and to believe it wouldn't let me fall. One more step, I thought, would bring me into the mountains, but still on the New Lakti side. If the boot left me in the midst of the Lakti guard at the pass, I'd merely step again.

The boot carried me up and up. No sign of people. Rocks flew in my wake, as if I were a boat on a sea of stones. Higher, higher, and over the final ridge to stop at last on a ledge in the land of monsters.

But I saw none. The Eskerns descended to a valley watered by a swift river. Across the valley rolled wooded hills. No life except trees and grass. What a beautiful place we Lakti—those Lakti—had fled.

I'd planned only to gaze on the old kingdom, but now I had to explore. While I exchanged magic boot for everyday, the mountain wind whipped across my face. My tassel slapped my cheek.

A ribbon of a path led downward. Sometimes the way was no wider than my foot and the drop vertical. At those moments, I leaned into the cliff wall and progressed with the help of my hands from one crack in the stone to the next.

Step follows step.

Hope follows courage.

I slowed my breath and stilled my trembling. In half an hour I reached the valley. If anything, the moon shone brighter than before. I followed the river for about a quarter mile. Soon, I'd don my magic boot to see more, but first I wanted to savor the land as the Lakti who once lived here might have. After a bend in the river, I stopped in astonishment. Beyond the other bank, not far ahead, a handsome stone manor house faced me. A complete house, not a ruin! A road wound from the east and ended in a wooden bridge and a path to the front door.

After a few more steps I recognized the house's crenellated roof and ivy and its five chimneys. Sir Noll's manor!

A figure passed behind one of the windows—slender, almost tall, a measured stride.

The door opened. There he was.

Halina! She'd spirited the house and Willem here, for some fairy reason.

I raced, bounded onto the bridge—

—into air, nothing beneath my feet.

I fell into the river, went under, emerged, and the manor had vanished, but Willem stood on the bank, smiling.

"Willem!"

His expression turned malicious, as I'd never seen it,

and his solidity thinned so I saw grass through him. A monster—a specter!

Then it was gone. Ahead, waist deep in the water: a grinning ogre!

CHAPTER TWENTY-EIGHT

THE CURRENT WAS carrying me toward it, and I doubted it was imaginary. I fought and scrambled out of the water, already reaching into my sack for my soaked boot. But two more ogres pounded toward me from the bank.

Hideous! Pocked, cloud-white skin; small eyes; no lips; smiles revealing broken teeth; twice my height, thrice or more my girth.

I'd never see the real Willem again. Or Drualt or Lady Mother. I was supposed to cook a barley soup for the Ships in the morning.

I drew Mama's kitchen knife.

The ogres laughed, sounding like boulders crashing together. The battle spell fell over me. Lady Mother spoke in my ear, *Courage, Perry. Strike hard.*

I ran at the closest ogre as it ran at me. I ducked its hand, stabbed its thigh through its breeches. It felt real and spouted seemingly real blood.

It howled. Jumped back.

But another ogre grabbed my knife arm and lifted me above its head. Using all my strength, I kicked its eye with one foot, its nose with the other.

It dropped me. I landed on the grass, the wind knocked out of me, but I jumped up anyway. Before I could run, the first ogre caught my wrist and pulled back a fist as big as a lantern.

With every shred of energy I had, I yanked free and ran, praying their huge legs were slow.

Not slow.

But I was quicker. The ogres' bellows diminished behind me.

Could a specter take the form of a living person? Or did my vision mean Willem had died?

As I ran, I wondered if the pasture around me teemed with ogres and other monsters a specter had made invisible, who would overwhelm me as soon as I stopped. But at last my lungs gave out. I fell to my knees. The ogres were out of sight behind me. I opened my sack and, quick as I could, donned my magic boot. Then I sheathed Mama's knife and stepped, heading away from the Eskerns.

During the step, I exulted. I'd overcome three ogres

241

and survived a specter, and nothing could catch me now.

The boot bore me up and down hills, through woods of oak and maple, beginning to leaf out. I flashed across meadows and through streams. The air, sweet, the wind, whooshing but not raw. All beautiful, except, for an instant, three gryphons in a meadow, tearing into the carcass of a horse.

Wild horses? Descendants of the Lakti's steeds? That we could tame?

The boot stopped at the base of a mountain, less steep than the Eskerns, pleasing in its gentleness. I'd learned Old Lakti geography. This was one of the seven Kilkets.

I checked the siege engine constellation, which had traveled only a little above the horizon. I still had time.

I surged over the mountain, up and down foothills, then ended in a field, divided by a stream, strewn here and there with round stones.

An owl hooted. Did that signify monsters or no monsters?

The bird subsided. If we did cross the Eskerns despite the monsters, we could build here. I picked up a round stone, tossed it in the air, caught it. We could line a road with such stones, as the Lakti did.

Oh! Perhaps they had. The stones' arrangement might not be haphazard. My heart picked up its pace. If a specter wasn't deceiving me, this had been a road! Ancient Lakti had walked here. Where might it lead?

I remembered to change my magic boot, but I didn't drop it into my sack, just in case. Willem's shell revealed nothing to worry me, so, all senses alert, I followed the stones.

I hurried through the pine forest that bordered the field. When I emerged, I gasped. A castle in ruins!

Of course this might be the work of a specter, too. Still, I approached. The drawbridge had rotted, so I crossed the dry moat and dashed between the gatehouse towers. The iron portcullis had frozen with rust, luckily above my head, but the big oak door hung crookedly, making a gap too small for me to squeeze through. I pulled hard, heard a groan, and won three inches. I was in.

The moon illumined heaps of broken slate atop chipped floor tiles. I stood in the great hall, where the roof had caved in. Grass pushed up here and there. A throne tilted on the dais, with two legs sunken through the boards.

As I surveyed the chamber, a shadow crossed the hall. I looked up at the blackness of a dragon, sharp against the starry sky. If I'd had a bow and arrow, I could have shot its unprotected belly.

It flew over again. Did it smell me? See me? There was no place to hide.

The dragon circled back twice more and then stayed away.

I pictured the hall restored. A king who resembled Willem filled the throne; a minister stood by, holding a stack of documents; the fireplace blazed; a hound slept; a cat stalked a mouse.

Returning from my imaginings, I picked my way across the hall and into the kitchen, where crockery was scattered in shards across the crooked worktable, but the metal platters, a dozen silver and a small gold one, needed nothing more than polish.

I thought of my family's poverty, the widespread poverty of the Bamarre, and the cost of weapons, armor, horses. Into my satchel went three silver platters and the gold one.

After that, I knew which chamber I most wanted to find, and in that chamber, which relic, if I were lucky. I stepped carefully to the tower at the end of the great hall, hoping to find the lord or king's study.

Instead, I discovered the counting room. Like all satisfying tales of treasure, gold and silver coins spilled across the floor, with here and there a scrap of burlap from the sacks that had once held them.

I grabbed fistfuls of gold and silver, added them to my sack, and hoped the seams would hold.

The study should be in a tower, too. I followed a corridor with gaping walls that opened on ravaged apartments. A few minutes took me to the next tower, and there was what I believed to be the study, judging from the leg of a desk or table and a fragment of filigreed wood that could only have been part of a chair back. And there, protruding from rubble, the corner of a book!

I dug cautiously, removing fragments of this and that, and soon reached my prize, which had been protected by the leather stitching, the leather-over-wood covers, and the bronze bosses on the corners of the covers. Lord Tove used to occupy himself with just such a volume in his study—the sole book he kept there.

But here was another, poking up from the debris, this one smaller and thicker. I freed it as well, and pushed the two volumes into my satchel without opening either one. The night was bright, but not bright enough for reading.

Outside, the siege machine constellation had almost half crossed the sky. I should start for home, but I hated to leave without seeing more, and my boot carried me so quickly.

Remembering my geography, I decided to travel east toward the Haun Ocean through what had once been the elf queen's land.

After six steps, the boot, to my surprise, took me through cultivated fields, where I glimpsed a few cottages, too small for people, but not ruins. Smoke rose from one.

Specters again?

The boot deposited me on a low hill, where I smelled

the sea. Not far off, a beach slid into the dark Haun Ocean, but before that another castle rose—with towers, battlements, moat, drawbridge, guardhouse—not a ruin. Distance made size difficult to judge, but I felt almost certain that this edifice was smaller than our castles.

Had the elves remained despite the monsters?

Had the Lakti been cowards to flee?

I started back, through the glorious countryside. How splendid it would be to live here, despite the monsters, in the kingdom of liberty.

Would anyone agree with me?

Would Willem want to live here, if we ever found each other?

I had no idea. And the Lakti guarded the pass. Might they let us leave?

No.

By the time I neared home, the siege engine constellation was close to setting. I took out the magic boot and buried my satchel with the castle treasure in the soft earth under the oak tree on the knoll that overlooked Gavrel. Then I pushed dead leaves over the spot and hoped no one would be able to tell.

My family was now wealthier than they had ever dreamt of.

I put the snail shell to my ear. A voice!

Mistress Chavi, the widow's daughter, said, "It's a sacrifice to give up your sleep."

"I'd hate to miss Lord Tove's daughter if she arrived at night." This voice belonged to Joram, the young man soldier, who in fact rarely lost sleep to guarding.

They'd slipped outside to woo each other!

How might I get home? Soldier Joram would be suspicious of any Bamarre out before dawn, even an old lady.

His sword clanked.

If he caught me, he'd question me for hours, at the least. Soldier Kassia would, too. They'd interrogate my family.

Would they send for Lord Tove?

They might, even though I was only old Nadira.

Soldier Joram said, "But if we do find her, I'll be sorry to leave Gavrel."

"Did you know Mistress Peregrine?"

He didn't say yes or no, although the truth was no. "Excellent athlete. Lord Tove and Lady Klausine adore her."

"A paragon?"

"No one liked her."

The brightening sky dimmed the last of the constellation. Might I run behind the houses? If I reached the privy, I'd have my excuse to be out.

247

I couldn't tell exactly where they were, so I edged closer to the village and halted not far from the first cottage.

"I could teach you archery," Soldier Joram said.

Now I could hear they were behind the widow's house.

Mistress Chavi tittered, a sound I hadn't known a Lakti could make. "I could teach you to embroider."

He laughed.

Why were they behind the house?

To avoid being caught. Several small spruce trees grew back there, beyond the backyard fence. They could hide in the shadows.

What would my family feel when they woke up in a few minutes and found my pallet empty?

They'd be frightened but might be glad I'd gone, except for Drualt.

Was there an excuse I could make to explain arriving by the road?

I could think of nothing.

Pink smudged the horizon.

The widow's home was four houses farther than ours. Perhaps I could reach our privy without being seen or heard, if they had eyes and ears only for each other. Once inside, I could wait for them to leave.

If they had been listening intently, they'd have heard me as I darted from shadow to shadow of trees and bushes.

The privy door hung ajar. I could squeeze in. I squeezed—

—and heard a squeal. Out rushed a hedgehog.

"Who goes there?"

I pictured Lord Tove's eyes glittering when I was brought before him.

What to do? I froze.

I remembered Lord Tove's fist.

My muscles bunched. Soldier Joram wouldn't have the chance to beat me.

He repeated, "Who goes there?"

Don't be hasty. Think.

If I were innocent, I'd recognize the guard's voice and be frightened, but not as terrified as if I were guilty.

I called, "Only old Nadira, begging your pardon." I hid my magic boot under my cloak.

Had they heard me come? I didn't think so, or he'd have shouted sooner. No crime in my visiting the privy.

Mistress Chavi stayed in the shadows, but Soldier Joram approached. I heard our gate latch lift.

He loomed over me and fairly shouted, "What are you doing here?" Guilt was making him dangerous. He knew he shouldn't be with the widow's daughter.

My family would be listening and would be frightened. I covered a yawn with my hand. "What a night, Master. Did you ever fall asleep in the privy?"

He crossed his arms.

"The hedgehog and I surprised each other. Voices woke me from my sleep, but I didn't want to disturb you and"—I whispered pointedly—"the young lady." I was becoming as crafty as any other Bamarre. "Beg pardon, I'm sure."

He stared, the realization dawning that I'd threatened to tell about the tryst. After a pause, during which I planned how to take his sword from him if I had to, he stepped back. "Go home, Grandmother."

When I opened the cottage door, Annet glared at me, and Mama and Poppi came down the sleeping loft ladder, both glaring too.

Why were they angry? For all they knew, I'd been home through the night.

Drualt hugged me.

I couldn't help smiling. "A little victory."

Poppi frowned. "Did you really fall asleep in the privy?"

People did. In the middle of the night, folks were half asleep.

I just shrugged, then added, "Begging your pardon."

CHAPTER TWENTY-NINE

HALF AN HOUR later, bleary-eyed, I chopped leeks in the Ships' kitchen and imagined leading a band of warriors (with Willem on one side and a grown-up Drualt on the other) against the monsters. After a series of glorious battles, the monsters would be wiped out or reduced to a very few. A squadron would guard the pass to keep out the Lakti.

I wished I knew more about the monsters. For how long could specters keep up their deceptions? How many could they fool at once? Was there any way to see through their wiles? I hadn't encountered a dragon or a gryphon except at a distance, but I wondered how clever they were.

And might more than the elves remain? Did dwarves

and sorcerers still live there, too? How did they manage against the monsters?

After the Ships, while we ate our evening meal, I announced, "Last night I used a magic boot to cross the Eskerns."

"Really?" Drualt bounced next to me on the bench. "Did you see monsters?"

Annet's eyebrows climbed her forehead. "Begging your pardon, if something happened to you, how would we explain your absence?"

I said nothing, just broke a chunk off the sesame-seed bread I'd baked for us in the Ships' oven.

Drualt said, "I'd rescue you."

Mama put down the cheese she'd been eating. "Where did you go?"

I told them about Old Lakti. Drualt's eyes never left my face. No one else looked at me at all. They were motionless, not eating, staring at their bowls. When I mentioned the gold coins and the platters, Poppi shook his head repeatedly.

After I finished, Mama buttered a slice of bread. "If we left the kingdom, what would the Lakti do without us?"

That was her first question? Concern for the Lakti? "Would you leave?" I asked.

Poppi corrected me. "*Begging your pardon*, would you leave?"

252

Annet said, "The Lakti don't eat us."

Drualt waved his bread. "We'd kill the monsters." He groaned. "I'm a dying ogre."

The parents I wished I had would have admired my courage. My imaginary mama would have said, *How lucky we are that you're here.*

My perfect poppi would answer, *The Bamarre must be free. You struggled to become more like us. We must follow your example.*

Poppi said, "While you're under our roof, Aunt Nadira, I forbid you from going back there, begging your pardon."

I wondered if Halina was hearing this.

Drualt grinned. Nothing discouraged him.

In early April, Goodman Marko the peddler returned with the latest stale news. King Uriel had died in a tournament in February. Weak-minded Canute was king. He had no wife or children, so Lord Tove had become crown prince. Lady Mother would succeed if anything befell him, and, even in my absence, I was next in line after her—the Bamarre princess of the Lakti.

I'd met the old king, who had been much admired for his wrestling, and I supposed I was sad, but it was an echo of grief. Nothing to do with me.

At the start of the spring fighting, the new king had formally declared war against the Kyngoll, and the

Lakti were now fighting along the length of the border. I suspected Lord Tove of using his influence to expand the conflict.

Three weeks passed. On a wet morning, Annet and I sat together at the Ships' kitchen table, skinning Lakti pea-beans, which were tiny. The task had already occupied us for an hour. I wondered if we'd do the entire job in silence.

No.

Annet begged my pardon.

She was about to find fault with me again.

"You never smile at any of us except Drualt."

A pea shot between my fingers and rolled across the floor. She wanted me to smile at her?

But my parents and she didn't smile at me, either. Annet herself had almost never smiled at me while I was growing up. No one had told me to smile when they were teaching me to be a Bamarre.

I knelt to pick up the pea. "Would you like me to?"

She shrugged.

A trumpet blared from the direction of the road outside. A woman's voice boomed, "Step outside, good people of Gavrel. Hear the words of King Canute."

My chest tightened. Mama opened the kitchen door. The vestibule was filled by His Master-ship, Her Mistress-ship, and their boys, whom we followed outside into a downpour. Annet held Mama's hand.

A herald and a dozen or more soldiers sat their horses in the road. The herald wore a livery collar—a brass chain from which hung King Canute's insignia, a bow and arrow, in worked silver. The soldiers flanked her. One of them held the trumpet we'd heard.

Along the road west of us, two oxen waited before a cart. A Bamarre drover perched on a bench behind the beasts, his face as fixed as a block of wood. The cart's contents, covered by brown sacking, mounded lumpily.

People hurried from their cottages. The Bamarre families grouped together, and the Lakti stood apart with the village's soldiers, Kassia and Joram.

Poppi and Drualt joined us, and Poppi took Annet's other hand. Drualt clasped mine and Mama's.

All the Lakti had assembled, but a few of the Bamarre were trimming trees in the orchard south of the village, and several, including Annet's Goodman Meerol, were weeding the vegetable gardens to the east. His Mastership told the herald to wait, and soon, the missing laborers arrived at a run.

The soldiers reared their horses and drew their swords.

A show of might.

The herald unrolled her scroll and addressed us with gentle words, at first.

"I am crossing the kingdom, north to south, east to west, out of the love our king feels for his subjects, especially his Bamarre. Know you all that His Royal Highness's mind has been toiling for them."

His Highness's mind, as far as I had ever heard, had never toiled for anyone.

"These are His Majesty's words: 'I am father to my Bamarre and my Lakti alike. The Lakti are parents to their local Bamarre, and parents must have broad power to raise their children well. Too long have my Bamarre been left to do as they like. This grievous laxity does not promote their well-being, so dear to my heart.'"

Someone shifted from one foot to the other. The rest of us didn't move. I felt Annet's eyes on me.

"'Therefore, I have created new strictures, called Beneficences, which I expect to be carried out faithfully.'"

The trumpeter blew a blast.

The herald shook her head, spraying raindrops. "'My Bamarre may no longer ply the trades of jeweler, furrier, or hunter, for these occupations depend on abilities possessed by the Lakti alone. Nor may my Bamarre own horses, for how can a noble beast be governed by a base being?'"

I stiffened, sure I was hearing Lord Tove's words in the proclamation. Drualt squeezed my hand.

Thunder rumbled.

"'Horses owned by my Bamarre must be sold on the

instant, and my Lakti must buy them at a fair rate. The purchase price will be held by the Bamarre's Lakti master or lord until the Bamarre proves need of it.'"

Even though none of us in Gavrel performed the prohibited trades or owned a horse, what liberties all the Bamarre had were being stripped away, and the Lakti's purses would grow fat. But, I wondered, why hunters?

Oh. Because hunters were skilled in archery.

The Beneficences continued, a deluge, like the rain. We were not to travel without written permission from a Lakti, and the permission letter had to be kept with us. This one seemed directed at me. If I looked like my true self and were seeking asylum without a letter, I'd be caught.

"'All land owned by my Bamarre must be sold to my Lakti and then rented back at a rate that is not unkind. I do not wish my Bamarre impoverished.'"

This affected every cottager. Of course we'd be impoverished or further impoverished. Someone sighed.

Ogres, specters, gryphons, and dragons would be easier to fight than this.

His Master-ship burst out with, "Hurrah for King Canute!"

Goodman Walde, Goodwife Dyrin's husband, called, "What about King Einar? Did he say yes to all this?" A brave man, to ask.

The question was tolerated. "Einar did not object."

Maybe he was never asked.

"'Disputes over purchase prices will be settled by Lakti judges, for how can judgment be delivered by beings who lack discernment?'"

Before, lawsuits had been settled by three judges, one of them a Bamarre.

I noticed that these Beneficences never called us *people*. We were *beings*. If you killed an animal, especially if it belonged to you, no one had a right to object. If you killed a person other than in battle, that was murder. What was it when you killed a being?

Lightning flashed. A loud crack followed.

"'No longer will my Bamarre confuse themselves over poetry. My soldiers will collect the volumes of poetry from each Bamarre household.'"

Thus prompted, the ox drover climbed down from his bench and pulled the sacking off his cart, revealing a mountain of books, which must have been taken on the way here, precious volumes now getting soaked.

Goodwife Dyrin cried, "You're stealing our essence!"

Two brave Bamarre. She'd called them thieves.

The herald merely waited.

The soldiers dismounted. What was coming?

"'We are engaged in a great war against the criminal Kyngoll. If victory is to be ours, as it will be . . .'"

My muscles tensed.

One by one, the soldiers threaded their way into the knot of us, and we made room for them. One positioned himself behind me.

Mama turned nervously. Annet tilted her head toward me, one eyebrow raised questioningly. Drualt looked up at me, too. The soldier shifted his weight from one foot to the other. His sword rattled against his thigh.

"'. . . my Lakti and my Bamarre must join the battle. Sacrifice must be shared. The Lakti already serve their lord. Youthful Bamarre beings will now serve as well.'"

The soldier reached for Drualt.

CHAPTER THIRTY

I HEARD CRIES of woe. Drualt ducked, while still grasping my hand. Our soldier, probably not expecting evasion, failed to catch him immediately. Drualt pulled me toward the edge of the crowd.

Escape was impossible.

"Dru!" I held up my free hand, hoping that the soldier would see an old lady controlling a youngster. "Stop!" I tugged back with my real strength.

He stopped. The soldier waited.

I spoke loudly. "If Kyngoll wins, we'll be enslaved. We have to help."

Drualt knew I meant none of this.

"Hug your aunt and say good-bye." I pulled him close and whispered into his ear, "Escape to the Kyngoll.

They'll help us." I wasn't sure of that, but I was certain they wouldn't kill children. "Tell everyone." I let him go.

Drualt laughed, as if I'd whispered something comical.

"What did you say to him?" the soldier demanded.

What? "Er . . ." I bobbed a curtsy. What? "When I was young, I cooked for soldiers." What else? "Beg pardon." What? "I once saw a Kyngoll prisoner. I told my nephew he was as ugly as a toad."

"Covered with warts!" Drualt laughed again, looking cocky. "I won't let the Kyngoll win. The Lakti can count on me."

Several soldiers laughed, too. Our soldier took my brother, who now went willingly.

Don't be reckless! I cried, "Be careful! The Lakti depend on you."

More soldier laughter.

Mama wailed, "Dru!"

The Bamarre lamentations were dampened by the weather, and no one in earshot—or anywhere else!—would help us. The Lakti stole fifteen of our youth, from eight to eighteen. Annet, at twenty-four, was too old to be taken.

His Master-ship complained, "You're depriving us of our most energetic workers."

"Everyone must help," the herald said.

Her Mistress-ship asked, "How will you use them, and

how long will the king keep them?"

"Five years. Others will join when they're old enough." She resumed proclaiming. "'These blossoms of the Bamarre will be foot soldiers armed with staves.'"

Armed with sticks! They'd merely slow the foe as they were mown down.

A realization struck me like a hammer to my skull: Lord Tove would be looking for me among the youths trudging to battle, and if I weren't in Nadira's form, I'd be among them. This Beneficence was directed at me.

Halina, can you be right that a Lakti-trained, awkward Bamarre has a chance to free us?

The herald finished. "'The Lakti are my sword and shield, the Bamarre my steed. Triumph to New Lakti!'"

After herding their captives together, all but three soldiers mounted their horses and set off with our youth and the herald, riding eastward. What would happen to those who couldn't keep up? And I feared that kindly Drualt would be punished for helping the weak ones.

The remaining soldiers ordered us to go to our cottages so that our poetry books could be collected.

His Master-ship protested. "That will delay our dinner!"

Inside our cottage, Mama hugged me and recited,

"Pawns from birth until we die.
Rebellions fail. We cannot thrive.
Obey, Bamarre, and stay alive.

"None of this is your fault, Aunt Nadira." She added, "We taught Drualt to be sensible."

I was glad she wasn't angry at me, but this was the first poem I ever despised. I quoted,

"Across the craggy Eskerns
In Old Lakti, where we transform
Our dreams into Bamarre reborn."

Poppi, moving as slowly as a grandfather, went to the chest and lifted out our two poetry books, the one they'd always had and my volume by Lilli. "We know many poems by heart."

Annet burst out in a furious whisper, "We've become slaves!"

Stay angry, Annet.

Someone pounded on the door. Poppi opened it, and the three soldiers faced him. Poppi extended our precious books.

A soldier took them. "Are there more?"

Without waiting for an answer, he entered, and the others followed. Baka growled from safety between Annet's legs.

Mama said, "Only these."

A soldier turned around slowly. I believed I could overcome them, even though they had swords. I widened my stance.

To my surprise, Annet came to me and clasped my hand, which stopped me from attacking.

The soldier must have concluded we had no more books, because he just said, "The king thanks you for your obedience," and led his fellows out.

As soon as the door closed, Mama collapsed on the fireplace bench, sobbing. Poppi patted her shoulder.

Finally, she gasped out, "The Lakti keep taking my children."

Annet squeezed my hand, or I squeezed hers. I told my family the advice I'd given Drualt. They knew my experience with the Kyngoll.

Poppi said stoutly, "He'll succeed, smart and strong as he is."

A few minutes later we heard hooves and went outside in time to watch the soldiers trot away, the cart and our poetry jouncing behind them.

Mama remained in the doorway. "We have to cook. Aunt Nadira, if you please, don't make anything delicious."

Small mischief, the poltroon's way to fight.

Or not. The distant bell that had rung before finally chimed clearly. Ideas tumbled over one another: the Bamarre, the Kyngoll, Sir Lerrin, Lord Tove.

"Begging your pardon, I'll cook as always today, but not tomorrow. Can the village gather here tonight, Niece? Nephew?" I meant the village Bamarre, which my parents understood.

"Of course," Poppi said.

Mama threw on her cloak against the rain.

We had less time than usual to prepare dinner, but I made honey toast and arranged the nuts on top in the design of a bow and arrow, King Canute's insignia. Let them think that our family were docile beings.

And I was glad to cook well. Silly of me, but I'd miss the satisfaction.

Meanwhile, Annet went from cottage to cottage, inviting everyone. We all probably would have met anyway, to complain and commiserate.

Back at home, I prepared my cheese puffs, and people filed in as soon as night fell. The Lakti, expecting no resistance, because there hadn't been resistance in more than a hundred years, didn't hinder us.

People greeted each other with the usual words: "Across the Eskerns." They hugged. Many wept. Annet proposed that we each recite a favorite poem, which everyone was eager to do. I stood at the fire, turning cheese puffs. The poems were all sad, and beautiful, and I felt proud to be a Bamarre and civilized.

I asked to recite last and, when my turn came, struck a different note.

> *"The sly Bamarre ant retaliates,*
> *Evades the boot above its back,*
> *Quiet valor. Oppression overcome.*
> *Bamarre bests the Lakti beast."*

I cleared my throat nervously. I didn't know how much convincing would be needed, and I'd never been skilled at talking. "Er, we have to act." Oh. I was giving an order. "Begging your pardon." Then I did it again. "We can't let the Lakti kill our Bamarre children. I'm sorry." How else could I put it?

A chorus answered, "To apologize makes you good."

"To forgive makes you wise." I swallowed. "I have something to say."

They waited.

CHAPTER THIRTY-ONE

TELLING THEM WHAT to do wasn't Bamarre.

A goodman pronounced my cheese puffs excellent.

What if I just announced what *I* planned to do? "Tomorrow I will burn the Lakti roast and pour salt into the soup and forget to put yeast in the bread, and I will be hours late with this terrible food."

No one spoke for a few minutes, until Poppi said, "Tomorrow I will rip out the seams of the widow's kirtle and tailor it an inch too tight."

I blinked in astonishment.

Mama said, "I will chop the rotted vegetables and give the good to the pigs. I will not sift the pebbles from the flour."

More silence until Goodwife Dyrin, whose son Vanz

had been taken, said, "I will forget to empty the slop buckets. When I am reminded, I will spill their contents." She grinned. "Oops!"

People began to smile.

Dyrin's goodman announced, "I will pull His Mastership's peas and leave his weeds."

My jaw slackened. They were doing what I wanted!

One by one, the villagers announced their own little rebellions.

Would my strategy work twice? When everyone fell silent again, I added, "I will not serve delicious food until our children are brought home. Only at the point of a sword will I cook edible food and, even then, no better than edible."

Several people echoed, "Only at the point of a sword."

Goodman Fiske, who kept the widow's orchards and whose two daughters had been taken, said, "I keep thinking about King Einar. Does he really know about the Beneficences?"

Among the villagers, our king was much respected.

Goodman Walde said, "Is Prince Dahn fighting with only a stave, too?"

His wife said, "King Einar should talk to King Canute, monarch to monarch."

Did I need our king in my plans, as unpleasant as he'd been to me?

Hoping the village would still follow my lead, I swore, "Freedom before I die. I will turn my efforts toward crossing the Eskerns." For an old lady, this wouldn't seem a far-off goal.

Now the silence lasted until Goodwife Petina, who cleaned for the widow, said, "Goodwife Nadira has a young spirit. My aching bones don't want to face a dragon." Petina was the oldest in the village after my seeming age.

Goodman Ornik, the shoemaker, said, "At least the Lakti don't feast on our flesh"—he chuckled—"yet."

Goodwife Petina added, "Crossing the Eskerns is just a saying, begging your pardon, Goodwife Nadira."

But Goodman Meerol said, "I'd go, if we could cross." He looked at Annet.

She nodded. "I would, too, but only if I knew Drualt was safe."

I was stunned she'd go at all.

No one was willing to leave while the children were in Lakti hands, and many didn't want to go, period.

Poppi announced, "Aunt Nadira told Drualt to escape to the Kyngoll."

I added, "And to tell everyone else to do the same."

This was greeted with consternation. The village really believed that the Kyngoll were worse than the Lakti.

Finally, Goodman Walde held up a hand. "We know

Goodwife Nadira loves her family. Why did you give this advice?"

"Er . . ." How might a Bamarre learn about the Kyngoll? "In my youth . . ." What? "I was a scullery maid in King Uriel's castle."

Wily Mama nodded as if she knew all about it.

"Everything we think we know about the Kyngoll comes from the Lakti." I spun a tale about overhearing Kyngoll prisoners talking before they were executed. "They said their prisoners were allowed to live. Away from the fighting, they were set free."

Silence fell again, but this time not the quiet of the Bamarre distaste for disagreement, but the silence of thought.

After a minute, Goodwife Dyrin said, "How could I have believed the Lakti?" She recited a rhyming aphorism I'd heard before,

> *"Been a fool. My mistake.*
> *Fool no more. Wide awake."*

She wept, while Goodman Walde rubbed her back, his eyes streaming, too. When she recovered, she said, "Vanz will reach the Kyngoll if anyone can."

Everyone straggled out soon after, in a lighter mood than when they'd arrived. We had something to do, and action, as Mistress Clarra often said, cures despair. I invented a couplet and recited,

> *"Enraged, the placid pig turns boar*
> *And gores the arm that wields the sword."*

Poppi sat at his sewing stool. "How will I work tomorrow without Drualt to lift my spirits? You have a plan, Aunt Nadira?"

I listed the steps I'd figured out so far. After just a few sentences, both Mama and Poppi began shaking their heads. When I proposed Annet's role in helping me, Mama stood and paced.

But Annet nodded. When I finished, she said, "Mama, good can finally come of Lady Klausine's theft." She turned to me. "You were such a serious child, always learning." She dropped her whisper to a mere breath. "Perry, I wish I'd . . ."

Wished she'd been kinder? Loved me?

She didn't finish her sentence. "Aunt Nadira, I listened when you studied strategy. I like your plan."

But dawn was too near to begin to spread Gavrel's rebellion. I did have time, however, to retrieve my buried treasure. With the magic shell to keep me safe, I left and returned in half an hour.

After curtsying to Mama and Poppi, I removed the

platters and the books from the sack and poured the coins on the table.

Poppi dropped a few coins into his palm.

Mama put her hand over her mouth, then lowered it, revealing a gleeful grin. "So much!"

How the Beneficences had changed her.

Poppi and Annet were smiling, too. I felt as if Lady Mother had nodded a dozen times. Good, I thought. Let them taste this and like it.

But Mama frowned. "What can we do with such wealth?"

Sounding smug, Annet said, "Some of the Lakti can be bribed."

She knew this from Lord Tove's castle? "No! Begging your pardon, no! Who?" I waved away the answer. "Never mind." It didn't matter.

"Shoni?" Poppi asked. "Don't you think the Ships would like a gold coin? Don't you think they'd do something or look the other way to get it?"

She thought they would. "But not the widow. She wouldn't take a bribe." Mama picked up the smaller book and opened it. "It's poetry!"

"*Lakti . . . poetry . . .*," Poppi said. "The words are impossible together."

Mama's eyes progressed down the page. "This one is moving. Listen.

"Hilltop floats above campfire smoke.
Blink by blink, sky lightens.
Dawn rises from circling peaks.
Mounting the gray stallion, I long
For my children, who won't remember me."

No one moved until Annet said, "Poor Lakti soldier, feeling sorry for himself before he kills more people."

Paging through, Mama said the poems weren't only about war. Some reflected ordinary life, and many depicted the lovely countryside. "They make me want to go there."

Hurray for poetry!

She closed the book. "May we see the other book, Aunt Nadira?"

I said, "I hope it's the Account."

Annet explained. "It's a record that a king or a lord of the castle keeps."

I added, "When Lord Tove wrote in his, he called himself 'Lord Tove,' not 'I.'" He even took it to war with him and wrote in it daily. When it was full, it was taken to the library and a fresh Account begun.

"If this is the Account, I hope it was written after the monsters came." I put my hand on the cover.

Annet coughed. Remembering my Bamarre manners, I gave it to Poppi, who spread it out. Mama and Annet sat on either side of him. As the youngest, I was at Mama's side and couldn't see it well enough to make out the words. Poppi turned pages, then read aloud,

"Out of a company of a dozen, the two brave knights left alive dashed into the throne room. They clasped King Josef's knees and gasped out their tale of a livid cloud that had belched forth gryphons—winged, slavering beasts—and dragons. Said Sir Ignace, one of the survivors, 'A mist flooded the Kilkets valley through which we rode, which mist resolved into huge, nightmare creatures, hulking ogres.' Sir Ignace covered his eyes, and his companion, Lady Selda, took up the recital: 'Then a miracle of deception lulled our senses. The music of lutes and flutes replaced the crackling of dragon flame, the gryphons' greedy squawks, the ogres' inchoate roars.'"

Specters!

"'Overhead, the heavens blued again; the gryphons were succeeded by sparrows, the dragons by hawks. I smelled roses and failed to recall that the month was November. The ogres became people to my eyes, and not merely people, but beloved comrades lost in battle, hale, in shining armor.'"

Poppi summarized what came next. The knights discovered their mistake by rushing toward their old friends. The two who lived had survived only by fleeing.

Mama said, "This is where you want us to go, Aunt Nadira?"

"The countryside is beautiful, Niece. The monsters aren't everywhere."

Poppi turned to a page dated a month later, which listed bodies recovered, living Lakti subjects borne away by dragons, livestock lost. The next page described the funeral of King Josef's wife and the king's laments. What came after, on the final sheet, written in January, was a proclamation, calling Josef's subjects to him.

That was his mistake, I thought. As they flocked to his castle, the monsters must have picked them off. We'd have to move into our new land cautiously, step by step, establishing safe havens before moving on.

The proclamation ended with these cold words:

> *"Long have the Eskerns limited our ambition. Let this exodus be an opportunity, skilled as we are in subjugation, to rule again, unopposed. No matter how small the numbers who attain our new land, no matter how numerous the years that pass, no matter how kind our reception, Lakti courage will conquer the Bamarre coward."*

Annet stabbed the page with a fingertip. "'How kind our reception.'"

I was shocked, too. They'd decided even then.

And Lord Tove might have been King Josef's son for his closeness to that king's beliefs.

Annet added, "Aunt Nadira, we should send *them* back."

Yes!

However, after a moment's thought I said it would be impossible to force an entire population through a narrow pass. I added, "They were the cowards for running away." And after only a few months. They'd hardly tried. "The elves stayed, and the monsters must have hunted them, too." Still might. "But the Lakti were afraid to fight a new kind of enemy."

Mama closed the books, and Poppi hid the treasure in our shed, in a barrel, under layers of green tassel yarn and spare tassels. "The Lakti won't poke in there for fear a tassel might leap out and make them Bamarre."

The next day dawned bright and warm, as if yesterday's rain had never been. I woke up wondering how Drualt was faring. If the soldiers kept gathering children, they wouldn't reach the fighting for weeks. But was there enough food? Was Drualt holding his temper? Were the soldiers holding theirs?

My family's drawn faces told me they were worrying, too.

A new fear cracked open, which I kept to myself.

Would Drualt, on Lord Tove's orders, be singled out for being my brother and sped to the battlefield?

At the Ships', our open rebellion had to wait, because I had made the pottage before the soldiers came, and only bread and cheese would accompany it. We wouldn't present our cooking until the midday meal.

But Goodwife Dyrin didn't delay. As if it were winter, she built a blazing fire in the solar before the Ships descended.

His Master-ship bellowed, "Are you trying to roast us alive?"

Mama cracked the door to hear.

"Beg pardon, sir. I've been chilled since my son was taken. I thought you must be cold, too."

"Don't just stand there! Douse it!"

Goodwife Dyrin entered the kitchen, sauntered to the iron sink, and pumped water into the bucket. "I'm not finished." She exited.

A moment later, His Master-ship cried, "You oaf! I'm soaked!"

Her Mistress-ship ran into the kitchen with the pail and thrust it at me. "Douse the fire. Dyrin is useless today."

I curtsied and made myself look puzzled. "Mistress, begging your pardon, a pail won't douse a fire."

Annet let out a cheep of strangled laughter.

"Put water in it, you dolt!"

I curtsied again. "Certainly. I didn't understand. I'll do so now." I pumped water, but stopped when the pail was half full. I couldn't remember when I'd had so much fun. "Is this enough, Mistress? Begging your pardon, is it a big fire?"

"Fill it!"

I let the pail slosh over as I carried it into the steamy solar, where Goodwife Dyrin was dabbing (actually poking) His Master-ship's wet tunic with a length of dry cloth and where the Ships' twin boys watched wide-eyed.

After thinking better of drenching His Master-ship for the second time, I put out the blaze. As soon as I did, I curtsied to Her Mistress-ship, who'd followed me in, and escaped to the kitchen before laughing.

After we recovered, we set ourselves to our mischief. I oversalted the soup, began the roast hare too soon, and turned the pepper mill over the blackberry tart until my arm ached.

As she'd promised, Mama set aside the good carrots, onions, turnips, and cabbage for the pigs and chopped the rotten. When she finished serving breakfast, Annet prepared His Master-ship's beloved egg-and-cheese pie, eggshells included.

Quiet reigned, except for an occasional shout wafting

through the windows as the twins play-battled under the tutelage of Soldier Kassia.

Noon came. Annet had cleared and washed the breakfast crockery and reset the table. For a festive touch, she'd plucked a bunch of the daisies that edged the road and put them in a tall tumbler. I carried in the roast on its platter. Cooked to three times a turn, I'd rescued it before it blackened. Now it glistened a dark gold and made even my mouth water.

Mama and Annet followed me in, bearing the rest of the meal on trays. As we placed everything, the Ships filed in. His Master-ship wore his preprandial smile. I curtsied and exited as usual, because Her Mistress-ship said my gargoyle face spoiled her appetite.

As I passed through the vestibule, someone rapped on the door. The widow's sharp voice cried, "Let me in! Don't—"

I sang at the top of my voice, "Victory over the Kyngoll!" to cover whatever warning the widow had been about to issue, and continued into the kitchen. I heard Mama and Annet take up the cry and repeat it.

But His Master-ship's outraged shout broke through our noise.

More pounding at the door followed. My heart took up the beat. Dyrin's mishaps had been taken as Bamarre stupidity, but the meal could be nothing except deliberate.

279

Someone let the widow in. I wondered what Goodwife Petina had done at her house.

At a loss for what else to do, I sharpened Her Mistress-ship's biggest knife and began chopping onions.

The kitchen door blew open. His Master-ship pushed Mama and Annet inside, and Her Mistress-ship tugged Goodwife Dyrin in by her elbow. The widow came, too, her face an exclamation point. I told myself I mustn't use the knife, but my grip tightened on it.

His Master-ship panted with anger. "What is the meaning of this?" He leaned toward each of us in turn.

We all spoke at once, a chorus of "Beg pardon." Then we stopped, unsure who should continue.

Not I, I thought. I was only the aunt.

Mama did, although her voice was frightened. "B-beg p-pardon. I lost my son yesterday. He may never . . ." She became truly sad. I could tell, and my throat tightened. She went on. "My mind is addled with it—"

Her Mistress-ship turned to her husband, her voice urgent. "Deegal, they may not be working in the fields, either."

"My orchards!" The widow rushed out.

"I'll go," His Master-ship said. "Make them cook dinner again. Don't let them out of your sight. See what Dyrin's done upstairs. Make her undo it." He followed the widow out.

I watched Her Mistress-ship's face as she tried to decide

whether to stay downstairs with us or go to Goodwife Dyrin's domain. Finally, she called Soldier Kassia in to watch us and left the kitchen with the goodwife.

When the soldier understood what had happened, she unsheathed her sword.

At the point of a sword. How quickly that had come.

CHAPTER THIRTY-TWO

SOLDIER KASSIA INSISTED we stay together. We cleared the dishes and dumped the dreadful meal in the pigpen behind the house. Back in the kitchen, we started an indifferent dinner for the Ships.

His Master-ship returned in two hours, his eyes bulging with outrage. We heard him storm into the solar and shout at his goodwife, as if it were her fault, that only Goodman Walde had gone to the fields, where, true to his promise, he had pulled peas and left weeds. Hardly stopping for breath, he yelled that the widow's laborers had pruned branches from her apple trees that had been loaded with green fruit.

Victory for us! Victory for the Bamarre!

When we brought in dinner, he told his wife to taste it first.

Flushing, Her Mistress-ship pronounced the meal edible but not good.

"Supervise them tomorrow, Wife. Make them make it good. I'll write to His Majesty and tell him what we're enduring."

Mama coughed. "Master . . . begging your pardon . . . ask him to return our children to us. They're your most willing workers."

My neighbors would stop rebelling if the young people came home. I didn't want the rebellion to end, but even more, I didn't want Drualt to reach Lord Tove.

His Master-ship actually nodded. "I'll petition him to return them or send soldiers, because *this*"—he gestured at the food, at us, at the room—"is insupportable."

I doubted Drualt and the others would be sent back.

Annet and I were going to have another sleepless night, and Mama and Poppi probably would, too, from worrying over us. During our own (delicious) evening meal, I asked for advice about how to present our rebellion to the families I'd visit—families rather than all the Bamarre in a village, because there would be no time for everyone to gather.

Poppi squinted. "They'll start by respecting your age, but it will be best if you don't order anyone to do anything."

I knew that, but I thanked him.

Annet said I should tell the revolt as a story, step by step, without rushing.

I was a terrible storyteller! I always rushed!

Mama said not to leave out how frightened I was, whether I really was or not. "Your fear will give them courage."

I nodded, but Annet saw my confusion and said, "If they're afraid and they know you were, too, but you rose up anyway, they'll think they may be able to."

Oh. I was going to say everything wrong.

Poppi said I shouldn't forget the part about the children going to the Kyngoll. "That will offer hope."

Mama saw my expression. "Recite a poem. You're good at that." She squeezed her hands together and looked at Annet. "Don't let me lose you again." To my surprise, she turned to me and added, "Not you, either, Aunt Nadira."

When the village quieted in sleep, I gave one boot to Annet, along with warnings about how to use it, and I lent her the magic shell, reasoning that she was less accustomed than I to danger. We both carried a pouch of dried meat for the dogs and a few coins for the humans, if need be.

I would go west, where the soldiers had already been, and she'd travel east, where her task would be harder. People who hadn't yet lost their children would be less ready for our message, and she'd have to deliver the terrible tidings of the Beneficences.

"Before you leave a family," I said, "tell the people to spread the rebellion to nearby villages—to save you time—and take another step in the boots." If only the boots would stop wherever their wearer wanted! Annet, not a fast walker, might have to walk miles to reach a village.

They were all frowning at me.

"Oh!" I'd given orders again. This didn't bode well. "Beg pardon."

We left soon after. I visited a family in each of three villages, knocking on only the humblest cottages to ensure the residents were Bamarre.

In the very first, I made my mistake before I spoke even a word, by banging on the door. I knew the timid Bamarre tap—light and quick—but knowledge sank beneath worry over my coming performance. The goodman and his wife believed me a Lakti impostor, and nothing I said, including my desperate poetry recitation, changed their minds.

Not that they expressed their suspicions. They listened. They nodded, but I was enough of a Bamarre to understand. And enough of a Bamarre not to try another cottage in the village. If one family believed me to be a Lakti, the others would be afraid to disagree.

In the second village, the goodman, his wife, and their grown daughter agreed with me—a child of the family had been taken—until I gave an order without noticing. "Spread the rebellion! We'll succeed only if . . ." I trailed off, seeing their faces. "Beg pardon!"

They chimed in with the first part of the saying, which I finished, but I saw from their faces that the damage had been done.

The goodman asked, "Does King Einar know about your rebellion? Does he approve?"

I admitted he was unaware of it.

The goodwife said, "Alas, the village is unlikely to act without our king's consent."

All the people who'd ever judged me—Lady Mother, Mistress Clarra, Annet, my parents—clamored in my mind to say I was disappointing them.

And I was failing Drualt.

By the time I reached the third village, the night was half over. Why enter a cottage if I was going to fail?

Mama had said I should admit my fear.

Willem didn't hide his feelings.

In Gavrel I'd succeeded when I'd talked about what I was going to do. But wasn't it prideful to talk about myself?

Yes, if it was boasting, but I had nothing to boast about.

I tapped on the door.

After a minute, a goodwife cracked the door. She held a babe against her chest.

"Across the Eskerns. Please pardon the intrusion."

She let me in, as the others had.

I took a deep breath. "I'm afraid. I'm afraid . . ." Afraid they wouldn't believe me, but afraid of what most of all? "Afraid I'll fail. I've failed before. Afraid my great-nephew will die."

She led me to the bench by their table.

Her goodman said, "Please sit."

Maybe I began with Drualt because he was my most important reason, more important than Halina or even the injustices of Bamarre life. I described how sturdy he was, how brave, how kind, and how young but how old for his age. Only Lakti toughness kept me from weeping.

The goodman and goodwife sat across from me. Both nodded with my words.

I didn't rush. I told them how many young people Gavrel had lost and how we'd decided together what to do. They laughed when I described Goodwife Dyrin's antics and our culinary insurrection—and sobered when they heard about Soldier Kassia's sword. I had to explain why soldiers were stationed in the village.

"Yet you still went ahead." The goodman sounded admiring.

I nodded. "But the sword came out quickly." Then I smiled. "There aren't enough swords to be everywhere."

The goodwife asked about King Einar, and I confessed that we hadn't consulted him. "We haven't had time."

Silence fell. I feigned Bamarre patience.

Finally, the goodwife grinned. "Soon I'm to trim the master's beard and cut the mistress's hair." The grin widened. "I can help them be ugly on the outside, too."

The goodman said, "Begging your pardon, Grandmother. We'll have to discuss this with the village."

Of course.

"We may persuade them. I'll try."

"Thank you. We're hoping other villages will join us." I didn't say we'd be crushed otherwise, but they had to know. "If you decide to join us, would you spread the word?"

The goodman nodded. "Begging your pardon, but it might help if you had a note from the king."

When I left, the night was too advanced for me to visit another village. At home, Mama and Poppi passed me back and forth for hugs! Annet nodded at me from the fireplace bench.

Poppi said, "I don't like staying behind. I'd be happier if I were in danger, too."

Where was the Bamarre coward?

Annet had succeeded with only one of the two families

she'd visited. "Both asked if King Einar approved, and both wanted a letter. I couldn't tell them how useless he is against Lord Tove."

Over the next week, the villagers became increasingly inventive with their mischief, and two soldiers couldn't be everywhere. Annet and I ventured farther and farther from home, begging people to join our outbreak. Annet had more success than I did, but I improved. Still, most families wanted King Einar's blessing.

Meanwhile, the widow's daughter set off on horseback, riding to King Canute to ask for aid.

At home, at the end of the week, I announced, Lakti-fashion, without discussion, "Tomorrow night, I'll go to King Einar."

No one disagreed.

The next morning, at sword point again, we prepared a mediocre meal. Soldier Kassia wouldn't leave me alone in the kitchen, so I entered the solar with Mama and Annet. While they were serving, someone rapped on the Ships' door.

I was standing behind the twins, across the table from his Master-ship, whose jaw tightened, but he seemed unsurprised.

He stood without complaining about the interrupted meal. "Come!"

I thought he meant just his family until Soldier Kassia herded us out into the road, where Soldier Joram had Goodman Meerol, the young man who was sweet on Annet, by the neck of his tunic. The soldier's horsewhip girdled his waist.

Goodman Meerol's narrow face was set. His eyes, which found Annet, gave nothing away.

His Master-ship told Soldier Kassia to assemble the rest of the village. While she hurried off, he asked Soldier Joram, "What is the offense?"

"He pruned green apricots and failed to harvest the ripe, except the one he was eating when I caught him." Soldier Joram pulled back his own shoulders. "I stalked him like a lion."

Proud of sneaking up on an unarmed man? And a reedy one at that.

The widow and the Bamarre who weren't in the fields joined us. The widow held a coil of rope.

I didn't doubt that I could snatch Soldier Joram's sword and that Soldier Kassia wouldn't be able to match my swordplay, but I'd be revealed as more than an old lady.

Soldier Joram had Goodman Meerol remove his tunic and undershirt. Then he drew his prisoner's hands through the rusted rings on the whipping post and bound his wrists with the widow's rope. If Goodman Meerol struggled, his wrists would bleed, as well as his back.

Lady Mother had kept me away from floggings, but I knew people died sometimes. Lord Tove had said Bamarre weakness had killed them.

Annet sent me a look of appeal. I shook my head. However, I'd count the lashes. If the whip landed fewer than twenty-five times, even the infirm survived.

I wouldn't let Goodman Meerol die.

Soldier Joram unwound his horsewhip.

Goodman Fiske, Goodman Meerol's father, cried, "He's sorry! Soldier Joram, please don't whip him!" He wheeled on His Master-ship. "Please have pity on my boy!"

If His Master-ship had given in, that would likely have finished our rebellion. I doubted anyone would have had the anger to continue.

But His Master-ship nodded at Soldier Joram. "Begin."

The whip was leather with a tip of brass that was fashioned into the shape of a star with seven cruel points. Soldier Joram snapped it on the ground and then on Goodman Meerol's back.

Soldier Kassia intoned, "One!"

CHAPTER THIRTY-THREE

SEVERAL OF US cried out, but Goodman Meerol made not a sound. Beads of blood dotted his skin, marking the line the whip had made. His back was to us, so we couldn't see his expression.

"Two!" Soldier Kassia grabbed Goodman Fiske before he could reach his son.

Goodman Meerol must have heard the motion and understood. "I'm all right, Father."

Goodwife Dyrin and Goodman Walde stationed themselves at Goodman Fiske's side, for comfort, I was sure, and to prevent rash action.

By the tenth lash, Goodman Meerol's back was scored by the whip. I reminded myself that Goodman Walde had herbs to lessen pain.

On the fifteenth lash, Goodman Meerol let out a short cry, followed by a weak "I'm fine."

Annet's glare bore into me. I ignored her anger. I had my own to keep down.

On the eighteenth lash I began to plan. Take Soldier Kassia's sword in one long, satisfying pull. Run her through and silence her numerical song. Leap upon Soldier Joram. Stop his whip arm forever.

After the twentieth lash, His Master-ship told Soldier Joram to stop. "Cut him free. Next time will be worse." He turned to Mama. "Come. I want to finish my dinner."

Mama and I went inside, but Annet helped Goodman Fiske support the bleeding man as they walked to his father's cottage. Goodman Walde ran to his own cottage for his healing herbs.

The immediate consequence of the flogging was that Goodman Meerol, from his sickbed, asked Annet to marry him, and she accepted.

And she forgave me for not saving him. "He might have taken years to find the courage to propose."

I congratulated her. "I wouldn't have let him die."

That night Annet visited more villages and I headed west under clear skies and a three-quarter moon, with the magic snail shell in my purse, because Annet and our parents ruled that I needed it more than she did.

Yes, I was at risk. We all were. We'd plunged into a swift river of danger.

Though I'd never been to King Einar's residence, I knew it lay three miles south of Lord Tove's castle. As the boot slowed at the top of a hill, I saw ahead the flickering lights of a town or a castle. The boot stopped in a forest, where I exchanged boots and set out. The lights proved to come from both town and castle, the castle my old home.

The drawbridge was up. Torch-bearing sentries paced the battlements.

Part of me wished Halina had never visited me and I was sleeping in my old bed with a resentful Annet nearby on her pallet. If the old Perry were wakeful, she'd feel secure in Lord Tove's love and might be smiling, anticipating a race.

Best of all, Willem wouldn't have been pushed from a tower.

How young she was, that Perry.

Lady Mother might be home now, running the castle. I wished I could talk to her. She'd oppose our revolt, but she'd be proud of me for starting it.

Too risky. I kept to the trees until the woods ended. The magic shell assured me that no travelers moved on the road ahead or behind, though traffic, even at night, was common this close to the castle. The houses on either side were closed up for the night. I expected dogs to bark, but I doubted their owners would let them out.

I ran, happy to be moving, imagining how I looked, a fleet old lady.

The king's residence—a large stone house—proved easy to find, because the yard was clogged with half a dozen carts, and the carts, when I lifted a canvas cover, contained King Einar's merchandise—shoes. The Beneficences kept his drivers, who were certainly Bamarre, from traveling without permission letters. Apparently, letters hadn't been provided.

A bas-relief on the manor door lintel showed an upside-down crown, representing Bamarre's sad estate. A lamp burned in what was probably the kitchen, if the house followed the same plan as the Ships'.

After my tap, a few minutes passed until a yawning maidservant opened the door. Behind her in the vestibule stood King Einar himself, holding a lamp. Behind him, in shadow, a woman stood. Queen Greta? I thought so. Young Prince Bruce was probably asleep in the nursery, and Prince Dahn might be sleeping, too. Surely, even Lord Tove wouldn't have taken a Bamarre prince to fight for the Lakti.

"Across the Eskerns." I curtsied.

The maid stepped aside.

I entered. "I am Nadira."

"Across the Eskerns." King Einar dismissed the

servant, who climbed the stairs.

Surprising me, his wife took my hand and preceded me into the kitchen, where the king hung the lamp on a hook next to a cupboard.

"More ill tidings?" King Einar asked. He stood, arms hanging, as if unsure what to do next.

Queen Greta led me to a chair by the cold fireplace. "Please sit, Grandmother Nadira."

The chair even had arms. His Master-ship owned no armchairs.

I sat and saw that the eyes of both my monarchs were red. What was amiss? The Beneficences? Or something worse?

Only a Lakti would question the Bamarre king, so I just waited.

Taking him by the elbow, Queen Greta guided her husband into a chair facing me. Then she pumped water into a tumbler and brought it to me. I thanked her and sipped.

Next, she filled a small bowl with almonds and another with strawberries and set both on a stool between her husband and me. Finally, she brought a stool for herself and sat next to the king. When she sat, her belly mounded. She was pregnant.

King Einar seemed to come out of himself. "Pardon me. What have you come to beg of me?"

Still pompous.

"Highness, I do have a request." I swallowed. "I would

like a letter. Two letters, if you please." One for Annet.

He nodded. "Letters."

What did that mean?

Queen Greta said, "Please eat something."

I made the polite response. "If you will join me."

She took a single almond, and so did I. It would be greedy to gobble more and rude to reveal what I wanted the letter to say without being asked. We sat in silence.

The king said, "It is good for us Bamarre to be together in terrible times."

Was this the beginning of a poem proverb no one had taught me?

Now the silence felt expectant, whether it really was or not. I racked my brain for a rhyme with *times. Crimes? Grimes? Slimes?* Most likely *chimes*, but what would the rest of it be?

I sipped my water. Maybe another poem would do. What? Something about royalty might please him. I spoke slowly, willing the words to come:

> *Those who descend farthest,*
> *Deepest, most uplift us,*
> *Ennoble our service—*
> *Monarchs of Bamarre.*

He nodded solemnly at the words. I dared to feel pleased until he frowned. "Your delivery is excellent. I've heard it before. Greta, do you recognize it?"

Of course she didn't. She hadn't been there the day Lord Tove slapped their son.

I waited. King Einar didn't deign to ask me when I'd recited in his presence, which saved me from having to lie. The silence stretched. I wondered why they'd been weeping before I came.

The king shrugged heavily. "Letters to the Lakti will do no good. They don't listen to me."

My tassel ticked across my forehead as I shook my head. "To your Bamarre."

Queen Greta said, "Will you do us the kindness of explaining what the letter is to say?"

I leaned forward in my chair. "We've started a rebellion in the east."

They said nothing.

"My great-nephew was taken."

Their eyes fastened on mine. I continued as if I were in a humble cottage. "Some villages have joined, but many want your approval in a letter before they do, too. We would like two letters, if you please, one for my great-niece and one for me. If you please, they'd say the same thing." He wouldn't have to think of words twice.

"In a rebellion, more of us will be killed," Queen Greta said.

Politeness prevented any contradiction, and she was right anyway. I nodded.

She added, "We're a precious people."

I knew that now.

"Lord Tove wants to wipe us all out," King Einar said.

His wife took another almond. "What will your rebellion accomplish, begging your pardon, Grandmother?"

Your rebellion, not *ours*.

"Our master dispatched a message to King Canute, asking him to send soldiers to his aid. If he does and then has to send more to other villages, his war against the Kyngoll will be hampered."

"So?" King Einar said, royally forgetting to be polite.

I bobbed my head in a sort of seated bow. "Majesty, begging your pardon, the Lakti respect only strength."

The king remembered his manners. "If you please, Grandmother"—and forgot them again—"that isn't an answer."

I exhaled a long breath. "If the war is going badly because of us, we'll have something to bargain with."

"Bargain for what?" King Einar said.

I squeezed my hands together, putting all my nervousness in them and managing to keep my voice calm. "For permission to cross the Eskerns."

"Not for the Beneficences to be rescinded?"

"For that, too." I hoped I wasn't about to contradict either of them. "Begging your pardon, if just the Beneficences are ended, we'll merely be returned to our old misery."

Silence.

Uneasily, I added, "Not everyone in Gavrel wants to cross. Most of all, we want our children returned to us."

The two monarchs exchanged a look.

Had Lord Tove taken Prince Dahn? "I hope your sons are safe and well."

Queen Greta said, "You don't know, do you?"

"Forgive me, I'm not sure."

"A week ago," Her Highness said, "Lord Tove himself brought us our son's body."

"Which son?" But I knew the answer. "Prince Dahn died fighting the Kyngoll?"

"Perhaps." King Einar stood. "Tove, the child murderer, took pleasure in his death. I heard it in his oily regrets."

I believed that. My chest hurt. My former father would relish Drualt's death, too. But my brother had abilities Prince Dahn had lacked, which might save him for a while at least.

Mama had taught me several Bamarre condolences. "When youth dies, joy dies."

They intoned the rejoinder together, "Bamarre survives."

King Einar took the lamp again. "Come."

We followed him into the solar, where he lit a candle

and seated himself at an oaken desk. A prepared quill lay next to a stack of parchment paper and a jar of ink. He spoke the words as he wrote:

> *"To my Suffering Subjects,*
> *Mindful of the Troubles that have been brought down upon you by the Lakti tyrant, I Approve and Authorize any Rebellion you see fit to engage in. However, out of concern for your Welfare, I urge you to obey the Lakti when your life is at Risk. We hope for two Withdrawals as a result of the Revolt: of soldiers from the Eskern Pass and of the vile Beneficences that have robbed us of our young people. Your Queen and I will remain here to Rule those who choose to stay, but Prince Bruce will . . ."*

Really? Promise of a king in the new land would make people more willing to leave.

". . . head the Exodus and, when he is old enough, lead the Battle against the Monsters. I remain your Monarch." He sighed. "Perhaps our son can be a real king." He nodded at his wife. "And perhaps our baby can be safe."

Queen Greta tilted the candle so that a gob of wax landed next to the signature and clotted there. King Einar impressed the wax with his ring, leaving his stamp—an entwined *B* for Bamarre and *E* for Einar. Then he and his wife repeated the process for the second letter.

He pushed back his chair and stood. "Greta, fetch Bruce."

The king and I waited in silence. When she came back with the prince, the boy's face was alert.

King Einar crouched to embrace his son, then looked up at me. "I wish I could remember when I heard you recite, Grandmother, but no matter. Take my son with you."

CHAPTER THIRTY-FOUR

"BEG PARDON?" I said.

The queen cried, "Einar!"

"It's his only chance, Greta. Son, listen to Grandmother Nadira."

The boy nodded. "Yes, Father."

How could I keep him safe?

King Einar stood. "What did Lord Tove tell you, Bruce?"

"He said that in a few years I would fight for the Lakti, too."

His father nodded. "What else?"

"And I might die gloriously like Dahn."

"Grandmother," King Einar said, "Tove won't wait years. He'll lower the age for us Bamarre to fight or invent another strategy. He wants me to be our last king."

The queen told me, "He tousled Bruce's hair! I couldn't stop shuddering."

"Go now," King Einar said.

"Wait!" Queen Greta rushed out of the solar, calling over her shoulder, "I'll be right back."

After we'd stood awkwardly together for a minute, Prince Bruce asked, "Where do you live, Grandmother?"

Better manners than his father. "In the southeast, in a village called Gavrel."

The king frowned. "You couldn't have walked the distance."

"I have a donkey. I left her down the road because I wasn't sure where your house was."

Queen Greta returned with a burlap bag, which she thrust at me. "He loves strawberries."

I put the bag in the sack with my magic boot and the king's letters, rolled up together and tied with leather lacing. Outside, King Einar and his wife watched us off. Prince Bruce didn't turn. His face was set, and I thought I saw the man he'd be someday: serious, brave, steady. Kingly.

At first I matched my steps to his. Our progress slowed until I realized he was pacing himself with me. I added *courteous* to my list of his qualities and walked faster.

As we walked, I thought about how often in my

experience children had been separated from their parents. But mostly, I worried about how we'd hide Prince Bruce from the Lakti.

When we'd gone perhaps half a mile, I stopped. "Your Highness—"

"You may call me Bruce."

I doubted his brother, even at the age of five or six like Prince Bruce, would have given me such permission.

But I couldn't omit his title. He was too exalted. "Prince Bruce, I have no donkey. I have this." I took the magic boot out of my sack. "We'll go very fast. I'll have to carry you. May I?"

He looked at my feet and at the boot. "It's too big."

"It shrinks." It probably would have fit him, too, but I didn't say so.

"It's magic?"

I smiled. "Yes. It's the reason we'll go so fast." I put on my boot.

He just looked at me solemnly. Drualt would have been laughing and turning somersaults.

"May I carry you?"

"I'm too old, Grandmother."

"These are special circumstances, begging your pardon. May I?"

He raised his arms.

I held him against my chest and stepped. He pressed

his face into my shoulder. His hand gripped my upper arm and tightened.

When the boot stopped and I put him down, he pulled back his thin shoulders. "Begging your pardon, Grandmother, have we arrived in Gavrel?"

"Not yet." We were in an orchard. A house must be nearby, and I wanted to leave before the residents could waken.

"How many more steps?"

"Just a few. Are you ready?"

He nodded.

"Which way would you like to face this time?" Perhaps he'd like this way of travel better if he could see ahead of us.

"As before."

The last boot step left us within a mile of Gavrel. I took out the magic shell. No one was about.

"What's that? Begging your pardon, Grandmother."

I held the shell to his ear. After a moment his face lit up. "I hear my heart!"

This magic he liked, calmer magic.

"Can you walk a mile?" I asked when he returned the shell. He said he could, but he soon flagged, and I carried him the rest of the way. The village was asleep, though Mama and Poppi were still awake, as I knew they would be. Someday we'd be able to sleep through the night again.

Annet hadn't yet returned.

Poppi squinted and Mama let out a quick yelp when they saw the boy.

"I have the letters. This is Prince Bruce, who will cross the Eskerns with us." If anyone managed to cross.

Poppi bowed and Mama curtsied.

Mama wouldn't let the prince sleep on a pallet. She followed him up the ladder to the bed in the sleeping loft and, when she came down, said he'd fallen asleep right away. I told them what had happened to Prince Dahn, which dismayed them, of course. Then they read King Einar's letter.

Shouldn't Annet be home by now?

Poppi rolled the letter up again. "Listen to your shell, if you please."

I didn't hear footsteps in it. Mama said we should all sleep, but we didn't move from the table benches where we were sitting, Mama and Poppi across from me. After a while, Mama unwrapped a loaf of bread and cut us each a thick slice.

I thought of putting on the boot and searching for Annet, but there was little chance I'd finish a step anywhere near her.

Had a Lakti caught her? Had she been attacked by wolves? Or had she just lost track of time?

Gradually, the cottage's dimness brightened. Annet

couldn't have merely forgotten the passing hours for this long. Something had certainly befallen her. We'd have to go to the Ships' soon, and how would we explain her absence?

When we heard Prince Bruce moving in the sleeping loft, Poppi brought him down. I cut him a wedge of hard cheese from our half wheel.

"Wait!" Mama rushed out and returned from the shed with a small gold salver, castle treasure, on which she placed his bowl. "We've never entertained a prince before, Your Highness." She blushed.

"You may call me Bruce."

I remembered the strawberries and took them out of my sack.

"Thank you," Prince Bruce said.

Poppi said, "I wish Annet were here to see you."

Mama looked close to tears. "She's our oth—our daughter, Your Highness."

"Is she fighting the Kyngoll, too?"

I said, "No. She should have been back by—"

Someone pounded on the door.

"A moment!" Mama cried.

Had some Lakti brought Annet home? Poppi scooped up Prince Bruce and rushed to the ladder. Mama took the gold salver and ran to the chest to hide it.

But the door burst open before the prince could climb.

His Master-ship stamped in. "I came— Who's that?"

Mama put the salver behind her back.

"Begging your pardon, Master," I said, before anyone else could speak, "he's Bruce, my youngest grandson. His mother sent him two weeks ago." Before the Beneficences required permission letters.

For a moment His Master-ship was silent, probably searching for a flaw in my explanation. Finally, "I see." Then, "Where is your daughter, Shoni?"

"Begging your pardon, Master, she stepped out to the privy."

"Fetch her. I want you all to hear my words."

Mama nodded. What else could she do? Managing to keep the salver from His Master-ship's sight, she started for the door.

In his piping voice, Prince Bruce said, "Beg pardon, Master. Do you like shiny things?"

"What"—His Master-ship's voice started out angry and turned careful—"shiny things, child?"

I wondered if the prince had seen King Einar offer *shiny things* to any Lakti. He was a wily child, to have picked this up.

"A golden tray."

I didn't know how this would go or what to prepare for. Mama, who could do nothing else, revealed the salver.

His Master-ship snatched it from her, turned it over,

walked to the window, and inspected it, an inch from his nose. "Where did this come from?"

Poppi said, "It's our relic from old Bamarre, from before the Lakti came, begging your pardon."

"You've kept it here?"

I saw what was coming but didn't see any way to prevent it.

"Yes, Master," Poppi said.

"Then it's mine, since the cottage is mine."

His because of the Beneficences, although they had mentioned nothing about belongings.

Prince Bruce's face was red. I thought I understood. He'd tried to save us and had only made us lose something valuable.

"Annet should have returned by now. Perhaps she heard my voice and fears to enter." He sounded pleased. "Fetch her, Shoni."

Mama nodded and left.

Annet, where are you?

CHAPTER THIRTY-FIVE

POPPI INVITED HIS Master-ship to sit.

He lowered his bulk onto the fireplace bench. "You think Shoni will not return quickly?"

"Begging your pardon, Master, my daughter has the gripes. If you tell us what you came to say, we'll inform her, too."

He considered this, and I held my breath.

"No. I want you all to hear at once."

We waited in silence. His Master-ship ran his fingers around the edge of the salver. Minutes ticked by. I turned an idea over in my mind.

"I'll see what's keeping your goodwife, Adeer, and that won't sweeten my words." He stood.

"Master, we have three gold coins," I said. "They're

hidden. Not here, begging your pardon."

Three gold coins were a substantial sum, even for the Lakti. A horse sold for two.

"Three . . . gold . . . coins. Give them to me."

"First we must agree on terms, begging your pardon, Mas—"

"I'll have you flogged!"

I shrugged. "I'm an old lady and haven't many more years." I added, thinking fast, "I'm the only one who knows where the coins are."

He'd been thinking, too. "I'll have the boy flogged, not you."

No! I'd just give him the coins.

But Poppi squinted. "Apologies, Master. Do you believe the village will let you whip a child, whatever the consequences to us?"

He was right. We wouldn't. There were enough of us to best the Ships, the widow, and the two soldiers.

"When King Canute sends troops . . ." He stopped, thinking about it. When the soldiers came—if they came—he would only lose by mentioning the coins. "What do you want?"

He agreed that he wouldn't concern himself about the whereabouts of anyone in my family and that no one else in Gavrel would be flogged by his order. He said he couldn't speak for the widow.

His conditions, to which I agreed, were that I would turn over the coins and our cooking would be as it had been before the rebellion. Left unsaid was that the rest of the revolt would continue and he wouldn't rescind his appeal to King Canute for aid. I promised to bring the coins when we came to cook.

Before leaving, he said, looking canny, "If there happen to be more coins or another salver, I may be disposed to help again."

That bloodsucker!

I asked, "Beg pardon, Master, what had you come to tell us?"

He grinned. "That you would eat a portion of whatever you prepared for us, but now I don't want you to. What will you cook for our dinner today?"

Annet returned half an hour later. On her last step coming home, the magic boot had landed her in a wagon rut in the road, and she'd twisted her ankle. She'd hobbled four miles and twice had had to hide in bushes to keep from being seen by parties of traveling Lakti.

As soon as she showed us the swelling, I left to fetch Goodman Walde, though I wanted to learn how she'd fared before her accident.

Instead, I witnessed the goodman's astonishment and joy over the prince. He was too awed to touch him, but he embraced the rest of us. "Bamarre's future; Bamarre's freedom. Maybe I'll still be alive when we win it."

Annet had to cough to remind him her ankle needed tending.

Word spread. While Mama and I were cooking, people visited our cottage to see Prince Bruce for themselves. They were sad about Prince Dahn's death and even more worried now about their own children, but the little prince still gave them hope.

They'd also been delighted with the king's letter, which assured them that what we were doing was right. Only old Goodwife Petina had asked how we'd come by the letter and how the prince had reached us.

Annet chuckled. "I told her she was safer not knowing and recited the good luck saying."

I knew that one:

> *Good fortune flies*
> *And won't come back*
> *If asked how or why.*

That evening, Mama and Poppi argued which of them should wear the boot in Annet's place. Each wanted to be the one to go into danger.

How the Beneficences had changed the Bamarre!

I broke in. "Mama! Poppi!"

Prince Bruce turned a startled face to me because of my Lakti-like interruption.

"Begging your pardon . . ." I curtsied to the prince. "Poppi should go, in my opinion. I'm leaving, and someone will have to cook." Meaning that if anything befell one of them, it should be Poppi.

Had I chosen death for him?

"Begging your pardon, where are you going?" Annet said from her pallet.

"To the Kyngoll." And then to Lord Tove.

I spoke over their protests, surprising the prince again. "The Kyngoll can help us. They'll be glad to know about our rebellion, and I'll ask them to look for Drualt."

My parents stopped arguing. Drualt, the child they'd raised, was more precious than I was.

Prince Bruce chimed in. "Why does the grandmother always have to go? She should rest. Beg pardon, but you're as bad as a Lakti to her. Goodwife Shoni can travel to the Kyngoll."

I had to grin.

Everyone else seemed frozen in surprise.

Finally, Annet said, "It's her lot, Prince Bruce, begging your pardon. Aunt Nadira has always been in servitude for us, more than anyone, even when she didn't know it." She added softly, "And I didn't know it, either."

"I don't want to stop!" I blinked back tears.

Annet held her arms out to me. I knelt by her pallet, and we hugged.

I left in the morning, carrying the magic shell in my purse and a satchel containing a magic boot, the magic tablecloth, and half of Prince Bruce's strawberries, because he wanted the Kyngoll to have a gift from him. Perhaps the tablecloth's return would soften Sir Lerrin toward me.

If he was still alive.

Although Drualt would be unlikely to be headed there, because it was so far west, I decided to return to the front where I'd been before, where I knew the terrain, and where Sir Lerrin's command had been.

The Kyngoll would know how to locate Lord Tove. I wondered if Sir Noll continued as his close adviser and if Willem might be with him. Willem, are you fighting again?

Keep up your shield! Don't forget the power in your back leg!

But he could be anywhere, and I might never find him.

The boot took me into the barrens and landed me just a few yards from the tower that had been my prison.

I walked north through an empty landscape, prepared to don my magic boot if the shell carried any alarming sounds. But, unless the war had suddenly ended, the Lakti had taken the fight north into Kyngoll. They were winning.

Suspecting that a boot step would take me to the battle more quickly than hiking would, I donned the magic boot again. In a blink I passed the town Willem and I had been taken to. Then I careered through a clash of swords, arrows, and spears and sped on.

The boot stopped on a road near three Maze cypress trees. I listened in the shell.

Hooves! Pounding the road behind me. I whirled. Dust. Figures in the dust. Nowhere to hide.

Tassel?

Tassel. Keep it on. Sir Lerrin had admired the Bamarre.

I occupied a bench in the Kyngoll mess tent, waiting for the day's fighting to end. A kitchen maid had been assigned to guard the grandmother, and the two cooks were supposed to watch me, too. No one would say if Sir Lerrin was fighting—or alive.

My tassel had been taken. The Kyngoll thought me a Lakti spy pretending to be a Bamarre, but too old to be dangerous.

Hah. Kitchen knives. Boiling water. Hot coals. More than enough for a Lakti grandmother to disable the three of them.

If I had been a spy, I would have gleaned valuable information. The camp was low on supplies. The sacks of flour, beans, and nuts were mostly collapsed. Supper was to be thin pottage. The riders who had overtaken me had been coming to join the fight, though all were either elderly or very young. The Kyngoll losses must have been severe.

Dusk fell. A horse whinnied. I heard hooves, voices. I wished I could listen in the shell, but I didn't dare take it out.

Instead, I removed the tablecloth from my sack. The kitchen maid frowned, but I kept it folded in my lap, and she relaxed.

After a few minutes, a dozen soldiers came into the mess, and then a dozen more.

"Good tablecloth, please set thyself."

It rose and spread itself, though it failed to entirely cover the long mess table. Dishes began popping out of the air. Soldiers crowded around, exclaiming, questioning, reaching for food.

My stomach rumbled. The food stopped arriving, then started again as more soldiers came. Finally, not an inch of tablecloth showed between platters and bowls.

I ate a cheese puff and decided mine were just as good.

"The Lakti are sending grandmothers to spy on us?"

I knew that grand, round voice. The second cheese puff lodged in my throat.

Sir Lerrin shouldered his way through the crowd. Alive, but thinner and with the beginnings of a beard. He was taller than I now. "Where did you get the tablecloth, Grandmother?"

He wouldn't believe the truth without a longer story, and perhaps not even then. "From my great-niece, if you please. She's glad to see you're alive."

He raised his eyebrows. "How does she know?" He didn't waste time on this. "You're Lord Tove's aunt? Or Lady Klausine's?"

"Begging your pardon, I'm a Bamarre. Your people took my tassel."

He filled a bowl from the table and told everyone they could eat, though, with Kyngoll independence, they already were. To me, he said, "Come." He carried the bowl out with him.

I slung the satchel over my shoulder and followed. Farewell, magic tablecloth.

Outside, a thunderstorm was on the way. I asked if Lord Tove was leading the force against him.

"I'm sure you know."

This camp, since it wasn't in a town, was more like Lord Tove's, but not as bustling. Sir Lerrin's tent sat in the middle. A soldier guarded the flap. Sir Lerrin led me in and then ducked out. I began to untie my purse strings to get my magic shell, but he returned. He seemed not to see my hand jump away as if burned.

The tent, strewn with fresh rushes, was furnished with a domed chest, three camp chairs, and a low wooden table covered with maps, which were weighted with the same wooden cat carving I'd used to bludgeon him.

He saw me look at it. "Your great-niece thumped me on the head with that." He sat in the chair that faced the tent opening. "Sit if you like."

I sat but didn't lower myself as an old woman would, as I had learned to do. If I was going to persuade him of the truth, I should act it out.

He said, "I see that Lakti muscles refuse to give with age. What I don't understand is why Lord Tove returned the tablecloth." He held up a hand to stop any argument. "Tove is the mind behind the throne. I understand the tassel and why he'd send an old woman even if she is his aunt or his wife's aunt, because he'd rather lose an aunt than a soldier."

Outside, thunder growled.

Sir Lerrin ate several spoonfuls from his bowl. "But why send you at all?"

I heard the tent flap open behind me. When I turned, my heart rose into my throat. Willem!

CHAPTER THIRTY-SIX

WILLEM'S EXPRESSION WAS closed, sullen even, unlike his usual frank look, but this glumness seemed familiar. When had I seen it before?

"Willem!" I jumped up, smiling, about to run to him.

He looked at me without recognition, and I remembered that I was Nadira. Absurdly, I hated for him to see me as an old lady, whether he knew or not.

"You know him, but he doesn't know you. Fascinating."

I didn't think to wonder why Sir Lerrin spoke of Willem as *he* and not *you*, and I did it too. "He's sad! What have you done to him? Begging your pardon!" I turned. "Master Willem, how do you come to be here?"

His expression didn't change and he didn't answer.

I ventured to answer for him. "You didn't want to fight and you—"

Thunder cracked outside. I jumped in my seat. Sir Lerrin put his hands over his ears. Willem didn't budge.

"He's deaf, isn't he?"

Sir Lerrin nodded.

"Do you know how it happened?"

"He said it was the result of an injury when he fell from a tow—"

"I was—"

"The Bamarre don't interrupt people." Sir Lerrin tilted his head. "I know that much." I heard his accent: *mush*. I opened my purse and took out the magic shell.

Willem's expression shifted into surprise and sharp attention.

"What's that?" Sir Lerrin said.

Willem put the shell to his ear and smiled.

I smiled back. In his presence I kept forgetting I was Nadira.

He swallowed. "Peregrine gave you the shell?"

"Not exactly."

"Is she all right?"

I nodded, glad he cared.

"Master Willem, that tiny shell lets you hear?"

Willem nodded. "Thank you for giving me refuge."

Sir Lerrin waved the gratitude away. "You recognized the shell as soon as the grandmother showed it to you."

"It used to be mine."

"Will someone"—Sir Willem leaned back in his chair— "do me the kindness of explaining the many mysteries?"

"I'm Perry, Lord Tove's daughter. The fairy Halina changed me into this." Blushing, I gestured at myself. Change me back, Halina, if you please. This is a perfect time.

Willem's lips flattened in an unbelieving line.

"Absurd," Sir Lerrin said.

"I was born a Bamarre. Willem knows that." I had to convince them. Being Perry was woven into everything.

But how? If I revealed things that only Willem and I or Sir Lerrin and I had known, I could have told them to Nadira.

Drualt could convince them.

"I have a younger brother. Willem, he was born years after Lady Klausine took me. He saw the fairy change me." But Drualt wasn't here. "He's on his way to the war. I told him to escape to the Kyngoll and ask for you, Sir Lerrin. I said the Kyngoll wouldn't kill children." But in battle, they might kill anyone marching with the Lakti. "Was I wrong?"

Sir Lerrin paced a circle around our chairs. "Why send you? Why does Tove need you? Do the Lakti have a weakness I don't know about?" He whirled on me. "Do you?"

I nodded. "The Lakti have a weakness he may not know about yet, either. In the east, the Bamarre are rebelling.

He'll need to send soldiers to put down the revolt. That will hurt them."

Sir Lerrin sat again. He put his head in his hands.

Minutes passed.

Willem considered me, his gaze level, unrevealing.

Sir Lerrin raised his head. "May I listen in the shell?"

Ah. He wanted to see if Willem had been only pretending to be deaf. Willem handed it over.

Sir Lerrin's eyes widened. "Fascinating!" Kindly, he passed it back. "How well can you hear with the shell?"

"As well as I used to be able to without it."

"Tell me about the rebellion, Grandmother."

But first I wanted my question answered. "If you please, are your soldiers killing Bamarre children?"

"Only when we must to save ourselves."

A reasonable answer, and it meant that Lord Tove probably had contrived to have Prince Dahn killed.

Sir Lerrin added, "The children distract us. The Lakti send them in at the start of every day. It's a brilliant strategy. We're heartsick from the first moment."

Lord Tove would call *heartsick* cowardice.

I described our revolt. "The rebellion is spreading. Our Gavrel master petitioned King Canute for help. More will have to ask, too."

"Master Willem, what do you think?"

"I never heard of an Aunt Nadira when I was at the castle. You never visited."

No one spoke. I hated the wasted time, when we could be doing something useful, like planning or even sleeping.

"I'll cross back," Willem said. "I should be able to find out if an old grandmother was sent to spy."

"You mustn't!" I cried. "You'll hold your hand to your ear! They'll find the shell. You'll be deaf again."

A tiny furrow appeared between Willem's eyebrows. "I can keep it in place under my cap. I'll stay outside."

"Outdoors forever?" My fears cascaded. "Do they know you deserted? They won't trust you. If you ask questions, they'll imprison you." My voice cracked. "Or they'll make you fight!" Couldn't I protect anyone? "Lord Tove will make sure you're killed . . ." Like he'd killed Prince Dahn. Sobbing, I pushed out, "Even your father won't be able to protect you."

Willem grinned. "Sir Lerrin, she's Perry."

How did he know now? I managed to say, "Because I'm crying? I almost never cry." I hiccuped.

"Because you didn't believe I'd remember about my hand to my ear. Because you thought I'd ask questions without being careful." His smile widened. "Because you know best about everything."

I smiled, too, and continued to weep.

Sir Lerrin coughed. "I believe you because the last time we met you had magical hair, so you *could* have become an old grandmother. Lady Pereg— not *Lady*. A Bamarre maid." Sir Lerrin shook his head. "How can that be?"

In as few words as possible, I recounted my history, while Sir Lerrin murmured, "Fascinating." When I finished, he said, "At every juncture, Mistress Peregrine turns bad to good." He stood and bowed deeply. "Once, I told you I was your friend. Now I'd be honored if you'd be mine. Your friends are lucky people." He sat again.

I swallowed against the tears that threatened to come back. "I'm glad I didn't kill you."

Willem and Sir Lerrin laughed, though I hadn't meant to be funny.

I added, "Is Lord Tove here, Sir Lerrin? I mean, have you seen him?"

"Yes. His camp isn't far."

"Perry," Willem said, "Lady Klausine is with him."

Could I get word to her?

I tried to think of a way, but in the middle of the Lakti camp? Impossible.

"Is your father with them?"

Willem nodded, looking unhappy. "He doesn't know where I am."

"King Canute is with them, too," Sir Lerrin said, "leading the archers. What do you hope for, Mistress Peregrine?"

"Some of us—us Bamarre—want to live as equals with the Lakti. Some want to cross the Eskerns and fight monsters for a new kingdom. I want to lead them, but the pass has to be open." I added to Willem, "I imagine you and me battling together. They're monsters, not people."

He nodded. "I could kill monsters."

I said,

> "Valor achieves.
> Courage succeeds."

Sir Lerrin puffed up his cheeks and let out a long stream of breath. "If you'd come a month ago . . . two weeks ago . . . I don't think we can hold out long enough for your revolt to help. Tomorrow's fight may be our last."

Oh, no!

Then I remembered Drualt, who wouldn't be killed in this war if it ended.

But if the Kyngoll surrendered, Lord Tove would soon discover that the unrest had started in our village. Drualt wouldn't survive. No one in my family would.

Sir Lerrin explained he had few trained soldiers left; spring planting wasn't taking place; supplies were low.

"What if we took the children?" I said.

"What do you mean?" Sir Lerrin leaned forward in his chair.

"If I wore my tassel, the children would run to me. The Lakti would be confused. They're not used to the unexpected."

"They'll kill you and the children!" Willem said.

I grinned. "Now who's worrying? Halina didn't take

away my strength. I'll fight if Sir Lerrin will give me a sword."

Willem asked, "Could you kill Lakti soldiers?"

Some in Lord Tove's army would be people from the castle, some I'd trained with. "I don't know."

Sir Lerrin said, "We'll protect the children and Mistress Peregrine. We can do that much."

"Ivar didn't protect me, even though my father was sure he would. I'll wear the tassel."

No! "They'll think a Kyngoll put on a tassel. The sight of a grandmother will make them feel safer."

"I agree. Mistress Peregrine will go." Sir Lerrin yawned. "We should sleep."

"Sir Lerrin," I said, "can you make sure Lady Klausine isn't struck down?"

"Not kill her when she's killing us? I'm sorry, Mistress Peregrine, but she's our enemy."

Before dawn, Willem and I waited in the mess tent while Sir Lerrin addressed his troops about our plan to save the children. Cheers erupted, so loud that Willem took the shell away from his ear.

When he joined us, Sir Lerrin said, "The thought of rescuing the children has given them heart, this"—he gestured at the tablecloth's bounty—"and the food."

After breakfast, Sir Lerrin supplied Willem and me

with horses, and the three of us cantered to the sentry tower, which lay between our camp and the battlefield. First, we looked through a northwest embrasure, where the Kyngoll were assembling.

"I still have a bit over five hundred archers, half on horseback; almost half as many knights on their destriers; four hundred in the knights' retinues; and over three hundred infantry with pikes and spears. Don't they look fine?"

Fine and numerous.

His voice tightened. "I count many of them as friends. I hope not to be friendless." He walked us across the tower, where we gazed out at the Lakti army, who appeared from here as an ant swarm, too many to count.

We all knew how well trained and determined each ant was.

Half an hour later, I stood behind the first row of the Kyngoll pike soldiers, who would lead the engagement. I'd refused Sir Lerrin's offer of a sword, because I'd realized the children wouldn't believe I was a Bamarre if I had a weapon.

In a moment, the center pike soldier would hold aloft my cap with the tassel. As soon as the fighting began, with its turmoil and confusion, the pikeman would toss me my cap and I'd emerge. The line of fighting would admit the children who came to me and close tight behind them. If I didn't get them all, as I probably wouldn't, the line would open again for a second go.

Sir Lerrin called the maneuver the Whale. The Kyngoll force would open its jaws, swallow the children, and show its teeth again.

I peered between the gap that separated two pikemen. Fifty or more children—none older than twelve, judging by size—led the Lakti. Lord Tove and Lady Mother may have been there, but I had eyes only for the children. I didn't see Drualt.

Our pikeman waved my cap. A young voice cried, "Look!"

The pikeman flung the cap. I caught it and broke through the line, crying, "Across the Eskerns!" I grasped a child's shoulders, saw her gray eyes, maneuvered her behind me, handed her off to Willem. Reached for a boy as a Lakti pikeman lunged, speared him, lifted—

Don't look!

The battle spell fell over me. Amid war whoops from the Lakti and the Kyngoll alike, I ran among the children, shouted our greeting, backed off with as many as I could.

I sensed a wind, jumped away. A spear vibrated in the ground.

Around me children milled with the fighting soldiers and were passed back when possible. I saw only the battle near the children. I grabbed a child's stave and used it to shove children toward the Kyngoll, who closed about them.

I whirled. Lunged into Lakti legs. A pikeman tumbled.

I saw two young bodies.

Saved a bleeding boy.

Pikeman on the ground. Grabbed his dagger.

Backed away with three children, my dagger out.

Returned.

Used every shred of my Lakti defensive training to jump, spring, twist, feint, kick, dodge. Twice, my cloak was slashed.

How long? An hour? Two?

Finally, no more living children were left. Seven young bodies, none Drualt.

Without more children to round up, Willem and I went to the mess tent, where the cooks had taken charge of the ones who'd been rescued. No Drualt among them, either.

"Perry," Willem said, "Lord Tove saw you. So did Lady Klausine."

They would have recognized Nadira. "Why didn't he kill me?"

"At first he tried to, but Sir Lerrin and his knights blocked the way. He could have kept trying, but he drew back and only watched. He's planning something."

Willem and I rode to the sentry tower, ready to return to battle if more children approached. From above, we might see weaknesses in the Lakti line that we could exploit and weaknesses among the Kyngoll that we could remedy, and we might have ideas for strategy.

But the Lakti held firm. The Kyngoll line, however, wavered and surged, wavered and surged—dismay, I thought, overcome again and again by courage.

Lord Tove and Lady Klausine were everywhere—I knew them by his steed's scarlet brocade caparison and by her horse's aqua one—engaging knights in swordplay, turning spears, unhorsing cavalry, directing their forces here, there. King Canute stayed with his archers, at the southwest end of the battle.

After we had watched for a few minutes, Lord Tove turned his horse. Its rump, his back, and his helmet disappeared into the mass of fighters.

Willem and I exchanged a worried look.

With Lord Tove gone, the Kyngoll rallied and advanced a few yards. Lady Klausine fought the tide, but unsuccessfully. I wondered if she was pretending to fight.

Willem's hand found mine. About an hour passed. The Kyngoll gained a yard or two more.

The Lakti line parted to admit Lord Tove with a child riding his armored shoulders. He raised a gauntleted hand, and the Lakti around him stopped fighting. Lady Mother galloped close and reined in her horse.

From here I couldn't be sure, but—

This could only be Drualt.

CHAPTER THIRTY-SEVEN

I RACED DOWN the tower stairs, leaped into the saddle, and whipped my horse to a gallop, Willem thundering after me.

I thought, Lord Tove, don't kill Drualt!

My mind raced. He wouldn't hesitate. He might kill a Bamarre child just for show or to strike terror into Kyngoll hearts, but he'd have a special reason for harming my brother.

I'd do whatever he wanted.

A few yards ahead were the backs of the Kyngoll spear soldiers, the infantry.

Willem cried, "Make way!"

An idea arrived, unfolded itself, though I didn't have time to turn it inside out and examine it. It was terrible.

It would likely be the end of me, but I had nothing else.

The throng ahead of us parted. Fighting around Lord Tove had ceased. Sir Lerrin rode toward him from my right. My horse and Willem's walked through to my former father, Lady Mother, and my beloved brother.

Drualt's face was merry. What was he laughing about now? Did he have a plan of his own? *Don't try it!*

When he saw me, he crowed, "Aunt Nadira, see how high up I am!" He was playing the innocent child, as he had in Gavrel when the soldiers led him away.

Willem's expression had dulled, although he held his shell hand to his ear. He was pretending, too.

Lord Tove had raised his visor, and Lady Mother had raised hers, too, so I could see their faces.

He wore his pleasant mask. "Look, darling, it's Willem with the grandmother from Gavrel. We can tell Noll his son is alive."

Willem bowed in the saddle, and I performed an awkward curtsy.

Sir Lerrin said, "Are you surrendering, Lord Tove, with this child as a peace offering?"

He grinned. "I merely want to make an exchange. You're collecting children. I'll give you this one, if I can have the Bamarre grandmother. The child will be much safer with you."

The threat I expected. I wet my lips and remembered

a Lakti saying against terror: *Fear melts my sword.*

Sir Lerrin said, "A child for an old lady? I'm not sur—"

"Begging your pardon, Your Lordship . . ."

Lord Tove's eyes snapped to my face. "Yes, Grandmother?"

Lady Mother watched me, too. One armored hand found the other. She feared for me.

"I'm old. We have a saying:

> *"Life's purse near empty,*
> *No need for safety."*

"Begging your pardon again, you may do what you like to me, but you won't get the information you seek, although I have it. Beg—"

"Then I'll kill the boy now."

No!

But I'd expected him to say that, too. I held up a hand. "Begging your—"

"Consider my pardon permanently granted."

"Beg— I have a proposal."

His eyebrows went up. "Yes?"

"I challenge you to a match to—"

"I? Against a grandmother?"

Drualt laughed. He didn't know that Lord Tove could best me in any kind of contest except a race, and this wouldn't be one.

I shrugged. "You'll probably win."

Drualt cried, "Aunt Nadira will win!"

Sir Lerrin said, "Grandmother Nadira, I can challenge Lord Tove in your place."

He'd do that? "Begging your pardon, Sir Lerrin, this must be between a Bamarre and a Lakti."

Lady Mother's voice sounded strained. "What is the prize if my lord wins, and what if you succeed?"

Bamarre-fashion, I thanked her for asking. "In the likely event that I lose and Lord Tove lets me live long enough to say, I'll reveal your daughter's location." Which Lady Mother already knew. "When she's captured, the heart will go out of the rebellion." I hoped this wouldn't be true.

"Certainly, you may overcome me," he said gallantly. "I'm not invincible. What will be the consequence if that happens?"

"There are more for you than for me, beg— But, considering my chances, I hope you'll accept them."

"Very likely." He nodded affably.

"Any Bamarre *beings* who want to cross the Eskern Pass may do so. The Beneficences will be lifted, and those Bamarre who remain here will have the same rights as the Lakti. King Canute and King Einar will share the throne as equals. The war with Kyngoll will cease, and all territory gained will be returned."

He nodded as I spoke, looking unconcerned.

Lady Mother nodded, too. Her nod uplifted me.

"Grandmother, Grandmother." Lord Tove sighed, seemingly at the foolishness of the Bamarre. "You give me too much power. King Canute has to agree to these terms."

"By your le—"

"You have my leave, my pardon, and all the permission I can offer. By your leave, you needn't ask again."

"Then I'll wait for the king's agreement."

Sir Lerrin and Willem edged their mounts closer to me in a show of strength. Thank you, my friends.

Lord Tove lifted Drualt off his shoulders and passed him to me. "Proof of good faith."

Drualt smelled like himself and like Mama's pottage and garlic. His arms were warm around me. Then I gave him to a knight behind us, who, I was sure, would take him to the other children.

Lord Tove walked his horse to King Canute, gesturing as he went to halt the fighting.

Could Willem hear the drumming of my heart in his shell?

We waited silently. Lord Tove and King Canute did not confer for long.

My former father returned, but slowly, greeting this soldier and that one on his way. When he reached us, he said, "King Canute agrees. He has more confidence in me than I have in myself that he'll never have to share his throne."

"But if he's disappointed, he will share it?" Sir Lerrin asked. "And everything else? I'd like to be assured before I release Grandmother Nadira from my protection."

"You have his promise and mine."

Now I had to do it.

Lord Tove turned to me. "What sort of contest?"

"I leave that to you to decide. I prefer to choose the location."

His pleasant mask sharpened as he appraised me. What might an old woman excel at? Might he really be at risk?

"I choose swordplay until first blood." An unimaginative choice, but he was unparalleled at it.

And he'd chosen not to fight to the death, though I was sure he planned to kill both Nadira and Perry.

Never mind. I was hoping for surprise and luck.

"What location?" he said.

"Across the Eskerns."

CHAPTER THIRTY-EIGHT

WAS THAT FEAR I saw in Lord Tove's eyes, when they flicked to Lady Mother? Did he know the chapter in Lakti history when his ancestors had been cowards?

"You expect me to grant one of the provisions of your victory before you win? The Bamarre aren't allowed through the pass."

He *was* afraid! But he couldn't change my choice! His Lakti custom forbade it.

Sir Lerrin snorted.

"Beg— We'll be in your custody, and there—"

Lady Mother broke in. "Tove, the rules of a match—"

"I concede. It will be where you say, Grandmother." His face brightened. "This has proven to be an interesting day. I long to embrace my daughter again."

That made my skin crawl.

Then Sir Lerrin and Lord Tove, with King Canute's approval, agreed on a truce until the contest ended. Heralds would be sent along the length of the border. Our Bamarre children would be safe—temporarily.

We still had to name the people in our parties. Lord Tove named King Canute, Lady Mother, and Sir Noll. The last two had divided loyalties, but I thought I understood his thinking. Sir Noll would hope to get his son back, and Lord Tove believed Lady Mother wanted to find me as much as he did.

I named Sir Lerrin and Willem.

Lord Tove nodded. "My daughter's deaf love. Who will be your third?"

I didn't know anyone else. "I'll stop at two."

Lord Tove agreed to pause in Gavrel, which was along the way. "Certainly. You will want to bid farewell to your family."

It would be farewell only if I lost. He meant to frighten me.

As I'd suspected, Drualt had been carried on a fast horse directly from Gavrel to the battle.

He was in his usual good spirits. "I was going to close Lord Tove's visor and block his air so he couldn't breathe. Wouldn't that have been funny?"

I smiled weakly, glad he hadn't had the chance to try it.

His face sobered. "I don't know where my friends are." He meant the others from Gavrel. "I was going to take care of them."

"The Kyngoll will. You're going home."

Sir Lerrin found armor for me. The breastplate and pauldrons were loose, but the faulds were tight, because Aunt Nadira had a plump belly. The smallest gauntlets were too big to be useful, so my hands would have to be bare.

We left the next morning, all riding together—the Kyngoll, the Lakti, and Drualt and I. Sir Lerrin was accompanied by two of his knights and two archers, Lord Tove by three of each. Drualt shared my saddle, sitting between my legs, a squirmy passenger.

By agreement, only the parties to the match would cross when we reached the Eskerns.

As we rode, Lord Tove led his Lakti entourage in singing, meant, I was sure, to unnerve the rest of us.

> *"Our might strikes fear in fighters*
> *When marching we draw nigh—*
> *Push past the meek resistance—*
> *Our enemy will die!"*

Since the words didn't mention the Lakti, we Bamarre and Kyngoll travelers joined in, too. Only Willem was silent. He still feigned deafness, though I knew he kept the shell tucked into his cap close to his ear.

At the end of the verse, in an effort to outdo one another, we all roared "will die!"

The villages and towns of the kingdom lay along its roads. We reached the first sign of rebellion on our second day, a red haze on the horizon. Bamarre field-workers had set their masters' farms ablaze, as we were told by a delegation of worried Lakti householders.

If the fires were widespread, both the Lakti and the Bamarre were in for a hungry winter. Lord Tove whispered instructions to one of his knights, who rode back the way we'd come.

Troops would have to be drawn away from the war if it resumed. Though I was happy for the Kyngoll, I feared for the rebels.

The ride to Gavrel took four days. Rebellion had blown across the kingdom. We saw burning fields everywhere. In the lowlands, dams had been breached and farms flooded. The local Lakti met us at every town and village. Lord Tove always said aid was coming and rode on. King Canute never spoke at all.

Lady Mother's eye was often on me. I think she longed for a private conversation—and so did I—but opportunity didn't favor us. Sir Noll gazed at his son as often as Lady

Mother looked at me. I wished I could interpret the meaning of his glance, but his face remained neutral.

Willem's eyes often met mine. He couldn't smile, because of his pretended gloom, but his glance was always soft. What other young man would continue to care for a girl in the shape of a crone?

As we rode, King Canute practiced his archery, littering the landscape with dead birds. He rarely missed, but when he did, he keened in a brief, painful wail.

When we stopped for the midday meal on our first day of travel, the king lowered his royal self next to me on the canvas that had been spread for us to sit on.

I jumped up, curtsied, and remained standing, uncertain what to do.

He gestured me down. "I like grandmothers," he announced. "Mine was kind."

I said I was honored and sat.

The king was often at my side, which seemed not to trouble Lord Tove. I decided he didn't mind anything King Canute did, as long as he—Lord Tove—made policy.

Too bad the king's mind was weak. He seemed gentle when not on the battlefield. His real enmity was directed against birds.

We reached Gavrel in the evening. Lord Tove and Lady Mother were met by the widow and the Ships, so Poppi had time to bring Prince Bruce to stay with another family. In our cottage, Poppi and Mama passed Drualt back and forth for embraces. I got almost my share as well, and a full allotment of hugs from Annet.

Drualt announced straight out, "Aunt Nadira is going to fence against Lord Tove. It's a contest."

They were horrified, even after I explained I'd proposed it only to save my brother. I described the agreement.

Poppi squinted. "You hope the monsters will give you an advantage?"

I nodded. "If we're going to live there, why not win our freedom there?"

"I'll be your third." Annet made a wry face. "I'm used to serving you."

She wouldn't be argued out of it. She left us to tell Goodman Meerol, who was still recovering from his flogging.

Mama asked Sir Lerrin if she, Poppi, and Drualt might ride the rest of the way to the Eskerns with us. Sir Lerrin applied to Lord Tove for his consent. Gracious again, Lord Tove agreed and commandeered two of Gavrel's three horses for the purpose. Mama and Poppi shared a steed. Annet sat her own, uneasily. Drualt continued with me.

Lady Mother's eyes lingered as often on Mama as on me. I thought she was comparing methods of mothering.

In another four days the Eskerns rose ahead. We

camped in a valley watered by a brook, where the Lakti had their base for the soldiers who patrolled the pass. The magic boot hadn't taken me this way. We would leave the horses here and continue on foot.

The morning dawned hot. After a quick breakfast, we began to climb, just Lord Tove and I and our parties, each group with a donkey from the base. Drualt begged to come, too, but Mama and Poppi wisely wouldn't hear of it.

The beasts, sure-footed and accustomed to these mountains, carried Lord Tove's and my armor, weapons for us all, flasks of water, and food in case we were delayed returning. The narrow path was steep. Sometimes we had to clamber onto waist-high rocks. I helped Annet when she flagged, serving *her* for once.

"Darling," Lord Tove said to Lady Mother, "the grandmother is a prodigy of strength."

"Exceptional," she agreed.

The morning was half over when, flushed and sweaty, we reached the pass, a notch in a cliff wall. The ten soldiers stationed on the rock shelf before the opening jumped to attention when they saw King Canute and Lord Tove.

We spent little time with them, all of us drawn to the crossing. The others blocked my view, so I looked up and saw only sky—no dragons or gryphons.

I wondered if specters could hide them from sight while we were still on this side.

Lord Tove entered the gap first and shouted, "The Lakti return!"

King Canute followed, then Lady Mother, who gestured for me to follow her. She meant to shield me! A lump rose in my throat.

I reached for Annet.

> *Each from the other drawing strength,*
> *Two sisters of Bamarre, hand in hand,*
> *Rising toward their longed-for land.*

CHAPTER THIRTY-NINE

THE GAP ENDED in a ledge barely wide enough to walk along—if indeed it was. Might a specter create the appearance of stone where really there was only air? Annet and I tested each step before we put weight down. Willem and Sir Lerrin, just behind us, were doing the same when I looked back to make sure. Lord Tove noticed and told Lady Mother to follow our example. Only King Canute strode with confidence, holding his bow with an arrow already nocked.

When my view wasn't blocked by a boulder or by Lady Mother's back, I saw low hills below, arid and rocky, unlike the pleasant valley I'd entered on my first visit.

At the bottom, which we reached in early afternoon, the ground was uneven and broken. Tufts of grass grew between stones—some pebbles, some small boulders.

Footwork was as important as anything else in fencing. I'd have to be careful not to turn an ankle.

"Give me a sword!" Laughing, Drualt popped out from behind a boulder. "No one heard me behind you! I was as quiet as a cloud."

He laughed through the scolding that Annet and I doled out. "Begging your pardon," he said, "I want to kill a monster."

Sir Lerrin smiled. "Plucky. I can give you a short sword." He went to our donkey's saddlebags.

An alarm bell rang in my mind. Was this my brother or a specter?

He seemed himself, jumping with excitement. He *would* follow us if he could, but could he really have gotten away from Mama and Poppi?

"Please don't, Sir Lerrin," Annet said. "He isn't old—"

"I am! Begging your pardon, I am too old enough."

I announced, "He may not really be my great-nephew."

It seemed to take a few moments for this Drualt to understand. "She thinks I'm a specter!" Laughing, he cried, "Woooo-woooo. I'm a specter!"

Exactly what the real Drualt would say.

"How will we tell?" Annet asked.

It would take hours to climb back and find out if there was another Drualt at the base with our parents.

We stood in an uneasy silence.

Lord Tove looked around at the barren landscape and up at the empty sky. "I propose we not give it . . ."

I thought he'd like to call every Bamarre an *it*.

". . . a weapon and begin the match quickly."

We had to armor ourselves first. Sir Lerrin lowered the chain-mail shirt over my head while Annet buckled on the sabatons.

How strange it felt to be served, as if I were nobility again. Sir Lerrin and Willem knelt to fasten the greaves around my shins. Drualt—or the specter—appointed himself monitor and checked to see if the armor had been pulled snug enough.

Lord Tove was ahead of me, with the cuisses already around his thighs.

"Oho!" King Canute roared. His bowstring sang.

Something squawked.

A swarm of gryphons flew toward us, excepting one that had outstripped the others, who plummeted.

We ran to the donkeys for our bows, quivers, long knives, and swords. The armor slowed me. I wished I had none or all. I pushed a knife and a sword into my belt and took a bow and a quiver of arrows. Annet, who knew no archery, just took a sword and a knife.

Lady Mother loosed an arrow and hit her prey. Hooray! Lord Tove killed another. We were on the same side again.

Annet stood next to me. Would she be able to wield her sword?

The creatures were almost overhead. As I took aim, the battle spell fell over me. I hit my mark—heard laughter, and the beast vanished.

"Some are spectral!" I shouted.

They wouldn't kill us but would waste precious arrows. How many gryphons were real?

I glanced around for Drualt, brother or specter, who was at our donkey, pulling out a weapon. When he finished, the beast, sensible creature, galloped off after its fellow.

The monsters were descending. I shot another arrow, and this time a real gryphon died.

"Oho!" King Canute roared.

Grinding laughter. Oh, no! An army of seeming ogres crested the nearest hill.

King Canute loosed an arrow, which hit its mark in an ogre's throat, but then the creature vanished. The king began his keening wail. Lord Tove shouted to the king, "Lakti needs you now, Sire."

The king fitted a fresh arrow, ignored a gryphon almost upon him, and shot a real ogre, who died a real death.

Willem, too, shot at an ogre, caught it in the arm. It howled. He fitted another arrow to his bow, hit its stomach, and it collapsed. He turned to me, and we smiled at each other.

It would be this way when we crossed for good.

But we'd need many fighters.

A gryphon flew at me, beak and claws extended. I drew my sword, stabbed upward, jumped away from the body.

Laughter. I glanced around. Drualt or the specter was dueling with a gryphon. It stuck out its beak. Still laughing, he parried with his short sword. The beast stepped back. He advanced. The monster tried again. He thrust under the beak into the throat. Blood spurted.

"Victory for Bamarre!"

The gryphon died.

My real brother. Had to be.

Now, how to protect him?

Lord Tove shouted, "Victory for Lakti!"

I ran to Drualt, half twisted an ankle on a rock, kept running.

An actual specter, not only its deceptions, had to be here. Might it be a gryphon or an ogre, or more than one?

A gryphon came at Annet, who swung wildly with her sword and—by luck or strength—lopped off its head. "Victory for Bamarre!"

Did Lord Tove notice how well the cowardly Bamarre were fighting?

A gryphon landed on my back, claws in my flesh, beak at my shoulder. Yii! I punched at it with my elbow. To no avail.

The weight fell away. I heard a thud. Lady Mother nodded at me.

The real specter would hang back, I thought. Waving my sword to keep the gryphons at bay—the ogres hadn't reached us yet—I observed.

There! A gryphon, wheeling, not descending.

Too high for Nadira's arm. I ran to King Canute. "Highness! There!" I pointed.

He took aim.

A high-pitched giggle became a screech. The gryphon changed shape, became vaguely human in form, thinned, vanished.

I cried, "Victory for King Canute!"

He cried, "Oho!"

A score of illusory gryphons vanished, leaving too many real ones. The army of ogres thinned, but the ones that remained charged while flinging a hailstorm of rocks.

A rock caught Lord Tove in his side. He staggered, stood, nocked an arrow, shot at a gryphon.

Too many monsters.

We dodged and fought on, Annet and I at Drualt's side.

The ogres closed in.

"The one on the right!" Drualt leaped forward, holding out his sword.

Annet and I sprinted. I whipped out my long knife.

The ogre laughed, displayed its own knife.

Drualt got under the creature's stabbing arm, pierced its thigh. The ogre groaned. Annet moaned. Her left shoulder bloomed blood, but she struck off the monster's hand. It screamed. I stabbed upward into its belly. It toppled.

How badly hurt was Annet?

Drualt, who failed to notice, darted at the next ogre. "Come and meet our might!"

Annet sank to her knees but cried to me, "Go after him!"

I leaped forward.

The creature raised a boulder above Drualt's head. Laughing at the monster's slowness, Drualt jumped from side to side. Bellowing, the ogre swayed.

Willem was there, too, advancing on the ogre's side, failing to see another monster, who reached out, picked my love up by his collar, swung a boulder toward his head.

No time!

But Sir Noll charged. With all his weight, he pressed his sword into the ogre's stomach. Willem tumbled to the ground. He stood and, limping, started after yet another ogre.

Drualt still danced with the ogre. Enraged, the creature kicked a foot at him, lost its balance, fell, and my brother jumped on it, stabbed its neck, crowing, "Victory for Bamarre!"

Annet lay on her side, extending her sword against a gryphon, which kept its distance, but another foe or a falling rock would finish her.

Only King Canute, my fearless brother, and I were uninjured.

Lord Tove held his side as he advanced on an ogre.

Blood trickled from Lady Mother's forehead.

Sir Lerrin's right arm hung uselessly.

Sir Noll's right calf bled, and, like his son, he limped.

Ten ogres still alive and eleven gryphons, though the gryphons had ceased attacking us to feast on the carcasses of their companions.

Too many ogres.

Momentarily free from attack, I saw two ogres circling Lord Tove, who, twisting from side to side, held both at bay with sword and long knife, but he was backing up, clearly unaware how close behind him the cliff wall was. When he reached it, he'd be finished.

Why try to save him, who despised us Bamarre, who would almost certainly kill me if I were revealed to him?

"Here!" I rushed to him.

An ogre whirled, knife in one hand, rock in the other.

I lunged. The monster struck my blow aside, and my sword clattered onto the rocks.

It leered and said something in its grating tongue.

I pulled out my long knife, but now I was the one backing

away. With my knife, I'd never get past its arm.

He thrust and sliced off the end of my sleeve. Thrust again.

I jumped away. My armored feet landed badly, and I fell onto my back. The ogre raised its rock. I was finished.

But the monster's face changed from monstrous glee to monstrous unease. It let the rock go, and I was able to twist aside.

All the ogres were stampeding toward the nearest hill.

The gryphons ceased their gluttony. One squawked, and the others rose, beating the air, flying south.

Drualt said in a wondering voice, "Are they really gone?" Meaning, had another specter made them seem to leave?

I stood, holding my knife at the ready, and collected my sword.

But no invisible rocks showered us, no beaks pecked, no knives pierced.

I rushed to Annet.

"It isn't too bad," she said, panting. "Not deep."

Drualt ran to her, too. "Sister!"

Willem stood by us.

Sir Noll said, "A miracle. We're all alive."

Lord Tove held Lady Mother's head and ran a finger along the trail of blood on her face. "Painful, darling?"

"No. Your side?"

"It isn't much. We can proceed with the match."

Sir Lerrin said drily, "Of course. The match—despite fighting together, despite being saved by your opponent."

Lord Tove turned to me. "I'm grate—"

"Oho!" King Canute aimed his bow.

In the southern sky, the size of my thumb, but bright, a flame.

A dragon!

CHAPTER FORTY

EXCEPT FOR KING Canute, we rushed to the cliff and began to climb, hoping for enough time to reach the pass.

After a minute or two, Lord Tove shouted, "Too late! Descend to level ground!"

I looked back. The dragon had grown to the size of my hand, its shape distinct: wide wings and narrow body. Flame and smoke obscured its head. We hastened back to the valley.

"Oho." King Canute drew his bowstring and waited, statue-still.

The rest of us fitted arrows, too.

Sir Lerrin loosed the first arrow, which arced and fell, the monster still too far.

The creature ceased flaming. Narrow head, long snout.

Lord Tove shot, and his arrow lodged in the monster's belly. Except for King Canute, the rest of us shot, too.

To no effect. The dragon flew on, its course unchanged, tiny arrows dangling from its neck and stomach. It began to descend. Its eyes were clear and faceted, like crystal. It seemed to smile.

"Oh-h-h ho-o-o." King Canute released an arrow.

The dragon shrieked, an arrow in its right eye.

Triumphantly, "Oho!"

A moment later, the dragon landed, flaming. We all drew back. Sweat beaded my face. The armor on my feet and legs scorched me.

It swallowed its flame and, using a claw, pulled the arrow from its eye. Blood streamed and pooled around its scales.

To my astonishment, it said in a fire-roughened voice, "Welcome to Old Lakti." It raised its wings and performed a bow that was a feat of balance. Then it stared through its one good eye, moving along the line of us. The eye stopped at Drualt. "Bold heart, little one. Merry heart, too. Rare." It moved on to Annet. "Ah, faithful. Loyal by nature and training. Exemplary." The eye continued to me. "Mmm. The instigator of everything. Much more than you seem." The eye passed on to Willem. The head nodded. "You'll do."

King Canute stood apart, another arrow nocked.

Grinning and showing saw-edged teeth, the dragon waved its head sinuously from side to side. "Sire, your second arrow won't hit its mark."

King Canute followed the head, his entire body swaying. The dragon's tail whipped out and circled his waist. He dropped his bow, which slid around the girth of the tail.

"I'd planned to dine on you all, but I see future benefit in letting you go, except for this one." It shook King Canute. "The last human I entertained was a King Josef, a charming man. How delightful for me to have you now." Its voice softened. "We'll amuse each other. I hardly regret my eye for the exchange."

King Canute moaned, "Oho, oh!"

The dragon flapped its wings once, pushed off with its back legs, and flew, tail out straight except for the curl at the tip that held the king.

We didn't shoot again. If we brought the monster down, King Canute would certainly be killed. The two shrank and disappeared. My throat closed in pity.

After a minute, Sir Noll said, "He'll shoot out the other eye or stab it out. He's brave and strong enough."

No one answered him. Even if he escaped, he'd be alone in a monster-ridden land.

Then I wondered what the loss of him would mean for my match with Lord Tove.

Lady Mother curtsied. "Lakti salutes King Tove."

Oh! The worst news for Bamarre.

Sir Noll bowed.

Lady Mother—now Queen Mother—continued. "May his rule be long. May courage and wisdom guide him. Victory for King Tove!"

Should I curtsy?

I did so. No matter which way the match went, he'd still be king, even if he shared the throne with King Einar.

Annet followed my lead. Drualt hesitated, then bowed.

"Your Majesty?" I said. "Beg— Will you carry out the match? You lost one in your party, and . . ." And now you're king.

"Do you wish to concede?" he said, smiling.

I shook my head.

"My wife and Sir Noll are more than the equal of Sir Lerrin, a deserter, and a Bamarre servant." He heard himself. "Apologies, Noll. I hope your boy regains his hearing and his senses. And, Grandmother, I want my daughter more than ever. She's moved closer to the throne."

The more reason to kill me.

King Tove's helpers and mine finished armoring us. Sir Lerrin drew the helmet over my head. Too big, it overlapped the gorget around my throat, more like wearing a pail. When he lowered the visor, I couldn't see.

"No!" I cried. "Leave it up, if you please."

Someone said something I couldn't hear through the steel. "What, beg pardon?"

Sir Lerrin raised the visor. "What?"

King Tove looked amused.

"I can't see with the visor down. Leave it up." My face as well as my hands would be exposed.

"You're sure?" Sir Lerrin said.

I nodded, and my armor clanked. None of it fit well.

King Tove and I paced away from each other, a distance of seven long steps. According to ceremony, I curtsied—and almost lost my balance. He bowed his head. A king needed do no more.

We each turned sideways to our opponent, bent our elbows, held our swords chest high, distorted reflections of each other—I, short and squat; he, tall and straight.

My power is in my back leg, I thought.

We edged toward each other. He thrust. I parried. I thrust. He parried, thrust.

A dot of blood on the back of my hand. Defeat for Bamarre.

Tears threatened. I'd known I'd likely lose. But I'd expected to do better, hold out longer. I didn't want to die, didn't want to lose Willem, lose my future here on this side of the Eskerns.

At least I won against the tears. Dry-eyed, I saw

Annet was weeping. Drualt, the only one who'd entirely believed in me, stood at her side, crying, too. I'd never seen him cry before.

Willem's eyes were wet, too. He came close and stanched the blood with his sleeve.

Sir Lerrin removed my armor. "You were valiant. We Kyngoll will do what we can."

It wouldn't be enough. They'd be defeated, too.

I faced King Tove, who had removed his armor. How I had loved him.

"Where is my daughter?"

I opened my mouth to tell him the truth and then had a different idea. Lord Tove had once had love in him. Perhaps I could make it grow.

"Queen Klausine, I remember your lessons in declaiming."

She nodded.

"You taught this grandmother?"

"I taught Perry, Tove."

Sounding charmingly confused, he said, "I hope someone will explain to this muddled monarch."

I tried to begin, but I had no breath. I bent over. Annet patted my back. Drualt's hand clasped my right hand; Willem's found my left.

"Is she trying to speak?" Lord Tove said.

I straightened and stepped away from the comfort. If

not the battle spell, something like it gave me calm and certainty. "Your Majesty"—I would not curtsy or beg his pardon—"you said you were grateful for my effort to save you from two ogres. If you truly are, please grant me a few minutes to tell you my heart, as a Bamarre would, and my thoughts, as a Lakti might."

"You'd like me to, wouldn't you, my love?"

Queen Mother said she would.

"Then speak as long as you like." His polite mask composed itself.

The words came in measured phrases, as if I were reading them from a book. "You're king. There's no need for secrecy now. In any case, Queen Klausine, Willem, and Sir Lerrin already know; Sir Noll has proven his loyalty to you and the rest of us are already ghosts." Ghosts because, unless my speech worked a miracle, he would soon kill Annet, Drualt, and me.

"Before you do away with Perry, you should know that during her childhood, when you were off with King Uriel or fighting the Kyngoll, she lived in a chilly place of walls, rules, and tests. She liked rules and tests, liked clarity, loved excelling. And she loved Lady Mother and sought to earn her approval.

"But she always looked for your return as for the return of spring or the sun after a long storm, for your warmth, your gaiety, humor, and, most of all, your unguarded love."

The mask seemed to dissolve. His face softened.

I continued. "Perry lost that, because of what she is, not what she ever did." I turned to Sir Noll. "Perry was born a Bamarre, is a Bamarre."

King Tove's mask hardened again.

"Majesty, you lost her, because of ideas you've hugged close and the cruelty they've birthed, not because of what you are." You are good! Can be good!

"You told me you aren't perfect—"

"I never told you that!"

"Told Perry, then, and the admission was part of your charm. Can you be imperfect again and change your heart? Can you truly reunite with your Bamarre daughter as fath—"

"May I speak? Then you may continue as long as you like, unless, of course, the monsters return."

We all looked about uneasily, but the sky and the land were clear. Remember that, I thought. An encounter may be followed by an interlude of safety.

As if I'd have the chance to use the knowledge. I said, "I'm eager to hear you."

"You'll be less eager once you do. The admission was to my Lakti child. To the Bamarre pretender, my disgust is as it should be. Perfect. Continue speaking, if you like."

I'd failed again to save us, but I drew a deep breath and

went on. "Do you know the price of tyranny, Your Majesty?"

He smiled and shook his head. "I'm sure you'll tell me."

"It is the loss of 'no.' Subjects say 'yes' to a tyrant, whether he's right or wrong. He may need a new way to see a problem, but no one brings it to him. There may be a route to greatness for his kingdom, which he can't spot and others can, but he'll never know. His rule will travel a rut, which will deepen and deepen, until his chariot of state can no longer move."

"Thank you for the warning."

I was running out of ideas, but I had one more. "We Bamarre don't speak of our power to curse"—because we didn't have one—"because we're kind and rarely exercise it, but I curse you with lovelessness. When—"

He chuckled. "A Bamarre sort of curse, not very troubling to a Lakti."

False. My former father loved to be loved. I shrugged. "I suppose. When you kill Perry or have her killed, however you arrange it, your queen will hate you and you will lose the power to command love in anyone else. Your charm will harden. A wall will grow around you, which you will have to climb to speak to anyone, and just from above. Life will lose its sweetness." I grinned, enjoying this final moment. "Even marchpane will turn bitter on your tongue. That is my curse. Long live the Lakti king." I saw his fury under the mask.

"Are you finished?"

"Yes, Sire."

"Then where is my daughter?"

"Here. I'm Perry."

He reddened. "If *you* had drawn first blood, I would have lived up to my agreement."

"I'm living up to mine."

A feather-light touch stroked my hair, my chest and back, my legs, down to my feet. Halina?

I began to burn inside. Oh, I'd forgotten the pain!

This time I kept my eyes open and managed to hold out my hands so I could see. The skin reddened. Tiny boils popped up.

I wrested my gaze from myself. King Tove drew back, drew Queen Mother back, too, and shielded her.

My bones were melting and my insides were boiling, or so it felt.

King Tove's expression changed from fright to eagerness. Ah, Perry was emerging.

He'd taken off his sword earlier, but he drew his dagger.

To kill me? Unarmed! In anguish!

I remembered Halina's warning to Drualt when I was becoming Nadira. King Tove would die if he came close.

Queen Mother, trying to save me, reached for his arm to hold him, but he shook her off. Willem sprang forward to stop him, but Drualt catapulted himself and made my love stumble. Annet held Willem to keep him from trying again.

In my agony I don't know if I could have moved away. I didn't try. If we both died, I would have killed a despot.

He approached, lunged, thrust.

CHAPTER FORTY-ONE

TRANSFORMING HURT TOO much to tell if King Tove had run me through and I really was dying. I fell backward. The heat receded, but my side hurt.

After a moment, I propped myself up on my elbow.

King Tove dropped his dagger. Tremors caused him to fall. He writhed on the rocks, jerked, and was still.

Queen Mother bent over him. "He's dead."

I'd let him die. What did I feel?

Relieved? Yes. He'd have killed me. And now we Bamarre might be less oppressed.

But sad, too. I'd never again have a father who loved me—who relished me!—as he had before he stopped.

The side of my kirtle was stained with blood, not bad, just a cut. King Tove's aim had gone wide.

"I'm fine."

I'd grown taller than Queen Mother again. Her expression was always hard to read, but I saw new lines around her mouth. Her eyes met mine levelly. I knew what she'd lost, what we'd both lost, except I'd lost him long ago.

If she'd been a Bamarre, I'd have hugged her. Instead, I stood next to her and linked my arm in hers.

She patted my hand. "You have your hair again."

I looked down. There was my shower of hair, without a single strand of gray. I glanced at Willem to see how he liked the change. He was smiling.

Sir Noll bowed deeply. "The Lakti salute Queen Klausine. May her rule be long. May courage and wisdom guide her. Victory for Queen Klausine!"

Queen Mother pulled her hand out of mine and stepped away from me. I saw her draw a long breath.

I hadn't thought! I curtsied. We Bamarre would have a just ruler, finally.

Annet, Willem, Drualt, and Sir Lerrin curtsied or bowed.

After he rose, Sir Noll pivoted and bowed again, this time to me. "And victory for Crown Princess Peregrine."

It took a moment for my mind to catch up. Sir Noll had learned I was a Bamarre, and yet he'd called me *princess*. Already he was proving his loyalty to Queen Mother by offering her the choice of letting me return as a Lakti or a Bamarre, in either case as crown princess or not.

Annet curtsied and Willem bowed to me. Drualt half bowed, half doubled up with laughter.

Sir Noll added, "Willem, I'm certain you can hear me." His voice broke. "Son, don't hold yourself apart from me."

Willem ran to him. Awkwardly, they shook hands, smiling and smiling.

Queen Mother unpinned my tassel.

I let her do it, seeing ahead to our return across the pass. To Annet and Drualt I said, "Beg pardon, I'm not deserting you."

Annet said, "I believe you."

Drualt laughed.

Queen Mother said, "Noll, I hope you'll agree that Tove was killed by a monster after Grandmother Nadira won their match."

Sir Noll nodded. "Tove disappointed me."

Queen Mother addressed Annet. "I'll lift the Beneficences. Perry, I'll live up to the terms of the match."

I nodded at her. For now I should help her rule. "Let us climb. Monsters may come again."

Sir Noll and Willem carried King Tove's body between them. I took the rear, holding my unsheathed sword, the protective princess. If monsters returned, I'd be first to fight them.

Luckily, none came.

On the other side of the pass, Sir Noll and Willem set down King Tove's body, to the dismay of the soldiers.

Mama and Poppi were there, too. They'd made the climb to rescue Drualt, but, fortunately, the soldiers hadn't let them cross. Mama held him and she and Poppi took a while to satisfy themselves that he was unhurt. Next, they embraced Annet, and finally saw me.

I backed away, hoping they'd understand. Mama, quick-witted as ever, curtsied to me.

"We have a new queen," I said. "Queen Klausine."

"Long may she rule!" Apparently, Willem had decided he didn't have to feign deafness any longer.

The soldiers bowed and curtsied. Mama and Poppi did, too, though both of them looked worried.

Willem added, "And Crown Princess Peregrine!"

Drualt said, "Mama, Poppi, you should have seen the ogres! I can't wait to go back. I helped kill one."

Sir Noll told the soldiers, "King Canute was carried off by a dragon. Then, after we'd acknowledged him, King Tove was killed by two ogres." Cleverly, he'd made the accession clear, so Queen Mother's crown couldn't be questioned.

Sir Noll didn't explain how the ogres had killed King Tove, whose body seemed untouched. Soldiers wouldn't doubt a knight, and the unknown power of monsters seemed to satisfy them.

But a soldier did venture two questions: What had happened to the grandmother? And where had I come from?

Sir Noll, seemingly an inventive improvisor, began, "The—"

I waved to silence him. On the climb to the pass, I'd anticipated these questions.

Then I hesitated. To explain myself to soldiers would be seen as weak, unbecoming Lakti royalty.

I wondered what King Tove would have done.

Ah. "You're brave to ask, and we always reward courage," I told the soldier, daring to speak for Queen Mother. "We left the grandmother in Old Lakti, where I'd been living and exploring since leaving my father and Queen Mother. I doubt she'll fare as well as I did."

Drualt laughed. I would have, too, if I could have, as I watched awe grow on the soldier's face. He didn't care that an old Bamarre woman had been abandoned, but he revered the new princess, who had crossed the Eskerns by an unknown route and had survived unharmed. How many monsters had she killed?

Before we left the pass, Queen Mother ordered the soldiers not to stop any Bamarre who wanted to cross. "Warn them of the danger and, if they are few in number, suggest they wait for more. But if they insist, let them go."

There was no earth for a burial at the pass, so we

continued to the base camp. We arrived near dusk and found a dozen Bamarre in the soldiers' custody. Spurred by the rebellion, these people had gathered here to make the crossing.

So few, and unarmed—except one with a pitchfork—they'd cross and be dead in an hour. We'd warn them after the funeral. Soldiers dug the grave, working briskly even in the heat. Sir Noll brought everyone together, the Lakti and the Bamarre, forcing the Bamarre to pay their respects to the creator of the Beneficences.

Before anyone spoke of my former father, Sir Noll delivered a few sentences about King Canute's steadfastness, enthusiasm, and excellent aim. While he spoke, I observed the Bamarre travelers: six female, six male; most young adults, one as old as Nadira, had appeared, and one a girl as young as Drualt. All appeared healthy, fit, alert.

Would I lead them? Or would I be just one of their companions? I wanted to lead! Few, if any, would be trained in battle.

Would they be glad to have me in their company, the partial Lakti, who usually said the wrong thing? They'd accept Willem sooner than me. He always knew how to behave.

When Sir Noll finished speaking, Queen Mother declaimed about King Tove's valor and the battles they'd fought together, the kind of praise expected for a Lakti king.

I spoke next. If I'd let my Bamarre side come forward, I'd have dwelled on his kindness when I was small and how he'd seemed to understand me better than anyone else. But all that had been betrayed, so I spoke as a Lakti. I told how he'd come when the Kyngoll had captured me and how proud he'd been that I'd rescued myself first.

I ended with poetry. Let the soldiers hear it from a princess:

> *"Exalted his departure . . ."*

Trying to murder me.

> *"Dispatched by monstrous ogres,*
> *Valiant, a soldier's death,*
> *Lakti's brave King Tove."*

The soldiers covered their surprise at the verse with a blank military gaze. If Queen Mother objected, she didn't stop me.

The Bamarre exchanged glances. A middle-aged woman, perhaps understanding how much was about to change, asked Queen Mother's leave to recite, too, for King Tove, and permission was granted. She spoke several stanzas, while I thought how King Tove would have hated this. She ended with these lines:

> *"High peaks like watchers waiting,*
> *The Eskerns take him in*
> *And welcome him, the Lakti king."*

After the funeral, the Lakti and the Bamarre separated again, each to prepare their evening meals. I knew better than to force them to stay together, but when Annet approached the Bamarre, I started to follow her.

"Perry?"

I turned.

Willem said, "You haven't told me about your months on the other side of the Eskerns."

He knew I hadn't spent months there, so why?

Oh. To stop me from going with Annet and frightening everyone. I called her back to me. "Tell them about our battle. Warn them not to cross until they're at least two hundred strong." Four hundred would be better. "And not until they have arms and armor."

"Begging your pardon, I know."

Of course. I looked around for Willem and saw him halfway down the hill away from the camp and the Eskerns. As I followed, I saw Queen Mother watching.

The sun had gone down, but light lingered, making

the grass greener and the rocks that littered the ground more somber.

He stopped at an outcropping of stone. "Your throne, Your Highness."

I sat. "I'm happy to share my throne." I moved over.

Then my words came back to me. Oh, no! *Share my throne.* Had I proposed to him?

If it was a proposal, he didn't answer. "Are you eager to cross the Eskerns?"

"I am." Just saying so made me want to jump up and battle a monster. "It will be simpler there, fighting an enemy we must defeat and won't enslave. Paradise."

He laughed. "A monster-ridden paradise."

"Yes! It was fun to fight them." I laughed, too. "Aside from King Tove and the imminent match and my likely death."

He was quiet.

I became uneasy. "Did you enjoy it, too?"

The pause lengthened.

I added, "Will you cross the Eskerns?"

"And be the only true Lakti there?"

That would trouble him? Everyone liked him.

He added, "I'll go. I don't want to be apart from you ever again."

Ah. He may not have minded if I'd proposed.

He grinned. "I think you don't want to be apart, either."

I blushed.

He went on. "I thought I'd like fighting monsters, but I didn't. Perry, I even hate to kill fleas."

Everybody liked to kill fleas!

He'd do what he hated for me?

Then I wondered if he'd be able to prevail against monsters if he hated hurting them.

As he often did, he read my face or my mind. "I'll fight them. I'll be fine, as long as I remember that my power is in my back leg."

I laughed.

He added, "Killing monsters is much better than killing people."

I reached out and took his hand, the prerogative of a proposing princess. As soon as I touched him, my heart sped up.

He put a hand behind my head, and gently pressed me toward him.

We kissed. Oh, my! Sweet, the long-promised kiss.

CHAPTER FORTY-TWO

WILLEM AND I rode side by side the next morning, enjoying our companionship. I caught several significant looks from Annet, but no one else seemed to notice.

We traveled under a blistering sun, and it was still only May. Often, we saw distant fires, spread by dry weather.

At every village we were met by angry and worried Lakti citizens. In some villages, fighting had broken out. A few of the Lakti had been killed, but more of us Bamarre.

Whenever we stopped, Queen Mother announced the lifting of the Beneficences. She promised the return of the Bamarre youth and rode on without waiting to see how her news had been received. Her purpose was to speed to the troops that King Tove had sent to quell the rebellion. I wondered how many of the Bamarre they'd killed. Hundreds, certainly.

After she called off the soldiers, she and Sir Lerrin would ride to the battlefront and sign a truce.

In the middle of the afternoon, a dark haze rose in the road ahead. When we got closer, it resolved to a mass of fifty or more Bamarre folk, raising dust, tassels swinging, marching to the Eskerns.

They stopped and faced us defiantly, but Queen Mother merely nodded and rode on. However, Annet stayed to speak with them. Half an hour later, she galloped up and rejoined us.

That night, Queen Mother drew me away from the campfire before we all lay down to sleep. By torchlight, she led me to the top of a gentle rise. Together, we faced out into the night.

I thanked her for protecting me from King Tove. "Begging your pardon, you shouldn't have taken me." All those years ago.

"If I hadn't, how pale my life would have been."

Mine would have had different hues, and I would almost certainly be in servitude right now. "You were an excellent Lakti mother." My nod to her.

I added, "I didn't tell Willem I was Bamarre until after Lord Tove had imprisoned me."

She took that in. "I see." Then, "You may marry him." Her voice was flat.

"Willem?" She approved? I smiled, though I would have married him anyway.

"Yes." She turned to face me. "I've changed my idea of a proper Lakti husband." Another pause. "And father."

I pitied her.

She smiled. "And a princess doesn't need an advantageous marriage."

Didn't she realize? "I'm going through the pass."

Her smile became a grimace.

I added, trying not to sound glad, "To fight monsters."

"Of course. You're a warrior, and we'll need other skills here."

Skills that neither of us had. I wondered how she'd manage but put the thought aside. We who crossed would have troubles of our own.

The next morning, I sat with Sir Lerrin while we broke our fast.

"I'm going to cross the Eskerns."

"Never be a queen?"

"Probably not."

He smiled. "We Kyngoll are willing to be wrong. We're not stiff-necked."

Stiff-necked about their superiority over the Lakti, I thought. Maybe he'd learn otherwise.

Later, when we set out, Annet and I rode side by side,

and I enjoyed the ease that had grown up between us.

"I'm really your sister, you know."

I didn't understand.

She smiled. "And Drualt's sister, too. I enjoyed killing the gryphon and chopping off the ogre's hand."

I smiled back. "Good." She'd be happy in the new Bamarre.

We rode in silence for a few minutes until she said, "I won't mind leaving New Lakti."

"It's beautiful beyond the Eskerns, not where we were, but farther south." Still, I thought, New Lakti is beautiful, too. I would miss it.

Three days later we reached Gavrel. To my family's relief and mine, the village had fared better than any we'd passed. In hopes of more gold when we returned, the Ships had been conciliatory to their Bamarre and had insisted that the widow and the two soldiers behave as they did. No fields were burning. No one else had been flogged, and no one had been killed.

Lady Mother and I parted there. She'd ride on to the battlefront and the future of the kingdom. I'd leave for the Eskerns from here. We stood awkwardly outside my parents' cottage while Sir Noll and Sir Lerrin waited at a respectful distance. She must have been reluctant to leave, and I could hardly bear losing her forever.

"What would we do if I were a Bamarre?" she asked.

"We'd hug. We'd kiss. We'd weep."

She held out her arms, and I went into them. She held me for a long minute, stroking my hair, my cheek, my ear. "Daughter, don't stop being a part-Lakti. It will keep you safe."

I promised. She mounted her horse and rode off without looking back. I wiped tears away before entering my parents' cottage.

I donned my tassel again. Poppi introduced me to the village as his stolen daughter, and Mama revealed that I had already lived among them as Aunt Nadira. The greatest source of wonder seemed to be that I had been raised a Lakti and had still been able to cook delicious cheese puffs!

Two weeks later, an hour before sunset, my family, Prince Bruce, Willem, Goodman Meerol (who had recovered enough to travel), and I reached the base camp. On the way, Drualt had won the friendship of Prince Bruce. My merry and bighearted brother, as no one else, could banish the worry stamped on the prince's face. When they weren't side by side, Prince Bruce followed Drualt with his eyes, finding comfort in my brother's robust form.

We'd gathered people as we marched through a

countryside that still blazed. At the camp near the pass we found even more Bamarre. In total, we were five hundred. A few had bows and arrows; some had rakes and pitchforks, some butcher's knives. I'd used the coins and plate from Old Lakti to buy arms, armor, and donkeys on our way here, but not nearly enough. Those with weapons would have to protect those without.

The Lakti soldiers followed Queen Mother's order and didn't trouble us. They must have been surprised to see their crown princess wearing a tassel, but no one questioned me.

Night fell. Willem and I sat with the Gavrel Bamarre, some of us on rock outcroppings, some on the ground. I was wondering aloud if the sorcerers had stayed in Old Lakti when I smelled peonies. A whorl of light spun in the center of our circle.

Gasps ran through the throng of us.

Drualt laughed. "It's the fairy again."

When she took her human shape, she beamed her brightest smile at me. "You didn't disappoint me after all."

Willem bowed low. Along with the soldiers, he was the first Lakti to see a fairy in hundreds of years, but when he straightened, his face was cheerful, not awed. "If you were surprised, you didn't notice that Perry always does what's right."

Oh, my!

He went on. "Will you visit us across the Eskerns?"

"Fairies will visit. I'll be among them."

"Can we conquer the monsters?" I asked.

"They still trouble the elves and dwarfs and sorcerers. But you'll prosper if you're determined, if you keep fighting back. I wish—"

Willem took my hand. "Will you come to our wedding once we're settled?"

Oh! I squeezed his hand.

But I wanted to know. "Halina, you started a wish." It might be important. "What do you wish?"

"I wish you very well."

Oh. Naturally. She didn't have to wish. She could kill all the monsters, but I knew she wouldn't.

"And I'll preside over your wedding." She vanished. The peony scent lingered, then dissolved.

I woke before dawn. Annet slept near me, but when I sat up, she woke, too. I gestured to her, and she followed me a few yards beyond the sleepers. We faced the black shape of the Eskerns and whispered together.

A few hours later, we began the ascent, led, as Annet and I had arranged it, by Drualt with Prince—soon to be King—Bruce. Hands joined, climbing together, Annet and I recited in unison:

"Out of a land laid waste
To a land untamed,
Monster ridden,
The lad Drualt led
A ruined, ragtag band.
In his arms, tenderly,
He carried Bruce,
The child king,
First ruler of Bamarre."

We reached the pass, crossed into Bamarre, and tossed our tassels behind us.

TURN THE PAGE FOR A SNEAK PEEK AT
GAIL CARSON LEVINE'S NEW NOVEL
OGRE ENCHANTED!

CHAPTER ONE

WORMY WAS DISTRACTED. I counted three symptoms:

- He kept forgetting to mash my inglebot fungus.
- He twice asked me to repeat why Master Kian's cough had seemed odd.
- Whenever I looked at him, he was wetting his lips, although—exasperatingly—nothing emanated from them.

Soon he'd need a remedy for chapping.

He was spoiling our daily companionable time, when we worked together in my apothecary (in a corner of Mother's kitchen) and chatted; we were old friends, though we were both just fifteen.

"Wormy, what did you notice on your way here?"

"Drag leg. Ferocious sneeze. Palsy. A gentleman who tripped over nothing." He named streets: "Moorcroft, sorry—don't know where the sneeze lives—Ashton, Westover."

"You're a miracle." He never missed anything.

Wormy was a healer's best friend. He knew almost everyone and where almost everyone lived, and he had a fine eye for symptoms, as well as for beauty, which—

shame on me—interested me less. He arrived midmorning every day, after working on the books for his parents' various enterprises. Not a coin remained unaccounted for when he was in charge, because numbers obeyed his every command.

Half my patients came from his observations. He told me about sufferers, and I tracked them down. Healing was my calling and my joy.

"Thank you." I patted his hand.

He blushed. He'd been blushing often. This blush seemed too brilliant. "Do you have one of your headaches?"

He shrugged. "Maybe." The blush faded.

I teased, *"Maybe* I'll treat you."

The blush flared again.

"Are you feverish?"

"No!"

Grimwood, my fever remedy, tasted bitter.

He smiled. "Grimwood cures as many patients by being

2

threatened as swallowed."

I laughed. "A good healer knows when to just mention a remedy and when to pry open a jaw."

A moment later we spoke at exactly the same moment. He said, "Evie?" and I said "Wormy?"

Ah. He was finally going to reveal what had been occupying him.

But he insisted I go first, and I didn't mind. Unless an emergency case came in, we'd be together the rest of the day.

I reached into my cupboard for my darkroot salve, a sovereign headache remedy. "Sit."

He sat on my stool and gazed up at me. I felt the satisfaction of an artisan surveying her good work. His chestnut skin glowed with health—and with his blush. His brown eyes were bright. "If you saw yourself on the street, Wormy, you'd have nothing to report to me. A headache is invisible."

"People are patients or nothing to you."

A mere dab of the ointment was all I needed. I began to rub it into his temples, my fingertips describing tiny circles, always going counterclockwise. "*You* are my friend. How lucky I am that you're also delicate, and you like my ministrations."

When we were eleven, I'd set his broken ankle. Before then, I'd treated only birds, rabbits, and mice. Afterward,

3

I'd made his stomachaches vanish, his headaches recede, and his fevers fade, and I'd spooned unpleasant concoctions into him to convince him he was well when he only thought himself sick.

Gradually, I'd garnered more human patients, but I'd always be grateful to him for being first.

He breathed deeply. Either that was the headache receding, or it was a sigh. If a sigh, why?

"What were you going to say, Evie?"

Oh, yes. "Wormy, am I peculiar?"

"No!"

"Who else my age wants nothing more than to take care of sick people?" I continued rubbing. "Who else reeks of camphor at least once a week?"

"Or worse," he said solemnly.

I nodded. "Pig bladder!" Stinky, but excellent when wrapped around a sprain. "I'll be an outcast! People will want peculiar me when they're sick and never otherwise."

He raised an eyebrow. "Some folk are friendlier at a gathering, a dance, even"—he raised his eyebrows and stage-whispered—"a *ball*."

I kept to myself at such affairs. "I'd rather observe for symptoms than talk or dance." Although I liked dancing. I lifted my fingers. "How is the headache?"

"Better, but it's still there."

I returned to rubbing

"You're not peculiar. You're remarkable." Wormy slid off the stool. "Evie?"

Finally.

Someone banged on the front door. Rupert, our manservant, would answer, but pounding meant an emergency.

"Wormy—"

"Go."

I put the salve on my worktable.

It was as well I went, because Oobeeg, a ten-year-old giant, couldn't fit through our door. Weeping, he gasped out his story. His mother, Farmer Aeediou, had had a brush with an ogre. She was alive because her hound, Exee, had sunk his teeth in the ogre's throat before it could say a word. Still, by the time the ogre died, it had lured her close enough to deliver a gash to her leg. With their honeyed words and irresistible voices, ogres could persuade people to do anything.

Calling behind me, I rushed back to the apothecary. "I'll get supplies. Don't leave. I'll be quick."

Untreated, the cut would kill Aeediou. Whatever Wormy had been about to say would have to wait.

Back in the apothecary, while I nested a pot of honey in my healer's basket, I told him what had happened. Where was my packet of turmeric?

There it was. Now I needed my flask of vinegar.

I smelled lilacs.

I turned to see and forgot everything in staring. A woman stood behind Wormy. How had she arrived without a sound?

She was a vision of health and beauty: yellow hair cascading to wide shoulders, garnet lips, blue eyes, and petal-smooth skin.

Wormy said, "Oh!"

She must have been dosed to create such perfection. What herbs? Periwinkle, for those eyes? Strawberry juice, for that skin? What else?

And what a smile. What teeth. I blinked.

"Young Master"—her voice rang out, as if her chest were as big as a castle—"speak your mind! Brook no delay!"

"Welcome!" I curtsied and wished my apron weren't shapeless and grease-stained.

"Thank you." She nodded graciously. "Continue, Young Master."

I remembered Aeediou. "Mistress, this must wait. Beg pardon. I have an injured—"

"I repeat: Continue, Young Master."

How dare she?

Wormy said, "Mistress, there's no hurry for what—"

Her voice gained volume. "Continue!"

Who was she? I gripped tight my manners and my temper. "I am Mistress Evora, called Evie by my friends, and this is Master Warwick." Wormy. "May we have the

6

honor of your acquaintance?"

She drew herself up even taller. "I am the fairy Lucinda."

Really?

Wormy bowed.

I curtsied. "Can you replenish my purpline? And give me a unicorn hair? Or sell both to me?" Purpline—dragon urine—cured almost everything, even barley blight, and lately there had been none in the market. Unicorn hair in a soup was nonpareil for fever. "I'd also welcome anything else for an ogre scratch, enough for a giant."

She seemed not to hear. "The young man will say his piece."

Wormy dropped to his knees, as a puppet might. "Evie, will you"—his Adam's apple popped in and out—"marry me?"

The woman clapped her hands. "So sweet!"

That was his secret? That he wanted to ruin our friendship?

"I relish proposals"—Lucinda jigged a quick hop-step—"and weddings and births. If I can, I come." Her hands embraced each other. "Proposals are the start—"

"No, Wormy, dear. Thank you for asking me, though." I put the vinegar in my basket with my next-to-last vial of purpline. "I must leave." But curiosity held me. "Why do you want to marry me?"

He stood up. "Because . . ." He shrugged. "You're you."

Did he think—being me—I'd say yes? He knew my ideas about marriage.

And I didn't believe he could truly be in love with me. As his healer, I made him feel better. He'd confused loving health with loving me. That was my diagnosis: imaginary infatuation, which would clear up as soon as we got a little older.

"And you can stop working so hard." His family was rich. "But"—his blush returned—"pretend I didn't ask."

"Why won't you marry him?"

I picked up my basket. "He's Wormy." Yes, I loved him—the way I loved my pet rabbit. I didn't even know how romantic love felt. We were too young. If Wormy didn't think he was, I thought we both were. I didn't know if I'd ever want to marry anyone. But I didn't have time to explain. "Good day." I'd be two hours riding to Aeediou's farm. A few farms owned by giants covered the rolling hills near Jenn, though most lay in the west near the elves' Forest.

"I urge you to reconsider. If you persist in breaking this young man's heart, you will suffer the consequences."

Wormy's jaw hung open.

I picked up my herb basket. "If I accept him, we'll both suffer the consequences." No one should marry before they were ready—and certain.

For a moment she looked puzzled; then her face cleared.

My mind emptied. The kitchen tiles no longer seemed to be beneath me. Somewhere, fabric ripped.

My mind filled again. I held my arms out for balance and felt the floor under my feet. My mouth tasted gamey and spoiled, as if I'd swallowed a three-day-dead squirrel.

Wormy's jaw was still unhinged. He extended my name. "Evie-ee . . . there's hair on your face."

Not what I expected to hear. I started to lift a hand to my cheek but stopped and held the hand out. Hair sprouted there. My fingernails were long and filthy.

My stomach rose into my throat.

"Evie . . . you're an ogre."

CHAPTER TWO

I LOOKED DOWN at further horrors. My bodice had ripped, but my apron strings held and were squeezing my stomach. Hastily, I untied them. The seams of both sleeves of my bodice had split. The hem of my skirt, which had hovered just above the floor, now fell a little below my knees. I had shot up a whole foot! My boots, which were visible now without raising my skirts, had come apart. When I lifted one foot, the sole flapped.

My stomach settled, though I didn't know how it could. And it rumbled. But I'd had a big breakfast.

How delicious Wormy looked: a little lopsided because he always hiked up his left shoulder, which just added to his appeal, and those rounded cheeks, those plump earlobes (the sweetest part), that flawless neck, that skin the hue of a goose roasted to a turn. How healthy I'd kept him, like a farmer safeguarding her livestock. How dear he was to me.

Aaa! What was I thinking?

The fairy Lucinda frowned. I sensed outrage, though I couldn't hear her thoughts. Her feelings buzzed, as if a quarreling crowd were packed inside her.

How could I tell? I'd never perceived feelings before.

She needed a dose of my bonny-jump-up syrup to calm her. Maybe she'd turn me back then. "May I treat—"

"Fairy Lucinda," Wormy said, "pardon me. Proposing was just a prank. We play tricks on each other, as friends do." I sensed his emotions too. He was frightened. Oddly, he wasn't in any pain, though he'd told me that his headache hadn't entirely gone away.

The fairy's outrage mounted. She glared at Wormy. What would she turn him into?

Had he really been jesting about the proposal?

"Yes," I said. "We have a merry time with our capers." My voice sounded husky, as if I'd been shouting. "We're never serious." Turn me back! And don't harm Wormy!

She surveyed us, her emotions still in turmoil. Finally, she decided. "No. I think he meant it. And you"—she poked a perfect finger into my large chest—"will remain an ogre until someone proposes marriage and you accept."

I gripped my worktable to steady myself.

Wormy went down on one knee this time. "Mistress Evie, please accept my *sincere* offer. I think—I believe—I'm certain—we'll be happy."

I sensed his fear and desperation. Kind Wormy. Perhaps the first proposal had been a prank, and now he wanted to save me from its consequences.

He added, "You can work as hard as ever. As hard as you like."

I did feel love coming from him. But we weren't *in* love. I definitely wasn't, and I didn't think he could be either.

Maybe I should accept him, become me again, and figure the rest out later.

It would be wrong to accept him just to be human and stop wanting to eat him. I couldn't do that to Wormy. Not to my dearest friend. Not to anyone.

Lucinda clapped her hands. "See how true his love is."

She didn't mind destroying a person's life? "Do you do this often?"

"Help people?" Her smile blazed again. "Yes, oft—"

"Turn them into ogres?"

"It's my latest inspiration."

She was insane. I turned back to Wormy. "No thank you." I was young. Eventually I'd find love with someone who loved me, too, someone who saw beyond the ogre.

"Oh." Now Wormy was sad as well as scared.

"But if you're ill, of course, I'll help you."

Lucinda's rage surged. I put my hands over my ears, which accomplished nothing.

I felt furious, too—at her and at Wormy for bringing this down on me, though he hadn't meant to. I doubted I'd ever been so angry.

"Then, foolish girl," Lucinda said, "if you don't receive a marriage offer and accept it, you'll remain an ogre forever. You have"—she tilted her head from side to side, deciding—"sixty-two days."

What kind of number was that?

Barely more than two months!

"Counting today?" asked Wormy.

"Certainly, counting today."

"Might she have a little longer? A year?"

Thank you, Wormy!

"Certainly not! Sixty-two is twice twenty-eight."

"Er . . ."

"What, young man?"

Wormy, the mathematician, saw my face—and my fangs.

"Er . . . er . . ." He collected himself and thought better of pointing out her error, which, if she corrected it, would cost me days. "Then the last day will be November twenty-second."

"I suppose."

"At midnight?" I asked.

"At four o'clock in the afternoon."

Why then?

She went on. "Who will want her anyway, even if she were human, defiant and contrary as she is?" She smiled. "You, young man, are exemplary. When you find someone who deserves you, I'll devise a marvelous gift."

"If I have to stay an ogre, will my human side disappear?"

"No. You'll always know what you lost." She disappeared.

And reappeared. "Do not think another fairy will come to your rescue, either, no matter how much you plead. The fools disapprove of me, but they fear their own magic too much to intervene." She vanished and this time stayed away.

A fly buzzed over my basket. I needed to eat. I wished the fly were a lot bigger, but I caught it and licked it off my palm. Tasted like venison.

"Wormy, why did you?"

He blushed yet again. "I thought we could spend the next few years discussing it."

A reasonable answer.

A fist pounded on our door, a large fist by the sound of it. Oobeeg! What would he do when he saw me?

"Wormy . . . Tell Oobeeg what happened. Tell him I'm me."

He left the apothecary. A bowl of late peaches rested on the kitchen table.

Ugh.

But I loved peaches.

No longer. I was angry they were even in my presence.

The stew for dinner bubbled over our low fire. I wondered if I could fish out the meat and ignore the flavor of carrots and onions.

Wormy returned and blushed. "Somehow I thought you would be you again."

"I am me." I forced my eyes away from his meaty thighs. "What did Oobeeg say?" The stew would have to wait. Aeediou couldn't.

"I couldn't tell him. The words wouldn't come out. I think the fairy won't let me."

Would I be able to say them? I grabbed my basket and left.

As soon as he saw me, Oobeeg screamed.

I tried to explain, but the words seemed to choke me. Oobeeg jumped on his enormous horse and spurred it. His terrified wail wafted back to me. I watched him grow a little less huge in the distance.

Aeediou would die without doctoring. Ogres are fast, so I started running, clutching my basket to my chest and stumbling in my broken boots. Ahead of me, the streets of Jenn cleared, as if Lucinda had cast another spell.

Beyond town, I stopped to strip off my boots. Luckily, the soles of an ogre's feet are calloused, so the dirt and pebbles of the road wouldn't hurt. I ran again.

Aeediou's farm lay ten miles from town. I hoped ogres had stamina. Ahead of me, Oobeeg crested a hill. As he descended, his height, especially on his mount, kept his head visible until, finally, all of him disappeared into the valley.

My mind returned to Wormy. Blockhead!

Edible blockhead.

Ugh! I wanted to leap out of my skin, as if the ogre were just a covering. I let go of the basket with one hand to touch my face, hoping for a miracle.

No miracle. Still hairy. Nincompoop fairy.

Why did I keep thinking this one or that one stupid? Was being angry part of being an ogre?

A side of beef hung in our shed at home, untainted by vegetables. I'd eat it raw. Mother wouldn't have to see.

As I streaked along, a new feeling mingled with the misery and rage—pleasure in the strength of my legs, the energy in my muscles, the depth of my breathing.

By now, Aeediou's large leg had probably swollen to three times its size.

Again I thought of Wormy's proposal. As a healer, I had seen too much unhappiness in marriage. Stomach complaints and worse were the result! The commonest cause, I'd observed, was youth. So I had decided that no one younger than eighteen should wed, no matter how in love they believed themselves to be. Many married at fourteen, and then—for example—one or the other grew ten inches! And height was the least of it.

My calves were aching when I finally reached a stile for giants and had to boost myself up each step with my arms. When I descended the other side, Aeediou's bull, an acre away, pawed the ground and lowered his horns.

I heaved myself up the far stile with his breath on my neck.

There was Aeediou's vast farmhouse—made of boulders, thatched with a mountain of straw. I banged on the door.

No one answered, but Aeediou and Oobeeg had to be inside. Exee trotted to me, clearly meaning no harm. His back, which used to be as high as my shoulders, now came up only to my waist. He rubbed himself against me. Did he know me despite my form?

I wondered how dog tasted.

I wouldn't eat a dog!

The door didn't open.

"Exee trusts me!" I cried. "Uueeetaatii (*honk*) obobee aiiiee." *I am a friend.* I knew a few words of the giants' language, Abdegi, which includes sounds as well as words.

Oobeeg's face appeared in a first-floor window, right above my head.

"I mean no harm. I'm—" The words *your healer, Evie* wouldn't come. "I'm a healer ogre. Aeediou needs me."

Oobeeg's face left the window. Was he going to let me in?

Five minutes passed.

Aeediou had to be in pain, which would soon rise to agony, and shortly after that, she'd be beyond my remedies.

Now was the time for ogrish persuasion. A born ogre would have had the door open before the end of her first sentence.

"Oobeeg, I won't hurt anyone." I tried to soften my voice, but it still came out rough. "I'm as kind as . . ." As what? "As a good human." In exasperation I cried, "If I were an ordinary ogre, wouldn't I have convinced you by now?"

Nothing happened. I was furious. Two stupids.

I couldn't reach the door latch, which hung too high for me even now. I saw nothing to stand on to get to it, either.

My rage melted as my own leg ached in sympathy with Aeediou's. I backed away and put down my basket. "Oobeeg! Aeediou! I'm leaving my basket and going away." I told them what was in it and how to use the ingredients. "Be generous with everything except the purpline. A few

19

drops are all you need. I want the rest back. Aeediou, don't stand up—Oobeeg, don't let her stand—until the pain is completely gone. Coat every bit of the wound." Now I was just repeating myself. "If you wait another half hour, nothing will help. I'm going now." They'd pay me next week. You can trust a giant.

Please, Oobeeg, be brave enough to go outside for my basket. Aeediou, please let your son go out and save you. Be well, both of you.

Also by
Gail Carson Levine

HARPER
An Imprint of HarperCollinsPublishers

www.harpercollinschildrens.com